The Threshold

Copyright © 2022 Mark A. Daniel

All rights reserved

The characters and events portrayed in this book are fictitious. Any similarities to real persons, living or dead, is coincidental and not intended by the author.

No part of this book may be reproduced, or stored in a retrieval system, or transmitted in any form or by any means, electronic, mechanical, photocopying, recording, or otherwise, without express written permission of the author.

The Threshold

Mark A. Daniel

Mark A. Daniel

I
1
1971

Davey watched in terror as his little brother sped down the road on his Big Wheel. He shouted after Tommy as loudly as he could, but his brother just looked back at him, ignoring the shouts in order to antagonize. Tommy could sense something more than the usual bullying in the tone, but he peddled on. He stared back at his brother in defiance, riding down the center of the road, oblivious to what lay ahead.

But Davey could see it all too clearly. Somehow he knew when the big truck turned onto the road that some form of destiny had taken over and he was helpless. Now all he was supposed to do was watch in terror and awe as those forces of destiny overpowered his life once again. But he could not stand by and watch. Instead, he ran toward his brother, screaming at the top of his lungs for Tommy to get out of the street, pointing down the road to the truck that was coming toward the both of them.

The man driving the truck swore profusely as the hot coffee burned his legs. The last corner had tipped over his "spill-proof" mug and now he could feel the hot liquid searing his thighs. Part of his reaction was to straighten out his legs, depressing the accelerator in the process. As he became more concerned about his burning legs than the road before him he made the turn a little too tightly.

The burning coffee took his eyes and his mind away from the road before him for only a couple of seconds, but that was all the time that destiny needed to do its work. His mind alerted him to the dangers of his distraction just in time for him to look up and see the little yellow handlebars disappear as his vision of them became blocked by the hood of his speeding vehicle. In that instant he also saw the look on Davey's face as the boy ran toward him, the look of total terror and defeat all wrapped up into one gruesome grimace.

Then there was the sick thud which came just before the squealing tires. He hadn't even been able to hit his brakes before he hit the kid. It was a residential area, so he was only going just over thirty miles per hour at impact. But he knew from the sound and the look on Davey's face that it was enough. The tires squealed and tracks of red appeared behind the truck. Davey watched as his brother was literally smeared down the road, trapped against the asphalt by the Big Wheel which was lodged under the left front tire. He watched the small and mangled body as it slid toward him losing bits of itself as it came. The man in the truck forgot for the moment the child under his tire and stared at the one who now stood like a statue before him. He pushed harder on the brakes, as if this could make him slow down faster. The truck slid slightly to the right as it screeched to a halt.

The small body broke loose and rolled under the tire which had held it to the road and disappeared from Davey's sight. Then he saw the white side panel of the truck just before it hit him and threw him back across the curb and into the bushes beside the road.

2
1991

Dave Chatburn awoke with the screams of terror and agony fresh on his lips. He stared into the darkness with his hands balled into fists while tears streamed down his cheeks. He relived the sorrow and guilt which had tormented him on and off for the past twenty years. Tommy was dead. He had been dead for a long time. Dave had talked about the guilt and 'dealt with it' as best he could. Now it was buried inside him and poked its ugly head out infrequently. He had not dreamt about it in over three years.

But tonight, it had seemed more real to him than it had since his teen years. Tonight, the grief was fresh, and the guilt was very heavy. He rolled over and buried his face in his old and soft pillow. His breath came in jerks, and he felt his face grow hot as he tried to hold in the sobs which he could not suppress. He brought his hands to the sides of his pillow and pushed its softness against each of his ears both to comfort himself and to hide his shame.

As the night wore on the images which had torn him without warning from his world of order and tranquility faded some, but only enough that he was able to stop the tears and begin thinking again of the things he had been told and which he had told himself over the years. Things which softened the pain and lessened the guilt.

An hour after he had been awakened by the dream Dave turned to his side and turned on the light. It blinked a few times before staying on. It always did that, even with a new bulb. It was four in the morning. He lay looking at the clock, not really seeing it as his thoughts remained scattered and incoherent. He got out of bed and walked into the kitchen where he made himself some coffee. He fought with the coffee maker which didn't want to start, but finally began spitting out the water after a little encouraging and pounding. As the coffee brewed he walked to his window and looked out into the night. The trees swayed softly in the northern breeze which had come to cool off the warm summer night. He watched them sway and listened to the cicadas sing as his coffee brewed. Finally, the coffee stopped perking. He turned back to the kitchen and faced the pot.

Why tonight? Had he seen something during the day that had triggered this? Had someone said something to him that had flipped the terrible switch once again? He racked his brain but nothing came to mind.

He shuffled his six-foot one-inch frame over to the pot of warm redemption and poured himself a full cup. It was not decaffeinated, but he knew that sleep was not going to be his anymore this night anyway. He took the cup of coffee into the back bedroom which he had converted into a small office and sat down at his old oak desk. He set the coffee down and looked at the calendar on the wall.

It was not a special day. Not one which might bring the memories back to him. It was not the anniversary of his brother's death; that was still three months away. It was not Tommy's birthday; that had been four months earlier. The date stared back at him defying any significance at all.

So why had the dream come?

He sat looking across his desk and pondering this question, but finding no answer as the morning made its way to his house.

3

The ringing of his phone brought him out of a sleep which had somehow crept upon him. His coffee lay spilled across the corner of his desk and had soaked into the carpet. It was cold. The morning light streamed through the window of the small room. He looked quickly to the clock by the calendar. It was nine a.m.

He answered the phone.

"I hoped to catch you there," came a familiar voice. It was his boss's secretary. "I tried your office, but only got your machine. Hope you don't mind me calling you at home?"

"No, it's okay," he replied. "That's why I gave you the number and put it on my business card." He tried to make it sound as if he had been simply doing some work at home, though he knew that this was not exactly in line with company policy. He hoped it would cover him for now, and that Katy wouldn't mention it to Stan.

What followed was a brief conversation in which Katy requested Dave's closing numbers for the month and Dave replied he would have to call her from his office with them. When he had finished talking with her he got up from his desk and went to the bathroom. He pulled off his slippers and his underwear and took a warm shower.

When he got to the office he checked the messages on his answering machine. There was the one from Katy, and one from the electrician who was supposed to have been in the day before to fix a burned-out light fixture, and a call from a contractor in Abilene who wanted a final price on the pipe he would be needing for the west wing of the new prison. Dave pulled his books from the top drawer of his desk and called Katy with his figures for the month. Then he called the contractor. Abilene was just forty-five miles west of his office in Cisco, but the phone connections were seldom good and it always sounded much farther.

"Hello, Dave?" came the familiar voice. This was a contractor with whom Dave had become familiar over the years. He always got this man's orders. This was due to a good overall relationship and dozens of rounds of golf and free lunches given.

"Yea, Bud, I'm calling you back on that order for the west wing of the prison."

"I was kinda hoping you were going to say that. The groundwork has been done and the pipe is going to be needed by the end of the week. Can you get me one truck load by then? And what the hell is this 'new pricing structure' you hinted at last Saturday?"

"Oh, you caught that," Dave joked. Today the connection was worse than usual and Dave could hear the popping and snapping of the static as it grew from background noise into a nuisance.

"You bet I did. I don't forget the bad news I hear on a golf course just because I'm winning. I made a quote to these guys based on your old prices. If you make me.....five percent more.....going to come out.....my pocket."

The static was getting worse now and Dave could hear pieces of other conversations in the background. He was going to have to hang up and call Bud back.

"Bud, I don't hear you very well. I'm going to have to call you right back."

"Are.....on one.....those damned car phone things....."

This was crossed with the pieces of another conversation which was becoming as loud as the one he was involved with.

"Betty.....lucky.....didn't lose.....too."

Dave could no longer make out Bud's voice and was about to hang up when the words which the other person had said struck a chord with him. He stayed on the line and listened. There was no noise now, and Bud's voice was entirely gone. Then the other voice came back. It sounded like the voice of a woman, though it was distant, and he could not be sure.

"It.....wasn't.....fault.....don't blame.....Nobody.....does but.....your father.....he's dead.....and.....doesn't.....matter."

The words ran around in his head. They echoed from somewhere in the past. Then as he sat listening to more static, he knew why. He had heard these words before. They were pieces of a conversation which he had been at the receiving end of once before, almost fifteen years earlier. The woman was his mother's sister, and she had been trying her best to help him rid himself of the guilt which he had slipped deeply into one summer three years after his brother's death.

But that couldn't be.

Then the static died down, but the voice returned. Now it was as if the voice was speaking to him.

"You've got to let go of this thing before it ruins your life, if it hasn't already," she said.

"Aunt Linda?" Dave said.

"I know, but now you owe it to him to make the most of yours. You owe it to him and your father."

Her voice was distant, but clear. But she could not hear him. It was as if he could hear just one side of that old conversation, but she could not hear him. It was too impossible, and in his mind he still held to the idea that it was coincidence.

"But little Tommy is gone, he has been for three years now, you need to realize there's nothing you can do to bring him back."

The notion of a coincidence disappeared as the conversation went on. He listened hard but could not make out any of the other end of the conversation, the end he had once been on.

Then there was another voice. It was the voice of a man this time.

"You can't punish yourself forever for this thing. If you do you'll never amount to anything. You'll end up like your uncle Jack."

Uncle Jack, of course, this was Uncle James's voice. This was a voice from a year earlier, a voice from the other side of the family, from the brother of his deceased father. Unlike Aunt Linda, however, Uncle James had died of cancer three years ago. Hearing the voice of someone who he knew to be dead sent a chill down his back. He wanted to hang up, but a morbid curiosity held him. Then he looked to his right and saw the answering machine resting on the corner of the desk. He reached forward and pushed the record button as the voice of his late uncle replayed its speech from the past. This voice continued for a few more sentences. The static was completely gone. The connection was better than what he normally got even on local calls.

He listened to pieces of past conversations from uncles and aunts, an older sister and even his Grandpa Morris. Three of the voices he heard were from people who had been dead for over a year. The common thread between these conversations was that all of them had taken place over the phone, and all of them concerned his bouts with depression when memories of his brother's death had been lying heavily on his mind.

Then there was a silence, one with no static at all. There was no noise, and there were no voices. He reached forward to click the receiver, but thought that by doing so he might break whatever odd connection had been made. Instead, he sat listening to the silence, waiting for what, if anything, might come next.

But there was nothing.

He did not wish to hang up, so after five minutes of waiting he turned the volume on his answering machine all the way up and put the handset face down on his desk. This way he could hear anything which came over the phone without having his ear to the ear piece. He left it this way and stood up to walk around the office. He looked at his hands and saw that they were shaking. He also noticed that they looked bloodless, and he imagined his face did too. He paced and listened.

Ten minutes later he jumped when the loud sound of a dial tone brought him from his state of semi-shock. He walked slowly to the phone and picked up the handset. He put it to his ear and heard the same dull tone.

Dave turned the answering machine off and placed the handset back in its cradle. He stared at it for a moment and jumped again when it rang.

At first he just looked at it. It rang three times, then he reached out and answered it. He brought the handset slowly to the side of his head. "Hello?"

"Jesus, Dave, I've been trying to call you back for almost half an hour. I've got to get to the site soon. What can you tell me about the pipe shipment?"

"Oh, yea," Dave replied, his mind coming back slowly to reality. "Let me call the plant and see when they can have it."

"I thought that's what you were doing," Bud chided. "Well, I've got to get out of here. Call me at the site. You got the number?"

"Yea, I have it here somewhere."

"Call me at the site, and what about the price? Are you going to make me give you guys the rest of my profit off this job?"

"No," Dave said, forgetting that he had resolved to do just the opposite. "I'll invoice you for the full amount, then I'll get a credit put through. But from now on you'll be paying the higher rate for your pipe, which is still ten percent less than full book rates."

"Sure thing. As long as you bump everyone up I'll still get the jobs I want. Just don't you dare undercut me with someone else."

"No," Dave answered, feigning offense. "Of course not, Bud. You're a good customer. I'd like to see you get all the jobs around here."

"Of course you would," Bud replied. "I always use your stuff on the job, even if some of that foreign shit is cheaper."

They exchanged final pleasantries and Bud hung up the phone and headed for the site. Dave called the plant to get confirmation on the ship date and to tell Stan that he would have to credit Bud the rate increase this time around since he had bid the job from the old rates.

Stan approved as usual and Dave called Bud back with the shipment date which seemed to be agreeable to him.

Then Dave sat in the silence of the office and looked at the answering machine which sat on the corner of his desk. He reached out and hit the rewind button and listened while the tape sped back to its beginning. It clicked and stopped, leaving him in silence again. Then he reached forward and hit the play button.

First he heard the messages which had been on the machine that morning, first Katy, then the electrician, then Bud. After that there was a long tone indicating the last message. Then there was silence.

For a moment Dave was suddenly sure that the voices had not recorded. The tape would be like those photographs which people said they took of ghosts, but which showed nothing. For a moment he thought that it was all perhaps a delusion of the guilt reborn.

But then the moment was over, and he heard the voice of his Uncle James. It was not as loud or as clear as it had been when he was listening over the phone, but it was definitely discernible. He could still tell who was talking and what was being said. He listened as the various voices repeated to him what he had heard a few minutes before. His mother would be able to tell whose voices these were; she would confirm what even now seemed unreal to him.

He listened to the voices until that of his Grandpa Morris finished its one-sided conversation. Then came a soft and static-filled silence which lingered as the tape continued to roll.

He stared at the machine and wondered what it was he had taped. He decided that he would call the phone company to see if these transmissions could somehow have been echoing around all these years. But he knew the answer already. Even if it was possible, why would he hear several conversations which had been spaced years apart, and all pertaining to his brother's death? He discarded that possibility.

He reached forward to turn the tape off when the static hissed at him. The hiss was loud, and he instinctively pulled his hand back, though he was unsure why this had been his reaction. He sat and listened as the static seemed to come in waves, first louder, then softer. He didn't remember that happening when he had been listening live. He wondered why the tape behaved this way now.

Then he heard the voice.

It was soft at first, and he had to strain to even tell that it was a voice. How had he missed this? He turned the volume up on the machine and listened as the voice began to take shape.

The voice was distant, and it whined as it spoke. At first there were no discernible words, but as the voice continued he began to understand a few of them. It was the voice of a child. He couldn't make out any sentences, but he could hear more and more of the words which made up those sentences. He took out a pen and began to write down what he could understand.

The first word he could get was 'door.' The next one was 'force.' He heard the word 'door' again before he made out 'danger' and 'brother.' He listened intently, trying to get more of the words. But he could catch no new ones. As the tape rolled the voice became a little clearer and he caught 'many' and 'evil' and 'stop.' He wrote the words down carefully, his hand shaking again as he did so. After another minute he caught 'dead' and 'take.' He noticed that the word 'dead' was followed by the word 'brother' and he began to wonder what this was supposed to mean.

He listened intently but could not make out any more of the words. It seemed that the important ones were being blocked somehow, hissed out by the static, as if something was trying to keep him from hearing them. He picked up on the pattern that the words were appearing in. Each time he came to an unclear one the static would pop again, and again he would be deprived of knowing what it was.

Suddenly the static stopped. There was a second of silence; then the child's voice said one word, clearly and loudly.

"STOP!" came the cry.

Then the loud dial tone.

His hand jumped from the paper and his head jerked up at the word. It sent a shiver of terror throughout his body. His throat tightening as his brain sifted quickly through its past and revealed to him finally the identity of the voice.

Through the static and hissing he could only tell that it was the voice of a child. But that final word, spoken clearly and loudly, had revealed to him the source of the voice which had spoken to him.

The voice belonged to his dead brother.

II
1

Sandra MacElroy walked slowly through the old Victorian styled home in a long dead part of Saint Louis. It felt cold despite the warm summer weather outside. The sunlight illuminated the red satin curtains which glowed on the eastern wall. The sunlight itself seemed muted not only by the curtains but by the damp and musty air which filled the old home. She walked with her eyes closed, her palms held upward before her. A middle-aged couple stood behind her, watching with wonder and terror as she made her way into the main living area. It was a large home for the area, but no one had lived in or near the home for over twenty-three years. The lot on one side of the home was covered with nothing but rubble. There were remnants of a house which had been the lodging place of street people for a few years before a fire meant to warm its transient residents burned it to the ground. On the other side of the big house stood an old abandoned warehouse. It was small as warehouses go, and looked out of place on this particular block. Denise and Sam Smalley had bought the warehouse too, and intended to tear it down and add the lot it occupied to the yard of the home they now stood in. Even then the yard would be only one quarter the size it had been when the house had first been built in 1897. They had intended to renovate the home and sell it, perhaps even live in it for a few years. But their first visit to the home after they had bought it had been at night. Then they had discovered something that explained why the street people had never claimed it.

The floorboards creaked underneath the carpet as Sandra walked. Though there were places where the floor had split, it was sound to walk on. Sam and Denise had checked this out with the help of a contractor. In fact, there were only a few structural problems, none of which were related to the foundation or the frame, all of which could be repaired in time. The house was in fairly good shape considering that it had remained vacant for so long. Despite this there were places on the walls where the wallpaper hung in strips, revealing old and chipped paint beneath. The chandelier which had hung majestically in what had once been a dance room lay shattered on a glazed brick floor which had lost its shine. All of the windows on the first floor had once been broken and subsequently boarded up. The boards had been removed and new windows put in by the previous owner as one of the conditions of the sale. It was one of many conditions which the seller, an old man whom neither Sam nor Denise had met during the entire process, seemed willing and even eager to meet. A few lines had been drawn, but all in all the house had been a good buy, considering of course that by the time they got the house repaired and renovated they would spend three times again what the house had cost them to purchase.

Sandra stopped suddenly and Denise's eyes went immediately to the old stone fireplace. This was automatic for Denise since it was there that she had first seen the apparition. She looked to that place again but now she saw nothing. Sandra seemed to be looking past the fireplace, toward the room which was full of old bookshelves, but very few books. Sandra stood still with her eyes now opened, looking toward the room and raising her hands a few inches more.

"There's something here," she finally said.

"No shit," Sam whispered to Denise. Denise gave him a quick confirming glance.

Then they both jumped as Sandra called out in a deep voice, "Wop!" She jolted as she said it, then she said it again, "Wop!" Her eyes fluttered and her head titled slightly backwards.

"What's she doing?" Denise asked in a slightly panicked voice. Images of what had frightened her so badly once before came again into her already confused mind.

"I don't know," Sam said. "I've never seen anybody do this for real before. I still can't believe we hired her." He paused and looked around the inside of the old house. "Of course, until last Tuesday I wouldn't have believed anyone if they had told me they'd seen what I saw."

"WOP!" Sandra called out again. Then her arms fell to her side and she stared blindly ahead into the room. It was clear that Sandra saw something, but neither Sam nor Denise could see what it was. They looked from the doorway to the girl, then back to the doorway. They stood and waited as she began to walk slowly toward the room.

When Sam and Denise had come to the house on the previous Tuesday night they had in fact heard a noise in the room Sandra was now walking toward. Sam had been going to investigate when Denise saw the thing at the fireplace. Then there was another, louder noise in the room. They had wanted to take a closer look but left the house when they heard a deep yet soft voice beckoning them to enter the old library. Now they stood watching Sandra walk toward that very room. Though they had left the door closed it now stood wide open. They could see the familiar red carpet through the doorway. Neither of them wished to approach that doorway now.

But Sandra did. She too was frightened, but it was an emotion she had grown used to ever since her childhood when seeing images from the past had been a recurring torment for her young mind. Then she had been labelled as a troubled child, one who craved attention and whose craving manifested itself in these silly displays of mock terror. But the terror had been real, and she had learned to bury it until her early teens when puberty had brought not only a strange blood which flowed between her legs, but simultaneously new and more intense connections with a world beyond the one which most people lived in. Through the years she learned to control and use this perception. But she had always been alone. She felt a great responsibility to use what she now referred to as her 'particular perception' for some good. But since most did not believe in her 'particular perception' there were limits to what she could use it for. She had been of occasional help to various police investigations, but her integrity always came into question when she could not maintain a hundred percent accuracy. It was as if everyone else expected her to always understand and correctly interpret the things she saw and heard and felt. Most often she could not explain the things she did understand to the average person since they did not have any common points of reference.

So now she spent her time giving seances and helping people who had 'ghost problems', either real or imagined. The seances were not held in a dark room with people paying a premium to speak to various departed souls. Her seances were always performed by appointment, at the dwelling place of the person requesting her services. She did these only by referral and never advertised, thus cutting to a minimum exposure to 'crackpots' or worse, curiosity seekers or the media. Her references kept her busy, and well paid. The couple whose home she now stood in had been referred to her by a couple she had worked on and off with for the past three years. Their situation fell under the heading of 'ghost problem.' She had known when she had first seen the house that this particular problem was not of the imagined variety. The cool electricity which coursed through her body now confirmed this. She had seen the 'shadows' as she called them when they had walked in the door. These shadows were not the ghosts themselves, but a soft and misty overlay of the house as it had been at some other time. With her physical eyes she saw the same flooring and walls and fixtures which the Smalleys saw. But with the eyes of her special perception she could see different, newer looking flooring. Indistinct shadows of furnishings where they had stood at one time filled the living area. She could only make out one as a piano, and there was a significant event surrounding the piano, but she did not know what this event was. All of the remaining images of the furnishings were too formless to determine what they had once been.

Now she stood in the doorway to a room which provided her with much sharper images than the living room had. The images hardened before her and an involuntary "Wop!" made its way from her chest. She had known it was coming, and she sensed another. They were harmless reminders that her body did not always comprehend its position between the two worlds which her mind and soul occupied.

The room before her became more solid, and then she could see that the red carpet was a deeper shade in one place, a deeper and wetter shade of red. She could hear a falling body as it hit the floor, but saw only a swirling mist as it collapsed before her. She walked into the room; her hands held out before her. They tingled and her fingers shook as she approached the indistinct mist and the red, wet carpet.

She got to one knee and reached into the mist. It was very cold, but it refused to solidify. This meant that she might never know who or what that mist had been. Its energy had been expended some time in the past, and there was not enough of it left in the present to make a distinct image. In the near future it would not exist even as a mist.

But she could feel the wetness of the floor and she knew at a touch that it was the blood of the thing which lay formless before her. She raised her wet hand from the carpet and looked at it. Blood covered it, and a small drop fell from her hand back to the carpet. As she looked at her hand the blood faded, though the floor before her remained wet with it. She stood and looked about the room trying to see more, but nothing changed.

Suddenly she felt a tremendous shock run through her body. Then she heard a shrill scream coming from the living room behind her. The scream had come from the world of the living, it was the scream of Denise Smalley.

Sandra turned around and looked through the doorway back to the living area. She could tell from her first look that it had changed. Already she could make out more of what had been the indistinct furnishings. She stood and walked back to the doorway and looked into the living room.

Sandra saw Denise standing near the center of the living room. Denise was standing in the middle of an old sofa that she could neither see nor feel. She stood with one hand over her mouth, the other pointing toward the fireplace. At her side stood Sam, muttering some indistinct and terrified words and staring in the direction which Denise was pointing.

Sandra looked to the fireplace and saw what now terrified the Smalleys. What Sandra saw was a very clear impression of a man dressed in late nineteenth century clothing. His hands were in his pockets and he stood staring in Sandra's direction. No doubt what the Smalleys saw was much less distinct, but certainly they could see at least the misty outline of a human.

Sandra buried her childhood fears and spoke to the man-that-was. Though she heard her own words, the Smalleys did not. She waited and repeated herself. Sometimes the images were crossed into present-time and would speak. Sometimes they would not. This one finally did.

"I'm so lonely," it said in a voice which revealed itself to Sam and Denise as a soft but meaningless whisper. Denise screamed through her fingers. Sandra heard the voice, and began to converse with the image in its own purgatorial language.

2

"So she was killed by the man?" Denise asked, her hands still shaking nervously.

They sat in the living area of Sandra's home which doubled as her office. The walls were decorated with ornate reminders of times gone by. The central motif was in fact late nineteenth century, since it seemed to be this era which most often visited Sandra. She assumed that this was based on geography more than anything else. In Boston her encounters might have been more ancient, and in Europe even older. In fact her trip to the castles of England had shown her the oldest apparition she had ever beheld, though it apparently had been completely invisible to those who had walked around and through it. But in Saint Louis most of the activity seemed centered around the late nineteenth century, and she had lived in Saint Louis all of her life.

"No, she was killed by the man's brother. It was apparently a murder driven by jealousy. The man I spoke with was the dead woman's husband. His brother had engaged in an affair with his wife. The man had discovered this some time before the murder, a few weeks before

I would guess." Sandra leaned forward and took her coffee cup from the small table which separated her from the Smalleys. They sat in the large sofa, spellbound by her words. It was a condition of her customers which she had gotten used to. It was times like these where the faces she looked into showed ample amounts of either wonder or disbelief, or a mixture of the two. Denise showed almost exclusively the former. Sam showed a little of the latter. "So one day the man returned to find his wife dead, killed by the hands of his own brother."

"You say you saw her body in the room?" Sam asked.

"Not really her body, more like an outline of her body."

"Were they important people?"

This was a common question. People seemed to think that ghosts were almost always the spirits of rather important people, or rather violent ones. In truth the mold was a random one, catching in it most often the spirit of the common human. This was the case here.

"From the clothing the man wore, and the furnishings in the home, I would say that he was upper middle class, but not necessarily 'well-off.' I would guess that the home had been inherited by the older brother, and most of the original furnishings sold off so that the money could be split or given to the younger brother." She took a sip of the still too hot coffee. "This is all just speculation on my part, however."

"So now what do we do?"

Sandra hated this question. People assumed that since she could often see and hear what went on in the realm of the spirits that she could somehow control it as well. In the years since her youth she had learned how to communicate with that world which had tormented her, though even this had most often been unsuccessful. Much more than that simple communication did not seem possible, at least not yet.

"I would say you have to decide if you can live with this or not."

Sam and Denise raised their eyebrows almost simultaneously. Sandra knew what would come next; it would just be a matter of which one said it. It was Sam who spoke.

"You mean you can't get rid of this thing?"

Sandra put her coffee down and looked into Sam's confused eyes. "I am merely an inspector," she reminded him, "not a repairman."

Sam had become caught up in the drama of the event and had forgotten or ignored Sandra's repeated explanation that she would be able to tell him what she found, but able to do little about it. Now he was sure that this had not been the case, that she had somehow promised to also rid them of the problem. That was why Sandra often asked for the bulk of her payment up front, especially with new people.

More disbelief crept into Sam's face. "You mean we're stuck with this thing?"

"There is no ill will coming from the apparition. Aside from a little door moving and some cold spots you won't notice him most of the time. From what I can tell, you would be lucky to see him a dozen times in a season. I couldn't live there because I can see and hear so much more, and all those images can be quite distracting. After a while it really wears me out. But there's really no danger here, and it could stop at any time. It will certainly become less severe as the years pass." Sandra paused for a moment and tried to read their expressions. "There seemed to be a substantial amount of residual energy coming from the spot in front of the fireplace. My guess is that he stood there for hours, perhaps even a full day while his wife lay dead or dying in the room. I would also guess that he died soon afterwards, probably within the same year. His troubled spirit probably returned to that place where it had so recently mourned, though again I am only guessing."

"So we're stuck with this thing?" Sam asked again.

"It's really not so bad," Sandra said.

"That's easy for you to say. You're not the one who's going to have to live with it."

"I live with that and more every day," she reminded the man sitting across from her. The disbelief was more prominent on his face, and she knew that she was losing him. A year or two from now he would write the whole experience off as a hoax of some kind, forgetting the genuine terror that had gripped him in that house.

But Denise's face still showed the wonder mixed with horror. She would agree with her husband that they should sell the place soon, though it would be two and a half years before they would finally sell it to another young couple such as themselves. By then the apparitions would be no more than a few cold spots to the new, less sensitive owners.

3

Sandra lay alone in her queen-sized bed as she had done most nights for over a year now. There had been a time, early last spring, when she had not been alone. But it wasn't possible to hide her special vision forever, and it was always this which drove them away. Over the years she had learned not to grow too attached to a man until she had explained her gift. Sometimes this worked. Other times she grew to love the man anyway, knowing what heartbreak it would bring. There had been a time or two when it seemed that things would work despite the gift, but her hopes had been dashed then too. It seemed that in the long run her particular perception was something too weird for a good man to put up with.

She was a very attractive girl, her long red hair surrounding a complexion untainted by the freckles each of her sisters had gotten. She kept herself in shape, and her special vision kept her mortgage paid and her house well furnished. She was a wonderful prize with a terrible secret, one which always proved fatal to the blossoming relationship. The bad experiences had made her wary. Now when she found a man she liked she went into the relationship with reservations and often ruined it before it got serious enough for her to reveal her terrible secret. For over a year now she hadn't even tried, turning down all offers and overtures, preferring the silence of loneliness to the pain of heartbreak.

She lay looking up at her ceiling, wondering again why she had been chosen for this gift which seemed at times a curse. It was a question which had gone unanswered for twenty-seven years, and it went unanswered again tonight. From time to time she liked to think that there was some very important, perhaps history-altering task for which she had been made. Perhaps something lay waiting in her future which would make her something more than a 'ghost chaser.' But then she always came back to herself and realized that her life was no more special than anyone else's.

She drifted to sleep with these thoughts in her head, as she did most nights.

4

Then she saw the demon on the wheel.

She found herself floating above a street, looking down on a scene with which she was unfamiliar. It was a sunny day, and she could feel the warmth of the sun, though she could not see her own arms or legs. She looked down and saw a street lined with homes which all looked very similar to each other and older model cars, though the cars looked to be mostly in good condition.

Then she saw a tall man walking into one of the homes and realized from his clothes and his haircut that this was not somewhere she had ever been. In fact, this place was not even in the present, but in the past. She had experienced dreams about the past before, but they were like her waking visions in that there were elements of the present overlain with those from the past. But this vision was pure and solid, as if it were from the present.

Then she heard the rattling of the plastic wheel and the grinding of the small stones which the little boy on the Big Wheel was riding over. The little boy rode down a sidewalk, his older brother watching him from the yard of the closest home. The older brother seemed dismayed, as if there were other things which he would really rather be doing.

Then the little boy turned suddenly down the driveway and into the street. Sandra floated over the scene and something inside of her stirred as she watched the drama unfold.

"Mom's going to kill you if she sees you in the street!" the older brother called out. The little boy rode on, acting as if he couldn't hear his older brother. The older boy watched for a moment, then looked back at the house. If his mother came out now he would be made to answer for his little brother's actions. It was always this way.

The older brother walked across the yard and called to the little boy who rode defiantly into the very middle of the road, ignoring the calls of his older brother.

"Hey!" the tall boy called out. "Get your butt out of the road!" he called.

The little boy looked back, but rode on. He looked back at his brother; a stare of defiance etched on his face. The look on the older brother's face turned first to anger, then to fear.

Sandra saw the truck as it turned the corner and she knew what was about to happen. She watched as the older brother began running after the little boy, screaming at him. She watched as the little boy looked back first in defiance, then in confusion. He could not understand the urgency in his brother's voice.

The truck came down the road heading straight for the little boy.

Then she saw the monster on the wheel.

The little boy's face grew and stretched. His teeth grew out of his face and his neck grew longer and twisted. The hands on the plastic handlebars grew long and crooked fingers with razor sharp claws on the ends. As the truck approached, the monster grew more hideous.

The older brother continued to scream and call out for his little brother. Apparently he could not see what Sandra saw. She tried to look away, but could not. She watched as the monster grew. Its warped and twisted body covered the small child's toy, and it stared back at the brother who looked toward it in terror not at what it was, but at what was about to happen to his little brother.

She heard the monster call back to the tall boy.

"Help me, Davey," it said. "You killed me, now you have to help me."

Then the terrible creature looked skyward and Sandra knew that it could see her. She tried to scream, but could not. The tall boy looked ahead at the Big Wheel and the approaching truck.

Sandra heard the beginning of a hideous laugh when the truck finally struck the creature and splattered its green guts everywhere.

The truck slid on and hit the tall boy, throwing him into some shrubs beside the road. The monster lay scattered in pieces across the road.

Then, as the picture froze and the images faded, she heard again the terrible gravelly laugh of the monster.

III
1

Dave awoke to utter blackness.

He lay still, listening to the heavy pounding of his own heart. His hands tingled and his eyes hurt. He lay listening for the sound of his brother's voice which still echoed in his ears. The dream was a fresh terror in his mind.

The dream.

It had tortured him again, only this time something strange had happened. This time his brother had spoken to him, had begged for his help, had accused Dave of killing him. This time the dream had seemed more real than ever, and the sweat which ran in a line down the side of his forehead and onto the pillow attested to this.

He turned his head to the left, but could not see the light of the clock which rested on the stand next to the bed. He reached out and knocked over the glass of water he had placed there that evening. He listened to the trickle of the water as it ran across the nightstand and onto the carpet. Normally when this happened he swore, but this time he simply moved his hand along until he found the clock. He had not knocked it off, so perhaps he had unplugged it. He felt along the top of the nightstand until he found the base of his lamp. Then he felt his way up to the switch which he clicked once clockwise. Nothing happened. He turned it again, but still there was no light.

Then he noticed that the dark was absolute. The glow from the lights of town did not softly light the back of his curtains as they should have. The power was out. He listened for the wind, but tonight it was warm and still. Sometimes when the power in Cisco went out it was because of a storm. Sometimes it just went out. Tonight another transformer had failed, the third in as many months. The 'experts' had looked the city's power system over time and again, but the problem could not be found, so the city simply kept a stock of the transformers and a special portion of the budget available to meet the problem. The transformers too had been tested, but they were manufactured by the same company that made the transformers for nearby Eastland and Cross Plains, and those towns had no similar problems with their respective power supplies.

Dave sat up in his bed and fumbled in the top drawer of the nightstand for the flashlight he knew to be there. He found it and turned it on, but the batteries had gone dead again. It seemed that this was always the problem. Batteries in Cisco seemed to have very little shelf life. Batteries which had been in the store for more than six months were never good. These had been fresh, but had been put into the flashlight last winter. Now it was summer and the batteries had long since passed their ability to light the small bulb. Dave dropped the light and got out of the bed. He walked ahead with his hands in front of him until he reached the wall. Then he walked along the wall to the door. Using the wall as his guide Dave made his way through the house to the garage where he kept his rechargeable flashlight plugged into the wall. He stumbled through the junk which had begun to pile up and found the flashlight which he used to guide himself back into the kitchen.

He walked to the counter by the stove and flipped the switch on the coffee maker to start the coffee, forgetting for a moment that it would not work without power. He cursed the machine and walked to the sink where he turned on the water. It ran for a little while before becoming hot. The power had not been off long enough for the water in the water heater to cool off. He got the old jar of instant coffee out of the cabinet and made himself a warm cup.

Dave sat down at the table and took a deep breath. He closed his eyes for a moment and again he saw clearly the face of his brother, looking back and accusing him. He opened his eyes and looked down to the table which was covered with the shadows cast by the odds and ends which rested between him and the flashlight on the counter.

What was this all about? What was happening to him?

When he had finally gotten home that evening he listened to the tape again. He had copied it onto a standard-sized cassette at the office and brought it home to analyze. He decided that for now he would not call his mother since she was not well, and the stress would only make her mind more restless. He knew what he was hearing, and after listening to it many times he knew that it was real, that he was not going crazy. But what did it all mean, and why the dream?

Dave sat and thought about it all as he drank the bitter coffee. He sat wondering about what he could do, or if he needed to do anything at all. When he had been a child, when his brother had still been alive, he had spent some time interested in the occult. His mother had not approved, so he had done most of his reading and experimenting in the attic or the woods behind the house. He had even bought a Ouija board once, but his mother had found it and burned it and grounded him for a whole month. He was sorry for having lost the board, but there was relief too because there had been some things which had scared him, some things which he didn't know whether to believe or not. Only when he actually saw the truck barreling towards his brother eight months after the burning of the board had he remembered that he had been told about the incident. That was where some of the guilt had come from, though he had never told this to anyone. Dave wondered how many other things he had been told by the mysterious board but had buried deep in his mind.

Dave looked out the front window into the darkness and wondered again about the dream. Why, after all these years, had it changed? Did the dream mean something that it hadn't before? What had his brother meant by asking for help? Was that supposed to be a reference only to the past, or was something deeper going on?

Dave stared into the darkness and he wondered.

As he stared, the lights of the city came back on and the growling coffee pot caused him to jump. He smirked at himself and then rose to empty his cup of lukewarm coffee.

2

Dave grabbed a book titled "Interpreting Your Dreams" and looked at the table of contents. It looked like it could hold the answers to some of his questions so he held onto it and began skimming the titles of the books which surrounded it.

It was Saturday and Dave had decided to pay the McKinney boy to do the yard work today while he tooled around in the library looking for some answers to his new questions. He had been waiting at the library's steps, unaware that it did not open until ten o'clock on Saturdays. He saw people inside the library he recognized, but none he normally associated with. He acknowledged each with a nod, but no words. It was as if the library inspired a new, more solemn kind of communication. He was thankful for that.

He gathered the books which seemed on the surface to promise some answers and walked to a table where he put them down and took a seat. He decided that he would stay at the library and do his work, a habit from his college days. If he checked out the books and took them home there was no doubt his questions would only be answered by another trip to the library, and there was always the chance he would lose one of the books, or fail to return it on time. This was something which had always been a silent but very real fear of his. It was one which in his youth he had shared with many of his friends, and which many of the children who came to this library felt as well. Dave was certain it had something to do with Miss Collier, the rickety old woman who had been the librarian for as long as Dave could remember. To the best of his remembrance, she had also always been rickety and old, though he knew that this was not possible.

Dave picked up the first book and began looking through it. The writing was both dry and simple, and seemed to concentrate more on speculation than fact. He found only vague references to some dream symbols, but nothing at all about the dead or dreams about them.

He shuffled through the books until he found one which went into some depth about dreams of the departed, but stopped short of offering a solid interpretation or explanation. Here too this book wandered into the realm of speculation and conjecture.

Then Dave felt a warm breath on his neck and turned around to see a lovely yet disturbing young girl with black hair and dark eyes looking at him.

"Fascinating stuff, huh?" she asked him. Her breath smelled sweet, like dried rose petals.

"Yea," he responded, his normally quick and conversational manner temporarily forgotten.

"Looking for something?" she asked. Her eyes were seductive and the question seemed full of double entendre.

"Yea," Dave answered. "I mean, I was just watching a show on dreams last night and it got my interest up." Her eyes seemed to pierce him, then she smiled and walked around the table where she sat across from him. She had a couple of books herself. It was a warm day, but she dressed in dark colors. She looked familiar, though he did not know her name.

"Mind if I sit here?" she asked, already seated.

"No, that's fine."

She was dark complected and although her clothing fit loosely Dave could tell she was well built. Her face was a little sharp, and created almost an eerie contrast with her full and probing eyes. She might have been twenty years old, or she might have been thirty. He could not really tell. He decided that despite her approach, which was quite forward for a town like Cisco, he would very much like to keep the conversation going.

"What are you doing here?" he asked. The question suddenly sounded too inquisitive, not casual enough, but it was out already.

"Just boning up on some old subjects," she answered. Her vocabulary seemed focused, and Dave could not help but take everything she said as a possible overture. This was not normally how he reacted, but this was a unique situation.

She raised one of her books to show Dave the cover. It was "Dreams and Their Meanings." His eyes registered the surprise.

"How odd," he exclaimed. "Did you see the same show?"

"Yes," she answered, knowing he was lying about the show, but also knowing that she could currently think of no better response.

"I'm sorry," he exclaimed as he remembered his manners, "I'm Dave Chatburn."

"Yes," she answered, "I know. You work with Henderson Pipe." She watched his reaction which was what she had hoped it would be. "I'm Colleen VanZandt."

She reached across the table and Dave took her hand in his, pumping it gently more than shaking it. The name seemed familiar. Then he remembered that VanZandt was the name of the family which had at one time owned over half of the land in Eastland County. Neither her clothes nor her jewelry seemed to indicate that she was from this family whose descendants still could be found in many of the towns in the county.

"How do you know me?" Dave asked.

"I make it my business to know about people here," she replied.

"What kind of business is that?" he asked.

"Just my business," she replied, slight annoyance registering in her lovely round eyes. "Actually, you have some of the books I need to do my research with and I was wondering if I could share them with you?" she asked. "These two stay pretty general and really don't address my questions."

"I'm having the same problem," Dave replied. "I think all of the books which get down to it have probably been thrown out by Miss Collier." Miss Collier, a devout and lifelong Baptist, was known to perform her own version of censorship from time to time, eliminating such books as were offensive or generally lacking in uplifting qualities.

"You're probably right," Colleen answered. "Why don't we head to Abilene and go to the public library there. We may be able to find more of what we're looking for." Once again her eyes suggested double meaning, and Dave accepted the offer.

3

They got into Dave's Grand Am and got onto the interstate. Abilene was a forty-five-minute drive, but it was the only city of any size within a hundred miles.

"So what did you think of the show?" Colleen asked.

"Oh, it was fine," Dave answered, hesitating for a moment.

"What did you think about the part where they talked about dreaming of the past?" she asked.

Dave looked to the girl, then back to the road. He felt as if she was fishing, but he wasn't prepared to spill his guts, so he continued with the game. "I thought it was pretty interesting."

She was silent for a moment. The sound of the road passing beneath the car became loud, so he turned on the radio to a country station. It was a song he normally liked, though today the words 'I'm just a ghost in this house' disturbed him, so he changed the channel.

"So, what do you do?" Dave asked, trying to change the subject.

"I work with people who are having problems."

"Are you like a counselor or something?" he asked.

"Something like that," she answered.

He looked at her again and smiled. "Do you always try to sound mysterious when you talk with someone?" he asked. Her eyes did not change at all and she did not answer. He looked back to the road and listened to the radio. It was a sunny day and the warmth and the light were comforting.

After a few more minutes she spoke again.

"Did you have a disturbing dream last night?" she asked him.

He debated on how to answer, then decided there would be no harm in telling the truth. "I had a bad dream, but I do from time to time."

"What was it about?" she asked.

"Something in my past. Something I don't like to talk about."

He could feel her eyes on him, but he continued to look ahead.

"I had a dream last night too, and I saw a young boy who looked a lot like you," she said.

"Really?" he asked, trying to figure out what her new game was. He supposed she was trying to get him into something, or maybe sell him something. Her questions seemed odd.

"Yes, and I saw another little boy too, only he got hit by a truck while the older boy watched."

Dave could not hide his shock and he felt a warmth run through his body.

"Your face is red," she said to him. "Did I say something to disturb you?"

"No," he lied, "not really."

They drove on in silence again. After a few minutes Dave spoke again.

"What was the little boy doing?" Dave asked.

"He was riding a tricycle or something like that," she explained. "He was riding down the middle of the road; he wasn't watching where he was going. He got hit by the truck and splattered onto the asphalt while the older boy watched."

Still he did not look at her. Who was she really? How could she know about his dream? He had spoken of it only to his mother and his psychologist, and that had been many years ago. How had she come to learn of all of this?

"Okay," he said finally, "what do you want?"

She continued to look at him, but did not speak. Finally he turned to look into her gaze which was both piercing and accusatory. Nonetheless he maintained his composure.

"I asked you what the hell you're up to," he said in a soft but firm tone.

"I'm trying to find out why we had the same dream," she explained.

Dave sat considering her words. How could she know about the dream? What could she possibly want from him?

But what if she was telling the truth?

This thought flashed through his mind and took him back for a moment. He decided that it was certainly a possibility, but most likely not the reality.

"I guess I'm just supposed to believe this?" he asked.

"I don't care whether you do or not," she replied. "I just think that something strange is going on and I'm curious." She smiled at him. "It's my nature."

"Did Doctor Hanlin tell you anything about this dream?" he asked. It was a trick question of sorts. Doctor Hanlin was the doctor who had treated him.

"Who's that?" she asked.

Well, if she was lying then that last tactic didn't work. What could he lose by playing the game? As long as it didn't cost him any money there really was no reason not to. And there was always the possibility she might have some of the answers he was looking for.

"Okay," he said. "I'm sorry I didn't believe you, but this kind of thing just doesn't happen every day."

"That's okay," she said. "Disbelief is common in my line of work."

"What line of work is that?" Dave asked again.

"I told you, I help people."

"Help them what?" Dave probed.

"Help them figure things out."

"Things like this dream?" he asked.

"Yea," she replied. "Things like this dream."

"So what's it gonna cost me to have my dream analyzed?" Dave asked.

"Nothing, right now," she responded. "I told you, I'm curious. I'll do my work and you can do yours. If we find anything interesting then it will benefit both of us."

"So when does it start costing me?" he asked.

"When it becomes work," she replied, clearly becoming annoyed.

"When is that?"

"Whenever I don't feel like looking into it anymore, but you want my insight. Or whenever we have to use my resources to get answers."

"What kind of resources are those?" he asked.

She was silent for a moment. "Just the tools of my trade. The things I use to make my living."

"Like what?" he asked, still curious at just what line of work that might be.

"You're too curious," she commented. "That's good."

"Good for who?" he asked.

"Good for both of us," she answered. Then she reached over and put her hand on his leg. "I think you'll be glad you met me."

He looked to her warm eyes and felt himself becoming excited. He thought then that he was glad already.

4

That evening they talked over dinner. They ate in Abilene at one of Dave's favorite steak restaurants. They had spent a good part of the afternoon reading and talking about what they had found, which had really turned out to be very little. Dave found that Colleen's knowledge of the supernatural seemed to be deep, deeper than the average person might possess. He wondered if this knowledge was one which extended to many realms, or if it was a result of a more than passing interest in the supernatural. He came to believe from her speech and clothes as well as her mannerisms that perhaps her expertise was a result of this more than passing interest, and he hoped to discover more about it over dinner. He also harbored a deeper hope that dinner might lead to discussions of things more physical than spiritual.

"You know this place well," Colleen said. It was a statement, not a question. She seemed to have offered many of these kinds of statements during the day, most of them right.

"Yes, my father used to bring our family here on Sundays after church. That was a long time ago."

"Your father is dead now." Another statement.

"Yes. So is my brother."

"And it was your brother who was the little boy in the dream."

Though they had worked together during the day he had never revealed that it had actually been him and his brother in the dream, nor had he suggested that the dream reflected any real-life events. Dave had simply portrayed that he had experienced this same dream and that he too wished to discern its meaning. Apparently she had seen through this for some time. Maybe he had mentioned just now that his brother was dead so that he could confront the suspicion that she did know.

"Yea," he admitted. He decided that now there would be no harm. "That was my brother in the dream."

"And you."

"Sure, me too."

"And this is something which really happened," she stated.

"A long time ago."

"So why has it come back?" she asked.

"I was hoping that you were about to tell me, or is this where you start charging?"

She smiled. "I would if I knew, but that is one thing I was hoping you could tell me. Has there been any significant event of late that would trigger these dreams? Has someone else close to you died? Has an important anniversary of some kind recently passed?"

"No," he answered, "I've already thought of all of that. There's absolutely nothing that I can think of."

The waiter came and took their orders and they discussed further the dream and the things they had found during the day. All in all there had really been nothing new uncovered, and their questions were as numerous as they had been when they had met in the Cisco library that morning.

5

After dinner Dave drove Colleen to her house. As they approached Dave saw a sign he had driven past probably a hundred times. The sign was in the shape of a hand and promised secrets of the future revealed. Suddenly he understood just what line of work she was in and he smiled in casual disbelief. The house was set at the edge of an empty field. The nearest house was two blocks away.

"This is your place?" he asked.

"You don't like it?" she responded.

"I didn't know anybody actually lived here."

"What did you think, that most people come to have their palms read during business hours? Most of my customers come after hours, mostly after dark. Many of them seem very nervous that I might let on that they've been here. They're afraid that the community will turn their backs on them like they have on me." She looked out the window at her house in a dreamy fashion. "You'd be surprised at some of the people that come in here. I even work with a preacher in town from time to time."

"I figured an old gypsy woman sat behind an old wooden table from eight to five in there." It was meant in a lighthearted manner, but Colleen seemed to take offense. "Well," Dave spoke again to relieve the tension he had created, "I never guessed I would spend a day like this. It's been very different."

She continued to look out the window. A large truck passed them by and shook Dave's car slightly. Dark clouds were forming in the west, clouds which would soon drop ample amounts of rain all over the Big Country.

Colleen opened her door and got out of the car without speaking. Then she turned and faced Dave. "Come by if you need any help with this," she said. Then she closed the door before he could reply. She walked slowly into the house and Dave wished he too was walking in. Instead he watched while she closed the door without looking at him. Then he put the car into drive and pulled away.

6

Colleen closed the door and fell back upon it. She had asked this man a lot of questions; she had looked through the books which should have been helpful. Still the dream remained fresh in her mind, fresh and as mysterious as it had been that morning.

She walked across the floor and into the back bedroom where a small black and white television rested on an old table with one leg which was shorter than the others. She turned the television on and walked to her single bed. Then she grabbed the bag of chips on the antique table next to the bed and stared into the television set, not caring really what time it was or what was on. She was in the watching mode and something as mindless as Wheel of Fortune was just the right thing.

She sat and watched the show as the storm moved into Cisco from the west. Her lights flickered from time to time and the picture on the television danced as the wind picked up and tossed the power lines about. She figured they would probably lose another transformer tonight. They seemed to go out on their own from time to time anyway, but they almost always went out when a storm came through.

Then she saw something on the television which stopped her hand on its way to her mouth. She held the chip a foot from her mouth and stared into the television at the odd show which no longer featured Pat and Vanna, but instead featured a small child riding away from the camera on a Big Wheel. She watched as the child rode away from her, and as the truck came around the corner in the distance. She watched in wonder and terror as the truck smashed the child into the pavement, then collided with the cameraman. The screen went black for a moment and then the sound came back. At first she heard whispers, whispers she knew were coming from a very cold and distant place. There were pleas for help and words of warning, but most of it was impossible to make out.

But then one of the voices explained that it would like to buy a vowel, and Pat and Vanna reappeared and continued as if nothing had happened.

Colleen dropped the chip and stared at the television for a moment. She wondered what was going on. First the dream, then this. She had always been in tune with the spiritual world, but she had never experienced anything quite like this. And why this incident from this particular man's past? And why now?

She decided that she had to know what was going on. She got off the bed and walked to the small table by the dresser where a phone rested. As she reached for it the phone rang and caused her to jump. She reached out and picked up the phone.

"Hello?" she said.

At first there was a silence, then a whisper.

"Don't let them through."

It was the voice of a child, though there was something horrible about it which she could not pin down.

"Don't let who through?" she asked.

"Don't let them through," the voice repeated.

She griped the phone harder, knowing that the voice she heard was not a voice from this world.

Then there was a brilliant flash of light and an immediate clap of thunder as an old oak tree less than a mile from her house was split in two.

"Hello?" came a voice from the other end. Now it was the voice of a man.

"Who is this?" Colleen asked.

"It's Dave, Dave Chatburn?"

She turned to face the window and looked outside as the rain began to pour down. "What the hell is going on?" she asked.

"I just had something strange happen to me," Dave explained. "I saw something on the television which shouldn't have been there. I thought since you do what you do, I mean, well," Dave's voice was beginning to break. "I don't know who else to tell about this. I don't even know if you'll believe me, but it's too much, it's just too much."

Colleen stared out the window. She knew what Dave had seen.

"I tried to call you," Dave went on, "but at first all I got was this small voice telling me not to let them through."

"I got the same thing," Colleen offered.

"What the hell is going on?" Dave asked.

"I asked you first," Colleen responded.

Neither one spoke as they both experienced some level of shock, some distant understanding of what was happening to the both of them. Then there was another flash of light and the lights went out and the phone went dead.

Colleen put the phone back in its cradle and stared at it for a moment. Then she walked slowly across the room. The sun was just setting and the room reflected the grey glow from outside. She walked to the bed and sat on its end looking out the window, watching the lightning as it streaked its white patterns across the sky. She watched the lightning and wondered what she was getting into.

IV
1

Sandra stared blankly at the price on the edge of the aisle before her. The sticker displayed the sale price for a four-pack of toilet paper, and even gave a breakdown of cost per roll. She stared at the sticker, but didn't really look at it. She had been watching it now for almost a minute while her mind wandered.

It was a cold and cloudy day in Saint Louis. It was supposed to warm up the next day, but then the weekend would be over and most of the citizens of Saint Louis would observe the warm and sunny day from the confines of the buildings they worked in. But today was gloomy. The clouds were thick, and even at ten o'clock in the morning it looked and felt like nightfall.

The night had been a restless one for Sandra. She had tossed and turned while terrible and mysterious dreams disturbed her sleep. She did not wake many times, but her sleeping hours were not very restful. She could not remember much about most of the dreams, except the one she had dreamt again about the monster on the Big Wheel. The other dreams were nothing but incomplete pictures in her now awakened mind. One piece of one of those dreams seemed as if it were about to shake loose, and this is what locked her gaze on the price sticker before her. A young man pushed his cart quickly around her, giving her a puzzled gaze. She blocked out the things around her and looked hard into that corner of her mind where the faint images had been stored, and suddenly that piece fell and exploded.

Her eyes widened and she took in a short and sudden breath through her nose as she remembered what had been hidden from her by her subconscious mind. She remembered that in her dream she'd been standing in the center of a dark and empty room. The walls were grey and featureless, much as the morning sky had been. She'd stood naked in the center of that room, holding her arms out in front of her. There was something terrible in the room, and the feeling grew. Then the darkness grew. The darkness was deep, but it was not empty. It had enveloped her slowly, and it was terribly cold.

Then a small strip of light had suddenly appeared on one of the walls. The darkness was drawn to that crack, and forced itself against it, leaving her alone again in the center of the room.

But then she had seen that she was not alone. Standing next to her was a little boy with one arm missing and a torn and bloodied face. The image was awful, but she'd felt no terror, just apprehension. The boy said something about the dark; he told her something important.

But that's all she could remember. The rest of the dream lay locked in that corner of her mind, and it refused to budge.

Finally she took her eyes from the price sticker, not even knowing what had been written on it. Later she would discover that she had forgotten to pick up any toilet paper.

She walked through the remaining aisles of the store in a preoccupied state, trying to see beyond the limited view she had been given of that one dream. But the view was blocked, and it was becoming clear it was going to stay this way. She walked down the final aisle and picked up her chocolate chip ice cream before finally going to the check stand. It was busy for a Sunday morning, but still not too bad. She was through the line in less than ten minutes, and the trip ended up costing her just thirty dollars and some change.

A young boy helped her take her groceries to her car and load them in the back. As she thanked him she heard her name being called out.

"Sandra!" came the familiar voice.

Another reason she shopped on Sunday mornings was that this was the best time not to run into people who knew her. She seemed always to run into them if she went to the store during the weekday evenings or any time Saturday. It was alright when she was wanting some new work, but not when all she wanted to do was go shopping.

Sandra closed her trunk and turned in the direction of the voice to see a very heavy woman of medium height and wearing horrendously colorful clothes coming toward her, waving an orange and pink polyester scarf. Sandra smiled at the woman as she put the name to the face. Sandra was good at this.

"Hello, Clara," Sandra called cordially. "How are you doing today?"

"Just wonderful," came the reply. Clara walked the rest of the distance to Sandra and seemed to be out of breath, even though she had not broken into so much as a brisk pace. "I just wanted to thank you for working with the Deaton family last month. They thought you were marvelous, and they haven't had a single problem since you came by."

The Deaton family consisted of an older couple and their quite young son. The "problem" had in reality been nothing more than overactive imaginations coupled with a desire for variety. This had manifested itself as an imagined ghost which was haunting their attic and whispering obscene things to Mrs. Deaton. Although Sandra normally just diagnosed problems, it was clear they wanted a fix. Since the problem was imaginary, Sandra obliged. She had brought out her bowls and fake potions and other props and had rid the Deatons' minds of their ghost. It was what they had really wanted, a good show to talk about at the next dinner party. Sandra grew tired of this kind of work, but it often paid well.

"It was really no problem," Sandra explained.

"Well," Clara continued, "I have a friend who lives in Springfield, Illinois, and she's been having some really weird things going on in her house." Clara looked around for a moment to make sure no one was listening. "She thinks it's her dead uncle who used to molest her. She thinks maybe he's come back to get her again."

"Really, Clara, I don't like to travel out of town much..."

"Oh, it's really not that far, just about two hours up I-55 and you'll be there."

"I really don't know when I could fit her in, and it would be an all-day ordeal..."

"I told her how good you were, and she has plenty of money. She'll pay anything to get away from this thing."

"Clara, I'd love to help, but..."

"Oh, wonderful," Clara interrupted again. "I'll tell her you'll give her a call." Clara dug in her purse for the piece of paper with her friend's name and number. After a little fumbling around she pulled it out and handed it to Sandra. Sandra said nothing, but simply smiled a forced smile.

"Will you please call her this week?" Clara asked with her best begging eyes. "This thing is about to drive her crazy."

"I'll try," Sandra said, trying desperately not to commit to anything, but knowing that somehow she already had.

"Oh, I knew you'd come through for me." Clara grabbed Sandra's hand and patted it quickly. "Thank you again, I don't know what I'd do without you."

"You're welcome, Clara."

Clara walked away, her mission accomplished. Sandra had managed to avoid this woman for three months, but it was always just a matter of time before Clara caught up with her. She knew it was going to happen soon because Clara had been leaving messages on her answering machine pretty regularly for the past two weeks. Sandra glanced down at the sheet of paper which Clara had handed to her. She really did not want to drive to Springfield, especially to put on another show for one of Clara's attention-starved friends. She stuffed the sheet of paper into the pocket of her pants, got into her car and headed for home as she debated whether or not to let poor Clara down.

2

Sandra drove past the rows of retail centers to the winding road which led eventually to her home. She passed at first small houses which were fairly well-kept with standard quarter-acre lots. A mile further down this road the homes and yards became larger. She drove past rows of trees and fairly well-kept yards, thinking again about her dreams, trying desperately to remember more.

Suddenly a child appeared out in front of her car. It was a small boy on a Big Wheel. He shot out from a driveway which was blocked by a large oak tree and was suddenly right in front of her. She reacted quickly, but not quickly enough. She hit her brakes hard but was still going over twenty miles per hour when she hit the child. She saw the child looking into her eyes just before he and his toy disappeared under her hood. She saw something odd in those eyes. It was not fear, but expectation. She opened her mouth in a silent scream as she heard the sickening thud and felt the impact. As her car travelled those final few feet before coming to a stop she could hear and feel the child and his Big Wheel as they were dragged along the road beneath her car. A small red streak appeared behind her car as it finally came to a stop.

Sandra cut off the engine and jumped out of the car, her heart pounding and her body trembling from the adrenaline. She ran to the front of the car.

She half expected not to find the child, but there it was. It was not the same child from her dream, this child had light hair and was a little smaller. She looked from the child to the house the child had come from. How could this have happened, and why now?

She looked back to the child.

But it was gone.

She looked down the road behind her car. All she could see was a Lincoln which was slowing down as it approached. She stood as the car drove around her. The man looked at her as if he was trying to figure out what her problem was. She stood and stared first into her car, then at the driveway where the child had appeared from. There was no sign the child had ever been in front of her car, or even that the child had existed.

She walked to her car door and stood still for a moment, listening. It was silent except for the singing of a lone whippoorwill. She recognized the vigorous deliberate call from a summer she had spent in Vermont.

But there were not supposed to be any whippoorwills in Saint Louis, or in the Midwest for that matter. She looked into the trees but could not find the bird, though she could tell where its song came from. She pondered the significance of this for a moment, then got back into her car. Her hands shook on the steering wheel and she sat still for a moment until another car came along and passed her. She started the car back up and put it into drive. As she resumed her drive home she tried to understand what had just happened, and what it all meant.

3

"It's dark in here. I like the dark."

The grimy man stuck his head in the garbage bin behind the department store, looking for some treasures which had perhaps passed by the eye of the unobserving store manager or clerk.

"It's dark in here. It's very dark, and I like it."

He repeated the statement in one form or another as he climbed completely into the bin, took one last look around, then began to dig.

The trip turned out to be a fruitful one. He found an old tape measure with a rusted but fairly readable tape. He also found an old wheelbarrow tire which was flat, but would look good next to the two others that were hanging over the television in his room. Nothing else had been worth taking. There had been an alarm clock which was only missing its hour hand and would have been valuable if he didn't already have five clocks which when used separately said nothing, but when combined could give a fairly good idea of the time of day.

He threw the two items into his shopping cart, on top of the other treasures he had found that day. Then he pushed the cart toward home. One of its wheels flipped from one position to the other as Joe sang his version of 'Bringing in the Sheaves', which was only similar in a few places to the actual version which he had been forced to memorize as a child. He wore two old shirts and an old jacket, despite the warm weather. He always wore them, even when he slept, and he couldn't remember when he had showered last, though he had stood out in the rain just last night for over an hour, and he had felt clean afterwards. His clothes reeked nonetheless from years of various body fluids which had soaked into them. He was short, and balding in odd-shaped patches which he blamed on the old microwave he had dug up ten years ago. It had a cracked glass and hummed oddly when operated. He also blamed that for his boils which appeared and reappeared in just about every place on his body. Currently he was experiencing a particularly annoying outbreak on his left thigh, and he stopped for a moment to scratch it fervently, breaking into a volley of swearing as he did so. He saw the moisture which meant he had caused the sores to bleed again. He cursed once more, then resumed his journey home.

    He hummed and mumbled as he pushed the old cart to an old wooden structure which looked more like an old abandoned general store than a home. That is in fact what it was, an old store which had been built in the early twenties. It had served the community during the big oil years, then had gone out of business during the depression. It had reopened in the forties as a hardware store which had changed locations in the early sixties. Then it had served as a low rent property for various failing enterprises for its last five years of operation. It had not been used as a store since 1971 and had been home to Joe since he had moved into it in 1973. Before then he had rented a small house in town from which he had eventually been evicted. He was not kicked out for not paying his rent; he always paid that and always on time. He was kicked out for what he had done to the insides of the house. This was why he had been kicked out of the past three houses, and why he now couldn't find anyone who would rent to him. Apparently his landlords did not share Joe's idea of art. Cisco was not a large city, and word finally did get around that a person was a bad risk, if he was one. Joe had gotten away with it for almost five years in the last place, until the landlord had popped in by surprise one day while Joe was out. Joe had always kept the main living area and the kitchen free of his collages of collections, saving this for the other rooms, including all of the bedrooms. Landlords usually would leave bedrooms alone, if you were home and kept the doors shut. But that time he had not been home; he had been scavenging. And the landlord had come over on a tip that strange odors were coming from Joe's bedroom.

But now he had his own place. When the store had been built, a second story had been put on. Much of it had been used for storage, though a fairly large area had been the living quarters for the family that had owned the store. Joe had occupied this now for almost twenty years, and had not been bothered. Apparently the people of town did not mind if he stayed here. It was away from any schools or businesses, and even further from any homes. An old set of abandoned railroad tracks ran behind the place, which added a homey touch for Joe.

He walked in through the front door, which was always opened, the top hinge rusted through. There was a puddle of water inside the door, and the floor was pretty wet from the previous night's storm. He walked down the center aisle of the old store, his torn and tread-less Reebok sneakers squeaking as he went. He walked until he came to an old set of wooden stairs which he had repaired. He wasn't bad with a hammer, and it had been sturdy except for the time in '84 when one step had finally rotted through and he had cut his ankle badly. The ankle had turned green in one place, and he still limped slightly. Next to the staircase was a wooden ramp with small troughs spaced about eleven inches apart. Each ramp was about six inches wide so both the front and rear wheels would fit. He pushed the cart onto the track, which was level at the bottom, and walked around to the front of it. He bent down and picked up the small metal hook which was attached to a long piece of rope and hooked it to the front of the cart. Then he walked up the stairs, grabbed onto the other end of the rope, and pulled his cart up to the second floor.

4

Joe sat in the old torn leather chair which would get stuck if you reclined back too far and watched the fuzzy picture on his old black and white television. He had hooked the television up to an old antenna, but still got poor reception. That's just the way it was in Cisco; he had never gotten good reception from any antenna. In the background the small generator hummed. He had no other electricity, so he had fixed an old gas generator and hooked it to a hundred-gallon tank. He would crank it up only when he needed power, and this was seldom. The tire he had picked up today completed the design on the wall behind the television nicely, and he smiled once again at his own ingenuity. He sat surrounded by his ever-growing collection of secret treasures which included a phonograph which had no speaker (but you could still hear the music if you got real close to the needle). He had several records, though most were warped beyond use. One particular record leaned against the phonograph. It was a collection of 'great oldies', but Joe only listened to one of them over and over. On those occasions when he felt so inclined he would put the record on and lay down on the floor, his ear as close to the phonograph as possible. He would lay quiet while his feet wiggled and moved behind him and Ford sang Sixteen Tons. He never tired of that tune, and he never would.

There was a broken mirror on the wall, a rickety old bookcase which held everything but books, three small tables with various items on them. His bottle collection rested on a long wooden shelf he had put up on one of the walls. There were at least three hundred bottles there, and no bottle showed up twice. These bottles were of assorted colors and had held everything from soft drinks to perfume. He had used a one-by-twelve for his shelf and had supported it with a dozen triangles made of two-by-fours anchored to studs. Above this shelf were pictures. Some were out of newspapers, others out of magazines, and a few posters hung here as well. There were pictures of old cars and young girls, and several pictures of junkyards with a handwritten inscription 'hidden treasures' scribbled at the bottom.

Joe sat and watched the old western on the television for about an hour, then he shut off the generator and sat down on the floor in the middle of his treasures. Outside the sun was beginning to set and as he had no western windows it was fairly dark.

But he liked the dark.

Joe crawled across the floor to an old musty smelling mattress and rolled onto it. He lay still looking at the silhouettes of his belongings which surrounded and comforted him. As he lay drifting to sleep he heard the loud snap of the big rat trap near his bottle display and a smile crept onto his tanned and wrinkled face.

5

Dave sat on his couch watching the Sunday night ABC movie. It was about a child who had been switched at birth with another little girl. Dave watched the show, but his mind wandered. Last night he had not slept well, but he had not dreamt. Still the events of the previous few days were heavy on his mind. He had not seen any more otherworldly shows on his television, but he kept a blank tape in his VCR just in case. He had called Colleen in the morning, but she didn't seem to have any new insight, and he just wanted to let it rest for a while. He figured if he just let it go that perhaps it would fade away and his life would become normal again.

Today the strategy seemed to have worked. He had seen no strange sights, nor had he heard any mysterious voices. He knew from the cassette of the phone voices that what had happened had not been just a trick of his mind. And if Colleen had really had these dreams then he was not the only one being affected. But he was not sure about her. He could not explain some of the things she had known about, like his dream and the vision on the television set. But he also did not understand how David Copperfield could walk through the Wall of China or make the Washington Monument disappear. The supernatural was Colleen's line of work. There was always the possibility she was trying first to gain his trust before she began taking his money. He decided that for now he would not give her that trust, as much as he really wanted to.

Dave watched the rest of the movie, then went to bed. He was tired from the previous night's restlessness. He got into his bed and set the alarm for seven o'clock. Then he rolled over and fell asleep, wishing one last time that he could go back and...

6

...the truck came around the corner, swerving slightly as it did. Davey watched in terror as the scene unfolded once again.

Only this time there was an awareness he had never felt before. He knew that this was a dream. He knew also that he had heard voices on the phone, and seen images on the television. It was as if his conscious self had been placed in this dreamland.

Then he noticed something else that was different. He looked down at his hands and feet and saw that they were those of an adult. He was dreaming that terrible dream, but this time he was there as an adult.

He looked back up at his brother. He was different too.

This time little Tommy looked very bad. His hands weren't much more than bones wrapped around the handlebars of the Big Wheel; rotted flesh dangled from his arms and legs. He looked back at Dave with one twitching eye, the other nothing more than an empty socket through which Dave could see hints of crawling things. The little creature's mouth moved. Dave knew what his brother was saying, but all he could hear was gurgling and hissing which continued until the truck struck the thing and exploded it all over the place. Rotted flesh and squirming creatures littered the road, a leg bone struck Dave in the face and his cheek began to sting.

Then he saw the man in the truck.

He had never seen this man's face in the dream before; he was always just a shadowy participant. Until now Dave hadn't even remembered what had happened to that man, but now as he looked into that face he knew.

The man behind the wheel was the same man who had been there before, Dave could tell this much. But he too had changed. The man was older now, about twenty years older than he had been when he had really run over Dave's brother. The truck slid toward Dave, and he got out of the way this time before it hit him. Then he watched as the man got out of the truck and fled, as he had twenty years ago.

Dave watched the man run off the road and into a misty void at the edge of the dream. Then he looked at the pieces of his dead brother which surrounded him. He heard a noise in the bushes and turned to see himself, twenty years younger, lying unconscious in those bushes. Then he heard more hissing and turned to face the truck.

The sound came from the rear tire, and at first Dave thought that perhaps air was leaking out of it. It was very loud, and the house and most of the street faded as the misty border of the dream closed in on him. He walked around to the tire and saw that the hissing was coming from what remained of his brother's mouth. The skull had been split and the top third of it was missing, including the rotted eye socket. The twitching eye remained and stared toward him as the shattered jaw twitched and jerked. He could see that there was no tongue left in the mouth, and he tried to turn away, but could not.

Suddenly the mouth spoke.

"You've got to stop them," it said in a rough and gravelly voice. "Before it's too late, you've got to lock the door. You've got to bolt it shut, Davey." Then it was suddenly the soft and smooth voice of his brother as he remembered it. "Please, Davey, please."

Then the head split down the middle and grey sludge oozed onto the street and gave off a rancid odor. The mist overtook the truck and then came for Dave.

7

"Who is it?" Joe called out.

There was no answer.

Something had awakened him. He thought he had heard a shuffling sound, then voices. Now it was just silence.

"Who the hell is in my house, I'll kill you in my house, I will."

He lay still listening for a response, but there was none. He reached back until he found the leg of one of the small tables. He worked his hand up the table to the top where he fumbled around for the old .380 he kept there. He knocked off an old spool which fell to the floor and rolled a few feet before coming to rest against the wall.

"I'll cut off your balls and eat them!" he called out as he felt the grip of the gun and took it from the table. It was loaded with old shells. He had not fired it in over two years, but he knew it worked, though the condition of the ammunition was questionable.

He rolled from the mattress and sat on the floor looking around his room. It was large and had many shadows of its own. But Joe knew these shadows, and looked for any which were different. He could get around in the room in the dark. Joe liked the dark, and it was his advantage. He had practiced over and over moving around his place in the dark, and he could do it with the best of confidence now. He did not need a light. Anyone else would certainly crash into one of Joe's many treasure piles, some placed in certain areas for just that purpose. If the intruder turned a flashlight on, he would shoot at it.

He stayed still, looking and listening.

Then he heard the whispering again and he turned suddenly to his left. He stared hard and listened. He wanted to speak again, but was afraid to give away his location, so he remained quiet.

Then there was a faint flow which appeared where the whispers had come from. He raised his gun quickly and fired. The shot rang out followed by the crash of glass as several of his prized bottles exploded. He fired again but the bullet was too old and did not respond. He ejected the shell and fired again as the glowing grew. Again the shot rang out and more glass exploded. He fired twice more before hitting another bad bullet.

Then he froze.

The glow had grown and he could see into it. He sat staring as a bizarre scene unfolded before him. He could see into the glowing, into a scene which went beyond where the wall should have been. Then he heard the whispering voices, only now he could make out the words.

"Joseph Coldren," they said. It was a name he had not heard in over a decade. It was his own name. There were many voices which said this, and they were soft and inviting, yet he was still terrified. "Joseph Coldren, we have come for you."

His eyes widened and he began to shake. He raised the gun again and pulled the trigger over and over, but the hammer simply kept coming down on the bad shell.

"The hell you did," he said in a trembling voice. "The hell you come for me, you sons of bitches."

He continued to click the gun nervously as a dreamy shape began to take form. It looked at first like it was going to be a woman in a flowing gown, but then as it took shape he could see that it was more than one person, and the flowing gown was nothing more than rotting bandages and torn clothing which floated out from their bodies. Their bodies were a mess of protruding bone and misshapen heads, fused together in various places.

Joe heard a loud popping and then the sound of static coming from his right. He turned to look and saw that his television had come on even though the power was off. The glow from the screen and the glow from the wall to his left lit the entire room brilliantly, and finally he dropped the gun and covered his eyes with his hands.

"Get away!" he said. A wet spot appeared at his crotch as fear ravaged his deteriorated mind. "Get away, I'm not coming."

"Joseph Coldren, we have come for you."

As he sat with his eyes covered and his body shaking, he suddenly understood what they were saying. They had not come to get him; they had come to help him. As this understanding came to him, he suddenly felt warm and his body stopped shaking. Then he heard a voice from his right. He turned and saw that the television screen was no longer filled with static. On it was a man. The man was wearing a white suit with a white tie. His blond hair was combed back and his eyes lacked any color. The eyes were simply smooth white orbs which looked out at him. The man was looking out at Joe with a smile on his face. Except for the eyes the man looked to Joe like a T.V. preacher. He was so clean, and his smile was full of both deception and promise. The man's mouth opened and his voice came through the speaker.

"Hello, Joseph Coldren." The voice was deep and mechanical. It sounded as if someone was holding a vibrator to the man's neck while he spoke.

"Uhn," was all Joe said.

"Sorry to frighten you so, but it was quite unavoidable."

"Sure," Joe replied. "Sure, whatever you say."

The man was still and just stared out from the television at Joe. Joe wondered for a moment if this might be a dream, but he knew that it was not. He had seen things like this before when he had experimented with drugs in his youth, but nothing so intense nor so real. He was not on drugs now, though his brain was damaged and didn't always work like it was supposed to. He knew this too. He also knew that he was getting worse. Perhaps this was all a part of that.

"This is neither an illusion nor a delusion, Joseph Coldren. This is reality as you have never seen it before."

"Sure," Joe replied. The man could read his thoughts? This was even more frightening.

"No need to be afraid, Joseph Coldren, we're here to help you."

"Sure." Joe could say no more. Although he knew what the man said was true, he could not fight off the fear, and he began to hum 'Bringing in the Sheaves' again. As he hummed the man on the television began to sing the words, the right ones, and Joe felt his fear slipping away. He watched the man's mouth as the voice still vibrated, but Joe did not care.

"I like that song too Joseph. It used to be my favorite."

The man was silent again and Joe's troubled mind began to function as well as it could. He stopped humming and asked a question.

"What the hell's goin' on here? And why do you call me by my old name?"

The man's smile broadened. "I call you Joseph because it is your name. We are here to help you. We have come for you."

"No, nobody calls me that anymore. Now they all say just Joe, and when they think I can't hear them they say Crazy Joe, and the kids sing that song about the buffalo, but nobody says Joseph no more."

"Joseph, look behind you."

He didn't want to turn from the disturbing image before him and face the more disturbing one to his left, but he felt compelled to follow this man's instructions. He turned his head slowly and once again saw the mass of undulating flesh with its many gruesome parts. It floated still just beyond the wall, as if it could come no closer. He could still hear the whispers which came from the mass, and he could hear moans of pain and anguish as well. He wanted to turn away, but knew that he should not until the man in the television told him to.

"What you see before you is a mass of suffering humanity. I am one small part of that mass, a part which has been chosen to speak with you directly. One had to be chosen; it was me. Look hard into the mass. Look hard and to the upper right and you will see."

Joe did look. At first he saw nothing, but then he saw a distorted and mutated looking reproduction of the man of the television. The man's head was fused at the ear with the deteriorating breast of a woman; his arm protruded from her ass. His waist and legs fused with those of another man, a small and weak-looking man who seemed to have no head at all. Joe tried to keep looking, but then he had to turn away as his stomach heaved. Nothing came up but some acidic bile which he quickly swallowed. Then he looked at the dark wall before him, not knowing whether to look at the television or the image.

"We have come for you because only you can save us."

Joe was frightened once again and would not look at the television. He began to hum aimlessly, singing no song in particular but his own little medley of all the songs he knew.

"We want you to help us, and we will give you the things you want."

Joe heard the voice but still he would not look. Then he saw colors on the wall before him, colors which were coming from the screen of his black and white television. He turned his head to see what was happening and saw the biggest pile of old radios and televisions, broken clocks and discarded mattresses he had ever seen. The treasures were not hidden; he could see them all. Then the picture changed and there was the image of a man on the television pushing a cart, only the cart was new, and the man's clothes were new. He knew that the man was him, only it was a better him, a Joe which once had been and which he longed for. This Joe was stronger, and his mind was good. People did not call this man Crazy Joe because they respected him. He pushed his cart with pride, and in the cart were treasures beyond his wildest dreams.

Then the picture faded once again to something which was unclear at first. It was large and smooth, but it had a small red center. Then the image backed away and he realized that it was the breast of a woman. As she backed from the screen he could see that she was young, and beautiful, and entirely naked. She moved and danced for him, and posed in erotic poses for him. He got hard as he watched and felt with his hand for his crotch.

Then the girl faded and the white flesh of her thigh became the white forehead of the man.

Joseph's eagerness returned. "What do you want me to do?" he asked.

"We will let you know when the time comes. For now just wait, and watch for us."

Joe sat looking at the man, imagining all of the things which would soon be his. Then doubt crept into his rotted brain. "How do I know you will do these things for me?" he asked.

"We will leave a sign for you, a little advance token of our thanks."

Joe smiled. It was like a present. He was going to get something nice and he didn't know what it was going to be. Then he began to wonder what would be asked of him.

"I have to ask you something," he said, lowering his eyes from the screen for a moment. The man said nothing. "What if I don't want to do what you ask? What if I don't want to help?" Joe asked.

The man did not answer. Joe waited, but heard nothing. Then the white glow which had filled the room turned red. He looked up to the television and saw something which brought the terror back.

There was a monster on the screen. It was like a big dragon, and smoke and fire came from its nostrils. He stared ahead and then heard a tremendous roar from behind him. He turned and looked and saw the full-sized creature where the mass of flesh had been. It rushed forward and broke the barrier of the wall. A few more of his bottles fell from that wall and shattered on the floor. The dragon came towards him fast and he tried to cover his face, but could not raise his arms. He screamed as the creature leapt, and he felt the searing heat of the flame and the claws upon his neck.

Then the room was black again.

Joe sat in the darkness mumbling to himself.

"Okay, okay, I guess that answers that question, ya know? Right. Okay, I guess I'll help you. This is really strange, ya know? Okay."

He rambled as he returned to his mattress, leaving the gun on the floor where he had dropped it. He laid down and closed his eyes, urging sleep to come on, alternately mumbling and singing to himself as he waited.

Finally, sleep did come.

And with it came the most wonderful, most erotic dream Joe had ever had.

V

1

Colleen walked slowly through the quiet green forest. Her feet did not quite touch the ground and she could not see them hidden beneath the thick ivy. It was very bright, but the brilliance did not hurt her eyes.

She walked along through the ivy which covered a smooth, featureless ground. For all she knew there might not even be a ground, just a misty border which existed only in her mind. The full green trees were spread far apart and reached upwards with strong and heavy arms.

Then she saw something which looked out of place. It was a door. It stood in the center of a small meadow. It seemed to stand alone, with no wall around it. It was as wide as two normal doors and made of iron. The door was divided into square sections which were all connected. There were six squares, and each depicted a different horrible scene. Each scene featured people or creatures or some odd mixture of both in awful positions of pain and disgusting torture. She walked slowly to the door, looking at it intently, both repulsed and intrigued by the hideous images.

One scene in particular disturbed her. It was on the square which was eye level on the right side, a few feet above the round steel ring which could be used to open the door. The image protruded from the door and featured a horrid creature which seemed to be a melting together of many deformed and disabled human beings. Bodies fused together and tore from each other at odd and impossible angles. She looked closely at each face she could see within the image and saw agony in each. One face in particular stood out. It was the face of a man. His head was connected at the ear to the breast of a woman; his right arm protruded from her rear end. This image was the only one which was not made entirely of steel. Clear white pearls, only a couple of millimeters across, were placed into the man's eye sockets. His face too showed agony, but it also showed determination and purpose. It was this face which frightened her most.

Suddenly a loud pounding sound came from the door. The pounding began slowly, then increased in intensity and frequency. The pounding came from many places on the door, as if a hundred hands were on the other side, trying desperately to break through.

Then there was an explosion and a flash which was brighter than the intense light which already lit the forest. A crack appeared at the top of the door and ran a third of the way down its front. Icy blackness shot through the crack, almost like light streaming into a dark room, only it was darkness streaming into the light Colleen stood in. She reached forward and covered the crack with her hand and she felt an icy coldness run up her arm.

Then she felt the door push outwards. A large piece of the darkness shot out from some invisible opening which had been created, and began to flow from the other side of the door. Colleen put both hands on the door and pushed as hard as she could, but the door was coming slowly open.

Then she heard a thousand screams and the door slammed shut.

She looked carefully at the door. The crack was gone, and it stood as before.

When she turned to leave the door she almost ran into the child who was standing behind her. She pulled back from the grotesque image, which was torn and rotted, and missing an arm. Then it spoke to her.

"Don't let them through ma'am, please don't let them through."

She looked at the child and realized where she had seen him before.

"You have to help my brother," the little boy said, flesh dangling at odd angles from his jaw. "He can't do it alone."

She felt revulsion, but she also felt compassion.

Then the vision faded.

2

Colleen sat on the edge of her bed looking out her window. She had opened it to let the cool morning air freshen up her dwelling. It was very early. The sun was just beginning to come up and she could hear a mockingbird singing in a nearby tree. First it sang like a scissortail, then like a cardinal, then it croaked like a frog. She wondered if the mockingbird had a song of its own, or if it was destined forever to borrow other songs and sounds.

She had awakened about an hour before dawn. She could remember most of the dream she had experienced during the night. She tried to understand what it meant. What did the door represent? What did the drawings on the door represent? What did the rotting little boy mean by 'don't let them through', and how did Dave Chatburn fit into all of this?

She rubbed her eyes and stood up. She still wore nothing but a long T-shirt and it crept up her legs as she stretched toward the ceiling. Then she walked to her small kitchen and grabbed a bagel and a glass from the cupboard, and a pitcher of orange juice from the refrigerator.

As she ate her bagel and drank her orange juice she considered what her options might be. She could continue to work on this on her own. Perhaps a seance or some other such ritual would help her find out more. But for this to really work she would need the participation of Dave, and he had not contacted her since the night of the storm. Without him she might only be able to scratch the surface. With his help she might be able to solve the mystery. He seemed to be the center of whatever was going on, he and his deceased brother.

She looked up at the clock and decided that it was not too early now to give Dave a call. She knew he worked in town, and wanted to catch him before he left for work. She walked to the old black phone and dialed his number. He answered on the third ring.

"Hello?" His voice was thick and groggy.

"Did I wake you up?"

There were some shuffling sounds as Dave checked the clock to make sure he had not slept in.

"I was about to get up anyway," he said. "Who is this?"

"It's Colleen. I wanted to ask if any more strange things have been happening to you."

He hesitated before answering. "Not really."

"What do you mean?" she asked, catching the hesitation.

"I mean I've had some more bad dreams, but nothing prophetic or anything. I think this thing is going to go away."

She knew he was lying but did not know why.

"Look," she said, "I have had some more strange things happen to me, and they seem to involve you. Why don't you come over tonight and we can try to work on this thing?"

"I've got to go to Abilene tonight and pick up some paperwork."

"How about tomorrow night?" she asked.

"Busy," he said.

"Okay," she replied. She understood that he did not wish to come over at all. She was going to have to do this on her own. "You've got my number. If you change your mind, give me a call."

"Okay. Bye."

He hung up without waiting for her to say good-bye. What was wrong? What had she done? She figured from the looks he had given her the day they had met that he would have wanted to come over even if he really hadn't experienced anything further. Now even that physical interest seemed to have disappeared. She wondered if perhaps she should go to his house while he was at work and try to find something which might help her understand what was happening. She decided that she would do this only if she couldn't get anywhere otherwise.

She finished her breakfast and got dressed.

3

About an hour after her conversation with Dave the doorbell rang. She walked to the door and looked through the peephole, expecting to see a bubbled-out version of Dave looking at her. What she saw instead was Bernice Wakefield. Bernice was a doting middle-aged woman who believed she had contracted everything from rheumatism to cancer, though the doctors could find nothing wrong with Bernice except a strong need for attention and too much fat. Colleen put on her grim and serious face and opened the door slowly, for effect. She could see the appropriate amount of both fear and concern on Bernice's face. Colleen did not speak.

"Hi," Bernice said, her lower lip visibly trembling. "Can I come in?"

Colleen let her in without speaking. Bernice had parked in back and walked around the house. Bernice did not want anyone to know she was here. Most of Colleen's customers were that way. Bernice came into the house quickly and looked once behind her to make sure no one was watching. Colleen had gotten too familiar with this procedure to take offense. Once Bernice was inside she seemed no less nervous, but her attention was more focused on Colleen.

"What can I do for you, Miss Wakefield?"

"I need to talk to my father again. I'm having a little trouble with a dog, you see, and everybody keeps giving me advice. But Papa was so good with dogs, and I really want to know what he has to say."

Colleen tried to keep her serious look, but it was hard. Bernice always came in with some new and interesting reason for getting in touch with her Papa, but this one was just plain silly. Still, a job was a job.

"Let's go into the power room," Colleen said as she turned from Bernice.

She led the woman down a little hallway to a small room. The room was painted completely black, though the paint was peeling in a couple of places, revealing a flat white finish underneath. There were no windows and only one door. A small card table sat in the center of the room, and there was a black steel file cabinet in one corner. One of the walls was decorated with various charts and symbolic trinkets. The three remaining walls were bare. They walked to the small table and sat down. Bernice faced the ornate wall and glanced briefly at the items which decorated it. They seemed dark and evil to her, and she wondered why they had to be there in order for her to talk to her Papa. She knew conjuring up spirits was wrong, but she had decided that consulting with her deceased Papa for practical matters was justifiable.

As you know there are many ways to contact the deceased," Colleen said, though she knew which way Bernice would choose.

"Oh, Papa always seems to do better with the board. I think it's because we used to have one, and when Mama was gone we'd dig it out and play sometimes." She looked around suddenly, as if she was afraid that someone might hear this dark secret she had shared only with her Papa and with Colleen. It had been harmless fun, and had really only been scary once. Colleen had heard this story before, and decided that she would quit asking Bernice which medium she wished to use.

Without speaking Colleen walked to the wall behind her and took the Ouija board from its place beside the pentagram poster. The poster was for effect; she had no interest in the Satanic nature of the supernatural. She walked back to the table and placed the board and the marker on it. Then she walked to the wall and turned the dimmer knob, lowering the lighting to a level which added properly to the mystic atmosphere but would not prevent the reading of the board. Then she sat down again. She did not speak much. This too was for effect. Most people seemed to be in a mysterious awe of the silence, so she had learned to use it.

She sat down at the table and placed her fingertips lightly on the edge of the marker. Then she looked up at Bernice who then reached out and did the same. Colleen looked ahead dreamily and her eyes fluttered lightly as she feigned contact with the spirit world. She began to hum softly and her body moved in small circles. Bernice watched the board.

Then the marker moved. It began moving in small circles as Colleen looked toward the ceiling. She did not have to look at the board; she had memorized where all of the letters were. Looking away from the board added to the believability for the subjects, so she had learned this too.

"Speak, Bernice." Colleen now spoke in a deep whisper.

"I," Bernice began. "I, well, Papa? Papa, can you hear me?"

The marker slid around the board. There was no answer.

"Papa, will you talk to me today?"

The marker slid softly across the board while Bernice and Colleen kept their fingers lightly on its edges. Suddenly the marker moved slowly over to the 'Yes' on the board. Bernice smiled.

"It's Papa," she explained, looking up for a moment at Colleen. Colleen kept her fluttering eyes on the ceiling.

"Papa," Bernice began. "How is everything up there, are you doing all right?"

Yes.

"Do you still get to visit the old house from time to time?"

Yes.

"What about Mama, is she okay?"

Yes.

"I have a problem I need some help with, Papa."

The board marker slid across the letters on the board. D-o-g.

"Yes, Papa, it's that dog I got last week. He's giving me some trouble."

P-e-e a-n-d c-h-e-w.

"Yes!" Bernice sounded excited. "I can't seem to get him to stop peeing the house and chewing on the furniture. He also barks a lot and bothers the neighbors."

The marker slid around for a moment before spelling out an answer. S-h-o-o-t. Came the response.

"Oh, Papa, you're always kidding. What should I really do?"

Colleen's eyes stopped fluttering and came down to the board. She meant to spell outside, not shoot. How could she have done this? The marker continued to defy her wishes and went for letters of its own design.

S-h-o-o-t y-o-u s-t-u-p-i-d b-i-t-c-h.

Bernice's eyes widened. So did Colleen's. Bernice took her hands from the marker and looked up at Colleen. "That's not my Papa," she said. Colleen knew she was right. Then Colleen felt a cold chill and she was unable to remove her hands from the marker as it slid about the board.

S-h-o-o-t a-n-d k-i-l-l s-h-o-o-t a-n-d k-i-l-l s-h-o-o-t a-n-d k-i-l-l...

The marker raced about the board spelling out the phrase over and over. Colleen was finally able to remove her hand from the marker and it stopped on the letter L. She looked up to Bernice, trying hard not to show her own dismay.

"I'm sorry, Bernice," she said. "We seemed to have run into a small problem."

"That's all right," Bernice replied. "This kind of stuff happens, I know. I'll still pay you the same. Can we try again?"

Then the marker moved.

The movement was slight, but Colleen caught it and looked back to the board. Bernice took this as a sign and reached forward to touch the marker.

"No!" Colleen called to Bernice. But it was too late.

Bernice's fingers touched the marker. Colleen watched as the woman's eyes began to flutter, then rolled back into her head. The heavy woman moaned once, then her head began to shake. Colleen kept her hands away from the board. The marker began to move.

S-h-u-t t-h-e d-o-o-r.

It stopped. Colleen stood slowly and walked to the file cabinet in the corner where she retrieved some paper and a pencil which rested on its top. She returned to her table and watched the board. Bernice let out another moan.

S-h-u-t t-h-e d-o-o-r, it spelled out again. Colleen wrote it down. D-o-n-t l-e-t t-h-e-m t-h-r-o-u-g-h.

"Don't let who through?" Colleen asked aloud. Bernice's head still shook; sweat appeared on her forehead.

B-a-d p-e-o-p-l-e.

"The bad people want through?"

Yes.

"Why?"

H-u-r-t a-n-d k-i-l-l.

"Why?"

A-n-g-r-y.

"Who are you?" Colleen asked.

The marker slid around aimlessly for a moment, then spelled out slowly and deliberately, T-o-m-m-y.

"Are you the little boy in my dreams?" she asked.

Yes.

"Are you the little boy hit by the truck in my other dreams?" she asked.

T-r-u-c-k.

"Is your brother named Dave?"

Yes.

"Why are the bad people angry?" she asked.

B-a-d p-e-o-p-l-e.

"What is the door?" she asked.

D-o-o-r.

"Are the bad people trying to come through the door?" she asked.

T-h-e-y c-o-m-i-n-g.

"Are the bad people trying to come through the door?" she asked again.

The marker became frantic. T-h-e-y c-o-m-i-n-g. T-h-e-y h-u-r-t m-e. T-h-e-y c-o-m...

The marker flew off the board and Bernice's hands fell to her sides. Then her eyes opened and a smile suddenly appeared on her face.

"Well, that was good," she said cheerfully. "I guess we got what we were looking for after all."

Colleen looked at the woman. She was showing no fear at all now, just her usual nervousness. Bernice did not know what had just happened. Colleen pretended that all had indeed gone well.

"I'm glad we got through for you," Colleen said. "I hope you found what you were looking for."

"I certainly did," Bernice replied. "Papa always comes through."

Bernice stood and Colleen walked her back to the front door.

"Oh, I almost forgot!" Bernice reached into her purse and brought out two twenty-dollar bills. "This is right, isn't it?"

"Yes, Miss Wakefield."

Colleen opened the front door. Bernice took a look to make sure no one was watching. Then she turned to Colleen.

"Thanks again, and," her voice raised an octave, becoming shrill and childlike, her eyes glazed over, "and remember, don't let them through!"

Bernice turned and walked out the door, then sneaked quickly around the side of the house.

Colleen stood with the door opened, looking out toward the road. She stood wondering again what she was getting into. Then she saw the dirty old bum standing across the street. He was standing behind a new-looking shopping cart which had a few items inside of it. He stood smiling a grim smile and staring at Colleen.

4

Dave sat at his desk staring at the sheet of paper before him. It was a listing of orders for the new month. He was supposed to be checking the rates and totals, but he was just staring. His mind was again wandering back to the dreams and to Colleen.

Colleen had called him this morning. She'd asked if he'd been experiencing any more dreams or occurrences. Dave decided that he was not ready to trust her just yet, though now he was almost wishing that he would have said yes just so he could see her. He remembered her soft face and deep eyes, and his physical yearnings stirred.

But they were quickly squelched by the memory of the dream.

He looked up at the clock. It was only eleven. He looked back at the numbers and tried once again to concentrate on the task before him.

Then he pushed the paper across the desk. He reached forward, turned on his answering machine, and grabbed the cassette tape he had made from the top drawer of his desk. He'd brought it to work today with the intention of listening to it again during lunch. Instead, he threw it and the paper he had written the final words on in his shirt pocket and headed out the door.

Dave got into his car and headed north on 183. Forty-five minutes later he was driving down the very road where it all happened. As he approached his mother's house, the house he had grown up in, he felt a shiver run through him. He came to the driveway and turned into it. Then he got out of the car and looked toward the street. His view was partially blocked by the large bushes which he had been thrown into so many years ago by the murderous white truck. Still he could see the scene; it was so fresh in his mind now that it was haunting his sleep and his television. He walked back to the street and looked down it. As he stood looking a small voice from behind startled him.

"Hey mister!" it said. "You know Misses Chatburn?"

Dave turned and looked. It was a little girl, about seven years old, riding a small bike with a pink frame. The handlebars shook as she tried unsuccessfully to look experienced at the task.

"She's my mom," Dave answered. "Where are you from?"

"I just live two houses down," she said as she rode past him, turning back in a circle and almost losing her balance. Her hair was in pigtails, and they swung out as she made the unsteady turn. "Sometimes I help Misses Chatburn in her yard. It's very pretty."

Dave looked back at the yard. It was very nice. His mother no longer mowed the grass or weeded the flower beds; now she paid a young boy to do that work. But she still insisted on planting her own geraniums and pruning her own rose bushes. She had always done these things and trusted no one else to do them properly.

When he looked back to the street he saw that the little girl had lost interest and was riding unsteadily down the road. As he watched he saw a big white truck come around the corner and his heart began to race.

"Get out of the street!" he shouted.

The little girl had already seen the coming vehicle and was headed for the sidewalk when her handlebars twisted and she went to the pavement. Dave started to run down the street, but before he could get there the truck pulled over. Dave stood in the middle of the road, his heart pounding loudly in his ears. He watched as the young man got out of the truck and helped the little girl up. The driver made sure she was okay before getting back in the delivery vehicle. Dave watched and cursed his own unsteadiness. Then he walked back to his mother's driveway. He heard the truck as it headed back down the road, its diesel engine rattling and moaning as the truck gathered speed.

Dave walked to the door of his mother's house. He knocked once then opened the door and stuck his head in.

"Mother, you home?" he called out.

His mother appeared around the corner of the hallway with a smile on her face. She looked very pale and very old today. He remembered that he had neglected to call first, and that makeup usually helped his mother hide those hard years. But her smile was sincere, and she welcomed Dave into the living room and gave him a hug.

"What brings you up to visit your old mom?" she asked in a playful scolding. "I was beginning to wonder if you were all right."

"I called you last Wednesday," Dave reminded her.

"But you haven't been over since June."

Dave sat down on the old couch. The springs had long since been destroyed by his own jumping feet years ago. "You have a car too," Dave reminded her again. He resented the fact that it was always he who came to visit her. And she was always able to make him feel guilty anyway.

"Can I get you a Coke or something?" she asked him.

He resisted the urge to ask for a beer and accepted. His mother had never accepted that he drank beer, and it had never been allowed in the house or the yard. His father had spent at least one night each week playing cards with some of his friends. They had rotated amongst the houses of the participants, with the exception of the Chatburn residence. The guys complained that it just wasn't any fun without the drinkin' or cussin'.

"So what brings you to Breckenridge on a work day?" she finally asked him.

"I brought something I wanted you to hear," he explained. "Do you still have that old cassette recorder that used to be mine?"

"If I do it's right where you left it last," she explained.

That's just about where everything which had belonged to Dave in his childhood was now, wherever he had left it before moving out. Tommy's things were like that too, locked up in a room which was old and musty. The door was only opened occasionally for a proper cleaning, then locked again. It had become a sort of shrine after Tommy's death, one which had haunted Dave and his father for many years.

"I'll be right back," Dave explained.

He placed his Coke on the coaster which rested near the corner of the coffee table and stood up. Then he walked down the hallway which led to his old room. As he walked he gazed at the old pictures which hung on the walls. There were no new ones. They were pictures of a family which had once happily occupied the Chatburn residence. Now they were little more than painful reminders to Dave of what had been, but was no more. He walked past the old pictures which included images of his now dead brother and father to his bedroom. The door was shut, but not locked. He pushed the door open and walked in. It smelled clean. His mother kept the rooms in order, even those she no longer used. He walked into the room and stood once again in a place which was so familiar, yet so strange. Some of his favorite stuffed animals sat in neat rows on the bed near the pillow, including the old pink dog with the zippered pouch in the back.

He walked to the old closet and opened it up. His clothes were arranged properly, pants first, then shirts. Many of the things were too small for him now; all were out of style except for the Levis. He looked at the bottom of the closet and saw the old box. It had no top and he could see all kinds of junk inside. He got down on one knew and began digging through the junk until he found the old recorder.

It was large and rectangular, and had the old big buttons at the bottom. He pulled it from the box and turned it over. The battery cover was still in place. He got out his pocket knife and popped open the cover. There were still old batteries inside, but there was also a rusty brown powder which covered almost everything. He stood and closed the closet door, being careful not to get any of the brown stuff on his hands. He carried the old recorder to the kitchen where he opened the trash can and dumped the old batteries into the garbage.

"Did you find it?" his mother called from the living room.

"Yes, but I'll need some batteries."

"There should be some fresh ones in the cupboard there over the coffee machine," she called out to him.

He walked to the coffee machine and opened the cupboard above it. Inside were several packs of different sized batteries which had apparently been on sale at one time. He got the 'C' cells and looked at the pack. The expiration date had passed, but this was not Cisco and there was a chance they would still work. He unwrapped the batteries and put them into the back of the recorder. Then he pushed the play button. The little rubber wheel came up and began to spin against the small steel one. It worked. He walked back into the living room and set the recorder down on the coffee table. Then he reached into his shirt pocket and pulled out the tape he had brought with him.

"I recorded this from the phone the other day, Mom. I just wanted you to listen to it and tell me what you think."

"Okay," she replied. There was a hint of wonder on her heavily lined face.

Dave started the tape player. It was silent for a moment, then there was some loud static. Then the voice of his mother's sister came on. It was not as clear it had been when he had recorded it, but you could still make out who was speaking and what was being said. At first Betty Chatburn listened, wondering when her son had spoken with her sister, and why he had decided to tape the conversation, and why it sounded so rough.

Then came the voice of her dead husband's brother James. She knew that James was dead; he had died as her husband had. Heart attacks had made widows of the women who had fallen in love with men of the Chatburn line. She listened to the broken pieces of the conversations and understood what they were about, but not where they had come from. When they had ended, and before the child's voice, Dave stopped the player and looked up at his mother.

"Did you tape these a long time ago?" she asked him.

"I just got them last Friday."

"But your uncle James and Grandpa Morris were on there. They're dead now."

"I know," Dave replied. He sat and watched his mother's face turn pensive.

"David, are you trying to tell me you taped these voices on Friday?"

"Yes."

"Where did you get them?" she asked.

"From the telephone," he replied.

Her lips pursed and her mind tried to understand. She believed her son; she always did. Now that belief was conflicting with her concept of reality, and it was confusing her.

"You haven't been messing around with that black magic stuff again, have you?" she asked.

"No, mom. This just happened. Thursday night I had that dream again, about the accident." His eyes lowered as he said 'accident.' "The next morning I heard this on the telephone. I wanted to know what you thought."

She sat silent; her lips still pursed.

"So," Dave asked, "what do you think?"

"I think it's the work of the Devil," she replied.

Dave had expected this. "What else?" he asked.

"I think that if you're being honest with me and haven't brought this upon yourself by dabbling where you shouldn't be, then perhaps he has chosen you for some reason. I told you if you went to church regularly these kinds of things wouldn't happen."

"I know, Mother. But it is happening, and I want to understand it."

"You shouldn't. The Devil counts on our curiosity to help him. You should put this thing behind you. You should burn the tape and walk away from this thing. Pay no heed to it, and go to church next Sunday. It'll do you some good." She had begun wagging that accusatory finger at him again.

Dave reached forward. "I want you to hear the rest of the tape." He pressed the play button.

At first there was just silence. Then the voice of the child.

She listened with first interest, then terror as she recognized the voice. She listened to the few static-filled words, but could not even make out as many as Dave had. When it was over Dave turned off the player and handed her the list of words he had brought with him. They were the words which he could make out, though listening now he could make out even fewer. It seemed as if the voices on the tape were fading slowly. Perhaps a month or year from now there would be no voices. He did not understand this, but knew it meant he would get no more from the tape than he already had.

"There are the words I could make out, and I think that this is the order they were in."

She looked at the list, then back up at her son. Her hands were shaking. She looked again at the list, then handed it back to Dave.

"I think that you're into something you shouldn't be," she explained. "Whether it's because you sought it out or not makes no difference. You need to get away from this thing, before it gets you into serious trouble."

"What kind of trouble?" he asked.

"Both spiritual and physical trouble," she answered, her brow now furrowed in deep lines of concern. "Remember what happened to your

Aunt Linda when she got into that cult stuff too deep?" He did remember indeed. "Well, that's what I'm talking about."

He looked at the tape, then to his mother. "Do you think Aunt Linda would understand what this was about?" he asked.

"I imagine she might, but I would rather you didn't bring it up to her. Her interest in this sort of thing is still unnatural, and she doesn't need to be dragged from her faithfulness, just like you need to refresh it."

"Okay," he said. His mother knew this meant that he was going to call his aunt anyway, but she said nothing.

Dave stood up from the couch. "I'd better be getting back to the office. I didn't let anyone know where I'd be, and they might be looking for me." He looked at his watch. It was exactly twelve thirty.

His mother walked with him to the door. "Come back some time with some better news, when you can stay a while."

"Sure, mom."

Dave kissed his mother and walked out the door. He could tell that she was still shaken. He took the old tape player with him. His mother watched him go and felt a warm tear run down her face. She wiped it away so he wouldn't see it if he turned around. But he did not. She closed the door as he got into his car to drive away.

5

But he did not drive away. He looked in the rearview mirror and saw a set of yellow handlebars sticking up from behind his car. They were moving back and forth as if a child were playing on the toy. He waited for a moment, hoping the toy would move, but it did not. He could not back out with the toy there, so he got out of the car and walked around it.

When he looked he saw that there was indeed a little boy on the toy. The toy was a Big Wheel. It was much like the one his brother had ridden on, only a newer version with a horn and clicking wheels. The boy sat, looking up at him. His face reminded him only slightly of Tommy, but his eyes were defiant.

"I need you to move so I can drive my car," Dave explained to the boy.

The boy said nothing. He just stared back with searing blue eyes. He didn't even blink.

"If you don't move, kid, I'm going to push you out of the way." Dave used a harsh and threatening tone. He had no time for a smart-ass kid like this one.

The kid stayed for a moment more, then rode his Big Wheel slowly away. He peddled out into the road and headed down it, his gaze still locked on Dave.

And a white truck came around the corner.

"Shit," Dave said simply. He knew what was happening. He knew what was going to happen. But he did not run after the child. Dave simply stood and watched as the truck swerved into the center of the road while the boy looked back at Dave. Dave tried to look away, but could not. He heard the clicking of the plastic wheels as the boy rode, and the revving of the engine of the approaching truck. He watched as the truck gained speed, and the little boy still did not turn to see it.

Dave watched in a resigned horror as the truck struck the child and scattered blood and body parts down the road. He watched as the truck skidded down the road toward him. He could see inside the truck, and there was no driver. He watched the truck come to a halt near the bushes at the end of his mother's yard.

Then the scene was silent except for the sound of the truck's engine. He could still see the blood which ran down the street in streaks. The Big Wheel was mangled and broken under the rear tire of the truck, but there was no body, just signs that one had been mutilated.

Dave stared at the truck which simply sat and idled. Then he walked slowly to it.

When he reached it he looked underneath. There was lots of blood, and a couple of severed fingers, but there was no body. He stood and walked to the side of the truck. It had no door, just an opening. On the side was the faded name of Sam's Delivery Service, followed by a slogan and a phone number. Dave reached out and touched the steering wheel of the vehicle. It was solid. It felt real. He looked back to his mother's house, but she did not emerge. He looked around and saw that no one had come out to see about all of the sounds. There was no one outside of their house; no cars were coming down the street. He looked back to the truck, then decided he would climb in.

He got into the truck and sat in the driver's seat. He reached forward for the key and turned it off. The engine coughed and sputtered before stopping. He sat and listened. It was completely silent. There were no birds singing, no children playing. The air was still.

Dave wanted to get out of the truck and go to his mother's house to see if she was still there. But deep inside he was afraid she would not be. Deep inside he was afraid that nobody in Breckenridge was home right now. All of them were in some other place, but not here. He looked down at the floorboard and saw that liquid was spilled there. He bent over for a closer look and saw that it was coffee.

Then he heard the engine start up and the truck began to roll.

He looked up quickly and saw that he was no longer in front of his mother's house. He saw her house, but now it was in the distance. He could just see it as he was turning the corner onto the street she lived on.

But how could this be?

Then he felt the searing heat on his leg and looked down to see that his pants had been covered with the hot coffee. He beat at the leg, trying to cool it off. Then he remembered that he was the only one in the truck, and that his eyes had not seen the road for several seconds.

When he looked up he saw Tommy. He also saw himself, several years younger and with terror filled eyes. He watched as his brother rode carelessly down the street, and he screamed out both from the truck and from the street.

But he was still far enough away that he could turn to the right and drive off of the road, avoiding the wreck with his brother. He grabbed the steering wheel and tried to give it a hard turn.

But someone behind him screamed a shrill scream and he felt a pain in his shoulder. In the rearview mirror he saw the bloody and mangled face of the boy who had sat defiantly behind his car. The boy's arms reached around him and his hands grabbed the steering wheel. The right hand was missing a few fingers, the fingers he had seen under the truck moments ago. Dave felt the boy's teeth sinking into his shoulder and cried out in pain.

He fought to steer away from the disaster, but the boy behind him was too strong. He tried to cover his eyes at the last moment, but the boy suddenly let go of the wheel and grabbed Dave's wrists so he would have to watch.

And he saw it all again from inside the truck that had killed his brother.

He felt the soft impact and saw the blood as it streaked down the road behind him. He saw little arms and legs rolling under the wheel outside the opening where the door should have been. He heard the cries of agony of the young boy who stood a few feet in front of the truck.

Then he hit the young David and his head flew forward against the steering wheel. He stayed this way, his hands now freed and at the sides of his head. He cried out in agony.

He kept his eyes closed until the humming of the diesel engine softened and he heard the slamming of a screen door.

Dave looked up and saw his mother standing in her doorway, calling out something to him. He looked around and found that he was in his own car now. The engine was running and his foot was pressed hard on the brake. He rolled down the window to hear what his mother was saying.

"I said are you all right?" she asked.

"Yes," he called back, "I just have a small headache." He paused and looked around for any sign of what had just happened. There was none. "Bye Mom."

She said bye and he put the car in reverse. As he drove away from the house he looked briefly at his watch and noticed that less than a minute had passed since he had walked out of the house.

He rubbed his shoulder which still throbbed from the bite of the child with the missing fingers.

VI
1

Sandra sat in a secluded room in her large house. The house itself was secluded by Saint Louis standards. It sat on just over an acre of land, and the neighbors could only be seen over the tall hedges from the second floor. She had grown to like the seclusion. She had bought the lot five years earlier and had a new house erected on it. She was the first and only occupant. There were never any ghosts here. She liked that too. This was a place where she could escape all kinds of people, both living and deceased.

She sat in a large room on the second floor. It contained very little furniture. No paintings or pictures hung on the walls. There were no windows, and no telephone was hooked up. It was a room which was designed to help her concentrate. There were no bright colors or frivolous objects to distract her, just comfortable furniture and soft tones of beige, burgundy and grey. She had come to this room to concentrate, to learn more of the secrets of the dream and the little boy.

Sunday night had brought her another series of dreams. The one she recalled best was again the one where she stood in the room with the dark images and the child. She finally decided that someone or something was trying to communicate with her. She decided that it was probably something of some importance, or the visions would have gone away by now. Instead of going away they had grown stronger and even presented themselves in physical manifestations, like the boy she thought she had run over yesterday. She decided that she would try to induce the images, that she would invite the little boy to come into the room and speak with her. This way she could learn what she needed to know. Then she would either solve the problem or find a way to stop the dreams.

The lights were dimmed, and she closed her eyes and began to breathe deeply. She relaxed in a soft leather chair, her legs propped up on a comfortable leather hassock. She laid with her head back, her eyes slightly opened and trained on the off-white ceiling. In her mind she opened the gates which she had learned to keep closed most of the time. Anywhere else this usually meant seeing things she did not wish to see. Over the years she had learned how to keep from seeing ghosts and images from the past everywhere she went. It was a kind of a screen she raised which filtered out the surreal and helped her to maintain the concrete. It was this screen she lowered now. In her new house, in this room, there would be no distracting images from the past. There would be no walls where walls had once been nor people standing where they once had stood. Instead this opened her up to the spiritual world in a way which allowed only those things which lingered to appear. Only things which sought her out would appear here. Here there was no background noise.

After about twenty minutes in this state she heard soft yet shallow breathing coming from behind her. She did not move, but maintained her relaxed and receptive state. The breathing continued for several minutes. Then she felt a soft pressure on her shoulder. Still she did not move. Then she heard a whisper. It was the whisper of a child. She could make out no words at first, but as she listened and waited a few became clear. Finally, after several more minutes, the voice became clear. It was still very soft, but she could hear the words. She opened her eyes more and could see the little hand now resting on her shoulder. She listened as the child spoke.

"Please help me," it said. "Help me stop it."

It said this several times. Finally, when she was sure the voice was strong enough, she spoke to it.

"Stop what?" she asked.

"The door," came the soft answer.

"Stop the door what?" she asked.

"Open."

She had learned through the years how to ask the right questions, and how to interpret the answers.

"Why?" she asked.

"Bad," came the reply.

"Why bad?" she asked.

"Hurt," came the child's voice.

"How can I help?" she asked.

"Door," came the soft reply.

"How help?" she repeated, hoping to get a different answer.

"Door. Stop door. Bad trick."

Sandra turned her head slowly until she could see the soft and faded image of the child. The sight was pitiful and horrible. The child was covered with cuts and torn skin. Dried blood covered one side of his face, and his right arm was completely gone. Gashes gaped open, some revealing white and rotting bone. She could smell a hint of death and decay, but it was more like old musty sheets than a dead body. She looked at the child and spoke to it.

"How can I do this?" she asked.

The child said nothing but pointed with his left hand. She looked where he was pointing to but saw nothing but an empty wall.

"What do you mean?" she asked.

"Go," the child said.

"Go where?" she asked.

"There," the child replied. He continued to point.

She knew from the way the house was built that he was pointing a little west of south. But where did he mean? Was the problem in southwest Saint Louis, or southwest Missouri?

"Where?" she asked.

The child said nothing but continued to point. Then he looked to her with sad eyes and spoke one last time.

"They got me now," he said. "Please help."

His eyes showed sorrow and resignation as his pointing image faded.

Then she knew that the child had come from a long way. His image did not belong with her and had sought her out for some reason. She did not know what this might lead to, but she knew it was important. Sandra decided that she would pack enough things for a week-long trip and get into her car. Then she would head just west of south until she got close enough to receive the child's image more clearly. Then she would learn what was wrong, and what she was supposed to do about it.

At least that's how she hoped it would all work.

2

Joe looked through his new shopping cart at the treasures he had accumulated that day. The cart was in very good condition. None of the wheels wobbled or went the wrong way when he pushed it. The wire was all straight; there were no dents or bent parts. Although it was a larger capacity cart, the wheel base was the same so he could still haul it up his ramp. It had been waiting for him that morning when he walked out of his home. Joe had stepped out the open door into the misty morning and seen the cart just across the street. There were no signs of anyone, just the new cart. He knew it was for him, and he knew who had left it for him.

Today his cart was filled with treasures mostly for him. The white man had urged him to get a few things as well. There were even a few things he had been required to buy. He didn't like spending his money, but he didn't want to disappoint the white man, so he had bought the things. They rested in their own corner of the basket.

Joe hummed another religious song from his past as he pushed the basket of treasures down the road, toward home. The sun was about an hour from setting, and he had to be somewhere this evening. But first he would go home and unpack his treasures. Then he would return to the house of the dark woman.

3

Dave sat at home with an empty dinner plate in front of him. The plate was a formality. He had stopped at the Dairy Queen on the way home and picked up a burger and some fries. He had been brought up eating on a plate in the house, even if it was fast food. He finished off the last fry and sat back. The food settled heavily in his stomach and a soft burp escaped him.

That afternoon he had decided that he would go to see Colleen. He'd called her a couple of times from the office, but she did not answer. He tried once already tonight, but again she wasn't home. Dave walked to the phone and dialed her number again. This time he let it ring ten times before giving up. He hung up the phone and looked at the clock. It was six. He decided he would just drive over to her place in case the phones were acting up again. He cleaned off the table, then he got his cassette and piece of paper he had written the words on and headed for the door.

4

"Hello?"

Colleen listened, but heard no one on the other end of the line. There was nothing at all, just dead space. It was the fourth time this had happened today, and she decided she would call the phone company in the morning.

The day had been an odd one, to say the least. Not an hour went by that she wasn't reminded somehow of Dave Chatburn and his dead brother. Early on it was the experience with the Ouija board. Once she simply saw a white delivery truck which reminded her of the one in her dream driving down the road. Around noon she had run into town for some groceries and had seen a man who looked a lot like Dave. And she had seen the old bum there too. She knew he had a name, but she couldn't remember it. He'd been pushing his cart across the store's parking lot, looking at her with a grin on his face. She'd found his gaze disturbing and was wondering if perhaps he had targeted her for some ill will. After lunch her television was on, showing a commercial for some hospital or other. The commercial had shown a bloodied child being wheeled into the emergency room of a hospital. It had been too graphic for the lunch hour. She didn't remember ever seeing the commercial before, and then she remembered that she had not even turned the television on.

The day had been full of events such as these. She wanted to know more, but her two attempts during the day to contact the spirit world had been fruitless. She needed Dave, but he did not seem willing to cooperate. She decided that the best thing to do was just show up at his house. But she didn't know where he lived. She went to the phone book and found his name. His number was listed, but there was no address. She tried calling him again, but this time he didn't answer at all. He had said something that morning about going to Abilene. Perhaps at least that much had been true. She would try again later.

Colleen went into the kitchen to fix a small meal. As she sat down to eat the sandwich there was a knock on the door. She threw her sandwich back to the plate. Why was it always like this?

She walked to the door and put on her somber face. It was dinner time, but she was not one to turn away business. She looked once through the peephole as she turned the knob.

Then she froze. She had turned the knob, but she had not yet opened the door. It was the bum. It was the old man she had seen that morning in front of her house, and again at the grocery store. He stood looking straight back at her through the peephole, a wicked smirk on his weary face.

She released the knob and it snapped back into place. Then she turned the dead bolt. As she did so the knob turned back. She barely had the bolt in place when the man began pushing hard on the other side. When the door did not open he began to pound on it. She looked through the hole again and he stopped pounding for a moment. He looked back at her. His hair was disheveled and strewn across his eyes in jagged patterns. Dark shadows of stubble and spit covered his face. He wore gloves with the fingers cut out. In his right hand he held a small object which was too distorted by the curved image to discern.

Colleen left the door and the pounding resumed. She ran to her room and opened the small wooden box by her bed. She threw aside the scarfs and lotion and grabbed the small handgun which she kept loaded for such emergencies.

The pounding stopped.

She walked slowly toward the front door, listening carefully for any sound or movement from outside. Then the television turned on and began screaming its accolades about a new formula which made Cheer better. The volume was too high, and she could not hear what she needed to hear. If the man was moving around her house, she could not hear it. She walked across the room and switched off the television. Then she listened.

But it was silent.

Then there was a knocking at the door.

She stood still. She waited for a few moments. He knocked again.

She moved slowly toward the door, her gun held out in front of her. If she had to shoot through the door she would. The police would probably congratulate her for getting rid of that nuisance of a man anyway. She walked to the door and listened. He knocked again. The knocks seemed less urgent. He was going to be very patient. She stood a few feet from the door. Then she called out to him.

"I've got a gun and I'll shoot you through the fucking door if I have to!"

At first there was silence. Then a reply.

"Uh, don't shoot. It's me, Dave." A pause. "What's going on?"

Colleen lowered her gun and walked to the door. From instinct she still looked through the peephole. It was Dave. She unlocked the door and let him in.

"What's going on?" he asked her again. "You look a little shook up."

"That bum was at my door," she explained. "You know, the shopping cart man."

"You mean Crazy Joe."

"Yes, that's the guy."

"He's harmless."

"He didn't look particularly harmless to me," she explained. Now that the excitement was over her hands began to shake a little.

She flipped the gun's safety back on and invited Dave into the living room. He closed the door and followed her to the hallway where she left him to return her gun to the bedroom. Dave went on into the living room where he sat on an old couch with bad springs. It reminded him of his mother's couch. In a few moments she returned from her bedroom. She looked different. He realized she had let her hair down.

She walked into the small room and took a seat across from him. All of her furniture looked old, and although some attempt at coordination had been made, there was a certain clashing of styles. He assumed correctly that she had picked most of the stuff up second-hand.

"So," she started, "you didn't have to go to Abilene after all."

"No," he answered, embarrassed now that he had lied. "I didn't have to do that after all."

"Good," she answered. She knew that something must have happened to Dave also today or he would not have decided to come. Since he was the focus of all of this and not her, she assumed that his experience had been even more distracting. "So," she began again, trying to sound conversational, "what kinds of things happened to you today?"

"What do you mean?" he asked, forgetting that she was supposed to be clairvoyant to some extent.

"I mean you look disturbed, and I can tell that you have been in contact with the other side today. What kind of contact was it, and when did it happen?"

"Well, I decided to go to my mother's house today and play my tape for her."

"Your tape?" Colleen asked.

"Yes, I didn't tell you about that yet. I brought it with me and I'll play it for you in a minute. Anyway, I went to play this tape for her and when I was leaving I saw this little boy on a Big Wheel behind my car."

Dave explained the whole experience while Colleen listened intently. He would not have told anyone else, mainly because they would have thought him crazy. But Colleen seemed to believe and to understand. Just a few days ago Dave would not have thought the experiences he was having even to be possible. Now he was explaining them as 'matter-of-fact.' He guessed that Colleen probably dealt with this kind of stuff regularly and had resigned himself to paying her for her services if that's what it took to understand this thing.

Colleen on the other hand had never experienced anything quite so concrete as this. All of her communications with the other side to date had been vague and somewhat induced at best. What she had been experiencing since the dreams started was much more concrete, but she had been prepared for it by years of work with the supernatural and it hadn't terrified her as badly as it might have someone else.

Dave finished his story and looked to Colleen for the answer. She just sat and looked back at first. Then her eyes narrowed and small lines appeared in her forehead as she thought about the meaning of it all.

"The spiritual world is trying desperately to get in contact with both of us for some reason," she explained. "It's trying to get in touch with you because you're the focal point. I'm not sure why yet, but it has something to do with your dead brother. It's trying to get in touch with me also, but probably only because I'm the closest person to you through which contact with that world might be made." She shifted her weight and put her chin in her hand. Her elbow rested on the small arm of the chair. "I think if we sat down and had a real live seance we might be able to get some answers. Beyond that, I'm not sure what to tell you, and I don't think this thing is going to leave you alone. My guess is that until you receive the message you will continue to be haunted by the dreams and images. Afterwards maybe it will stop."

"Maybe?" Dave asked.

"Sure. There's no guarantee that it will stop, especially if there's some task you're supposed to perform."

"What kind of task?" Dave asked.

"I'm not sure. Maybe something like exhume a body and solve a mystery, or something like that. It's never the same thing."

"You've done this before?" he asked.

"Sure," she exaggerated. She had performed seances before, and told people what they had to do to stop a haunting. But she had never been quite so involved in it personally, and she certainly hadn't ever dug up a body.

"Okay," Dave said. He decided he needed to get this over with. "Let's do it. How much will it cost?" he asked.

"I told you I'd start charging when it wasn't personal. I'm still trying to figure out my part in this," she explained. She liked Dave. She knew that she should charge him the standard forty dollars for the seance, but she would be able to make it up somewhere else. Maybe he'd buy her another dinner.

"Can we do it now?" Dave asked.

"We need to wait until it's completely dark. The best time is near midnight. That's when it's easiest to communicate with the spirit world." She was lying. She decided that she was interested in this man. Things were happening to him which turned her on in a bizarre way. She figured she could keep him around at least until midnight.

"Should I go and come back then?" he asked.

"Why don't you stay here, in case they decide to contact us first?"

Dave was hoping she would say something like this. Her dark eyes showed again the playfulness they had on the day they had met in the library.

"While we wait, why don't we get a pizza?" Dave suggested. "I'll buy."

"Sounds good," she agreed. "Let's order one and stay here."

"Okay."

Dave grabbed the phone book and looked for the pizza section. He liked how things were going, and then wondered just where that might be.

5

Sandra drove her car down Manchester Road. In the trunk of her car she had packed enough belongings to cover her for a week if that became necessary. There was no telling where she might be going. One possibility was that she would be going nowhere, returning to her home after a few hours of driving around. Already she had been driving for thirty minutes with no indication of whether or not she was headed in the right direction. She simply continued to drive south and west, keeping her mind and eyes opened to anything which might be a sign, but there was nothing. So she drove by instinct.

She drove through Rock Hill and Kirkwood and eventually through Des Peres, staying on State Highway 100 the entire time. As she approached loop 270 she debated getting on it and heading back around to I-44 North which would be the quick way back home.

But as she looked at the entrance ramp she saw a little boy. He stood looking in her direction from the side of the road. His face was tattered and one arm was missing. With his remaining arm he pointed up the entrance ramp of 270 south. She drove past the boy, not stopping, and got onto the loop heading southward.

Five minutes later she saw the boy again. This time he was standing on the shoulder of the highway at the interchange with I-44. He stood pointing down the ramp which led to I-44 South. She took the exit and headed toward the Missouri countryside, wondering just how far she had left to go.

VII
1

"It's pretty dark tonight. That's good."

Joe walked through the darkness of the night. He toyed with the small pistol in his right pocket. He carried the pistol from time to time, when he didn't feel secure. The things he had been seeing and hearing lately had certainly made him a little nervous. Still he walked with a smirk on his face and hummed when he wasn't talking to himself. He had been to the house of the witch woman, and had almost gotten her to open the door. He was supposed to have given her a message and a present. The present was in his right pocket, and he could feel one of the claws from the dead animal's foot as it pressed against his leg. But then the guy had come and Joe had fled. He would have to try again later, if that's what was required of him.

He walked toward his home. As he walked he came to a tall wall of sheet metal which had been painted orange. The wall had been built in response to a city ordinance which had been designed to hide the mess of old cars and trucks which lay rusting in the junkyard behind it. But the wall itself was a considerable eyesore, certainly not what the city council had intended when they had passed the ordinance. It was the owner's way of getting in the last word, which he always did one way or another. The wall was about a hundred yards long. As Joe got about two thirds of the way past the bright barrier he heard a sound coming from the other side of it. It was the sound of old metal creaking, as if an old car door were being opened. Then there was a loud 'pop.' He froze for a moment and tightened his grip on the gun. Then he listened.

The sound was louder the second time and it startled him. He pulled the gun from his pocket and began to walk quickly away from the wall.

Then he heard someone calling his name.

He recognized the voice, and relaxed his grip on the pistol. It was the White Man. Joe was at the White Man's mercy, so the gun was superfluous. Joe didn't think his gun could harm the man, and the rebellion it implied might simply make him angry. Besides, Joe was working for the White Man now, and already his rewards had been substantial.

He heard his name again. It was coming from behind the metal wall. Joe walked back to the wall and looked it over. He knew that the voice intended for him to look over the top of the wall, but he didn't see how he was going to be able to do this. Then he felt a hand on his shoulder. He turned quickly, but there was no one there. Then an old crate which rested against a lamppost across the street caught his eye. Joe grinned. He knew that this was what the ghostly hand had meant for him to see. He was getting used to the White Man's methods now. The White Man even seemed to have a dark sense of humor. That's what the dead animal in Joe's pocket was all about, as far as Joe had figured it.

"Okay. I got to look over there. Okay."

Joe retrieved the crate and brought it to the wall where he got up on top of it.

"Okay. I'm lookin' over there now."

The crate creaked as he mounted it, but it seemed stable enough to hold him. When he stood up on top of the box he could see into the junkyard. It would not be possible for him to climb over the fence, especially since the top of the sheet metal was so sharp. But he could see in. He looked into the yard and saw hundreds of cars. Most were old. Some were new but in bad shape. He saw a late model Oldsmobile with its front end pushed crooked. Even in the dark he could make out a little blood where the edge of its windshield had once been.

Then he realized that he could see much more detail than he should have been able to see in the dark. As he looked around he realized that it was because there was a dim light coming from within the yard. He looked for the source of that light, and after a few moments located it.

There was one vehicle about eighty feet from the fence which was casting a soft and eerie glow. The glow seemed to be coming from all over the vehicle. It was an even hue and it emanated in all directions. He would not have noticed the light had he been simply walking by the yard. But now he did see it, though he did not understand it.

"Hey, that's not right."

The vehicle which seemed to be the source of the glow was a very old truck. It was big and white and the name of some long-forgotten delivery service was written in faded red paint on its side. The tires were gone, as were the hood and one of the doors. They had been salvaged for some other truck which now lay somewhere else in this same yard. Joe heard the creaking metal again and saw that this sound was also coming from the old delivery truck. He watched as a small portion of the front left fender snapped outwards, eliminating a dent which had been there moments before.

Joe spoke with himself and watched in amazement as the snapping and popping continued. There seemed to be an invisible man working on the body of the old delivery truck, and he was doing a fine job. Joe watched as the large dent in the passenger door creaked and moaned before snapping out, leaving the door almost smooth.

Then the snapping stopped. There were still a few small dents left, but no major ones. The truck was now silent, but the glow remained.

Then there was a loud rumble as the engine turned over once. Joe flinched and almost fell from his box at the sound. Then it turned over again, just once. Joe stared in amazement at the truck.

Then it started.

Joe stood looking at the truck as it rumbled for a moment. Thick black smoke puffed out from the exhaust pipe, and the truck shook with the heavy rhythm of the engine.

Then it coughed and cut out again.

It did not start up again, and the glowing faded away.

As Joe stared at the truck he understood what he was supposed to do. He didn't like the idea of spending his money on the tires and parts which had been stripped, but he figured that some of the reward for his dedication to the White Man might be monetary. He also knew that he really didn't have any choice.

But he would have to wait until the morning when the yard opened before he could do what he was supposed to do.

The darkness returned in its purest form and Joe jumped down from his box. Then he kicked the box over and began singing to himself as he resumed his walk home.

2

Dave held Colleen close and looked into her deep dark eyes as midnight approached. Those eyes seemed so full of mystery. Her skin was so smooth, and her lips so soft. He kissed them again, and again he felt his heart respond.

One cold slice of pizza rested on the coffee table next to the two of them. The old television lit the room dimly with the black and white version of David Letterman. Letterman's voice droned in the background, his words both unclear and unimportant to both Dave and Colleen.

He explored and tested. She did not resist his wandering hands and he felt the soft skin on her stomach. He could feel her stomach rise and fall as she breathed. Even now her breath reminded him of rose petals, as it had when he had first met her in the library.

He kissed her again and as he did his hand moved slowly upward. She let out a sign of pleasure, and he knew that she would not resist. He felt the tension and anticipation build inside of him.

Colleen yielded and waited, feeling warmth in his touch. She did not know if it was real warmth, or if she just imagined it. Either way it did not matter right now. It felt good. She felt needed and wanted in a way she had not in a very long time. She let his hands wander up her blouse, across her breasts. She felt her own excitement as his hands passed softly over them. She grasped his strong shoulders. His shirt was opened, and she ran her own hands across his chest. He was not a heavily muscled man, but his chest was nice, and it felt good under her hands.

They kissed and explored together. Their clothes streamed easily from their bodies and they moved together on the couch.

They touched and caressed.

And then he was inside her.

As they moved together they both felt the power and the wonder of the encounter. It was deep, somehow magical. They were isolated from the world. There was nothing which could destroy their togetherness.

Almost nothing.

Suddenly they both heard David Letterman's voice loud and clear. It cut through the emotion and the passion and struck them both cold.

"It's time for you to stop fucking around," he said. It was still Letterman's voice, but his face had become blurry. They both looked toward it and saw the hazy image of another man. "It's midnight. Time to reach out and touch me!"

There was a loud laugh, then a soft 'pop' as the screen went black, leaving the room in utter darkness.

Their magic was gone, replaced by a much darker one.

3

Sandra drove down I-44. She had been doing so for almost three hours now. She had seen no sign of the child since she had been directed southward, but she felt that she was headed in the right direction.

She had already passed through Springfield, Illinois, and was about an hour from the Oklahoma border. She knew now that she would pass into Oklahoma, but how far she would travel after that she did not know.

It was dark out. The clouds obscured what moon there was. A spot of rain appeared on her windshield.

She was tired. She had driven much farther than she had thought she would, and she had no idea when it would be over, or what would be waiting for her when she finally did reach her destination. The music on the radio had gotten bad for her some time ago, and now she scanned the AM stations looking for talk shows which could hold her interest.

She found a local program where a man's medical problems were being discussed so she left it there to listen.

"So you get these headaches when you drink diet soda?" the host asked.

"Yes," the man answered.

"Do you notice getting them when you drink coffee or tea?"

"Sometimes when I drink ice-tea," the man answered.

"What do you use to sweeten your tea with?" the host asked.

"Lo-calorie stuff."

"Okay," the host began, "I think I know what your problem might be."

"Good," the man said, sounding relieved.

"I think you're seeing too many ghosts."

The radio was silent for a moment. Sandra kept her eyes on the road, but they showed the same confusion which the man calling in to the host must have been experiencing.

"I don't understand," the man said.

"Well," the host continued, "it's like this. You've probably been seeing ghosts of one kind or another all your life. Most of what you've seen, however, has really been nothing more than images of the past. Your contact with the present has been limited, and harmless."

"Okay," the caller answered, "but how does this give me headaches?"

"Well, lately I'll bet you've been seeing some pretty disturbing things. Like the boy on the Big Wheel for instance."

Sandra's eyes went instinctively to her radio. Then she realized that she had lost the talk show. Something very different had taken its place. Something meant for her. She left the radio on and listened.

"So what does this mean?" the caller asked.

"Well, this means that even though you are different than most people, and your experiences have seemed to be dramatic, they are really small potatoes when compared with what really lies out there, very small potatoes. These recent manifestations may be something much bigger than you've ever dealt with before, and much more current." The host's voice seemed to be changing gradually. It was becoming deeper, and rougher. "These headaches are just your body's way of warning you."

Sandra felt a sudden chill run through her body. The air around her seemed heavy. The rain began to fall harder on her windshield. She reached forward and turned the vent on to let some fresh air in. Then she felt a small pain in the back of her head.

"I would venture to guess," the host continued, "that these headaches could be just the tip of the iceberg." With the mention of the word 'headaches' Sandra felt the pressure inside her head build. The pain spread to her eyes and dug its way into her brain. The voice got deeper. "What I mean to say is that maybe the headaches are a warning of some kind. Maybe you are being warned to mind your own God-damned business!" The voice finally settled in on a deep and gravelly tone. "Maybe there's worse pain waiting for you. Maybe you should just turn around and leave it all alone, while you're still able to. It can only get worse from here."

Her eyes returned to the radio. At the final words the pain in her head grew suddenly until it was so sharp she cried out. A small line of blood trickled from her nose.

She put one hand to her face and felt the blood as she looked back to the road. Her vision was blurred by the pain. As it cleared she saw an old white delivery truck sitting across both lanes of the freeway and she hit her brakes. The road was wet and she knew that she would not stop in time. The car turned slowly sideways as she slid toward the truck. She watched as the white side grew in size as she approached it. Just before she hit it she saw into the driver's side and saw the man. He was dressed all in white and had the most evil eyes she had ever seen.

Then she went through the truck.

Her car came to a complete stop about fifty feet from where the truck had been. Her car was turned sideways and now it was her car that blocked two lanes of the freeway. She looked to where the truck had been. Now there was no truck at all, just a spot where the rain fell to the wet pavement. A small drop of blood ran down her face and fell from her chin.

The engine of her car had died. She turned the key and it coughed but would not turn over. She tried again, but the engine was not responding. After a few more tries she knew she had flooded the engine, so she stopped to let the fuel clear out.

In the distance she saw a pair of headlights appear. She wondered if the approaching vehicle would be able to see her. As she wondered this her headlights flickered once, then went out. Her windshield wipers stopped too. She smelled smoke. Something in the electrical system had shorted out. She turned the key again. This time there was no response at all. She looked back up the highway and saw that the vehicle was a large one, and it was getting closer fast.

She pulled on the door handle, but the door was locked. It was a power lock, the kind where you couldn't manually pull the lock up, even from the inside. It was supposed to pop up when you pulled the handle, but it would not.

The big truck approached. There was no way it would see her car in time.

She tried the window, but it too was electric and would not roll down. She looked around the car for something she could use to break the window, but there was nothing handy. She tried the door and window on the passenger's side, but it was no use.

She tried not to panic, but it was very hard.

Then the radio came back on.

"And so, you see," the gravelly voice continued, "you need to leave things like this alone. They can only get you into lots and lots of trouble."

She tried to ignore the voice and figure out a way to get out of the car.

"In fact, you may not survive this little warning. But that's probably for the best anyway."

She climbed into the back seat and tried the doors and windows, again to no avail.

The truck was approaching too quickly.

"You aren't going to get out," the radio explained. "You've been a very bad girl."

The truck would hit her in seconds.

She sat down in the back seat and quickly pulled the seat belt across her chest.

"It won't help," the voice taunted.

She buckled the belt and then bent over in the crash position she had seem numerous times both on the brochures in airplanes and in the movies.

The inside of her car lit up as the headlights of the oncoming truck illuminated it. She braced herself and waited while the voice on the radio laughed a hideous laugh.

***

The car appeared out of nowhere. It was just sitting in the middle of the freeway; its lights weren't even on. The truck driver hit his brakes and turned the steering wheel hard, trying to avoid the collision, though he knew that there was no way he was going to miss the car. The big truck slid across the wet pavement toward the shoulder. As he slid off the road he thought for a moment he might miss it after all, but then the left side of his steel bumper collided with the right front fender of the car. The windshield of the car exploded and the car spun off the highway, across the shoulder and into the mud. When it hit the mud the tires on the left side of the car grabbed hold and the car flipped over and began rolling toward the fence which separated the highway from a large corn field. The big truck smashed through that fence and created four large trenches as the tires plowed through the wet field before finally coming to a stop. The truck leaned heavily in one direction, almost tipping over before crashing back to all eighteen wheels. The car flipped over the fence, then flipped three more times before landing upside down in the field.

The truck driver sat inside his truck for a moment, trying to realign his mind with reality. A minute later, after realizing that he was not seriously hurt, he jumped from his truck and hurried over to the car. His feet sank into the mud as he trudged through the small rows of the immature corn toward the vehicle. It was dark, and his headlights pointed into the field, away from the car. Still the reflection of that light was enough for him to see that there was someone inside the car. The body was hanging upside down suspended from the back seat by a seat belt. As he approached the car he could hear an odd gravelly sound coming from it.

As he drew close to it he realized that what he was hearing was uncontrolled laughter.

And it seemed to be coming from the radio.

4

Dave and Colleen sat in Colleen's 'power room.' Only this time Colleen felt more power than she had ever felt before. It felt as if all her previous contacts had been nothing more than self-deception, and that was in fact what they had been for the most part. Dave felt the power too. He was disappointed at having been pulled from the enjoyable task of making love to Colleen, but now that seemed less and less important as the moments went by. The room was dark except for a single tall candle which sat in the center of the table. Dave and Colleen sat on opposite sides of the table, looking into each other's eyes, hoping the other would give a clue as to what was supposed to happen next. Colleen felt as much at the mercy of the outside forces as did Dave. They both simply sat and waited.

"Now what?" Dave asked.

"I'm not sure."

"I thought you did this kind of stuff all the time," he commented.

"Not exactly like this," she explained. "This is very concrete, more so than I'm accustomed to."

"So shouldn't we be holding hands and chanting, or something like that?"

Colleen sat and thought. That didn't sound like a bad idea, and she wasn't so concerned at the moment with maintaining an air of either authority or even credibility. She had a feeling that whatever was going to happen was out of her control anyway.

She laid her hands palm up on the table. Dave looked surprised, then he reached out and took her hands in his. Hers were soft hands, and the palms were sweaty. So were his.

She closed her eyes and he followed suit.

And they waited.

After a few minutes Dave began to grow impatient. He was beginning to wonder if Colleen knew what she was doing. As he prepared to ask the question he felt a cool breeze whisper across his neck.

And he remembered that the room had no windows, and only one door.

He remained silent and waited.

Then he felt the table shake softly. He opened his eyes slightly to see if Colleen was doing this. When he did he noticed that the room had gotten brighter, and that the candle had gone out. The source of the new light seemed to be somewhere near the candle, actually in the air above it.

He looked at Colleen. Her eyes were opened too now, only they were all white, as if the irises had rolled back into her head. The table shook more firmly. Dave's hands were still on top of Colleen's. Their hands rose together about a foot. The table still shook, and Dave felt the fear grip him hard. His chest felt tight and he wanted badly to get up and run.

But he waited. And eventually she spoke.

"Davey," she said. "Davey, are you there?"

The voice was Colleen's, but it was high-pitched, like that of a small child. He knew who it was supposed to be, but Colleen's voice was a poor match. Still he answered.

"Yes. I'm here."

"Davey it's me, it's Tommy."

Dave said nothing. He wasn't sure what he was supposed to say.

Suddenly the table shook violently, and Colleen called out in a shrill voice, "Davey! Davey, where are you?"

Dave looked at the table and felt his heart race. He could hear it pounding in his ears. The table began to slowly turn. One of its legs brushed up against his. He decided he should answer.

"Yes, I'm still here Tommy."

The table stopped turning but returned to its almost nervous shaking.

"Davey, I need your help."

Dave waited. When the table seemed to become agitated he answered, "What do you need Tommy?" he asked. His voice was shaking.

"I can't talk to you very long, so listen carefully."

When Colleen stopped speaking Dave took this as his sign to answer. "Okay, Tommy."

"There are bad people here. Lots of them. They're trying to get out."

"Out of where?" Dave asked.

"Out of here. Out of where I am."

"Where are you Tommy?" Dave asked.

"I'm where you put me. I wasn't ready to die. Neither were they."

Dave felt a knot in his throat at his brother's accusation. "I'm sorry, Tommy. I'm sorry." His voice still shook, only now there was sorrow mixed with the fear. "I didn't mean to put you there."

"You can make up for it," the voice continued. "There are bad people here, and they're trying to get over there."

"Over where?" Dave asked.

"Where you are."

"Why?"

"They want to hurt, Davey. They want to hurt and kill. You have to stop them."

"But how?" Dave cried out. "How can I stop them?"

"You have to use the magic, Davey."

The words rang a bell, though he was not sure why. "What magic?" Dave asked. "What do you mean, magic?"

"Remember when we used to play together, Davey? Remember you used to tell me about the magic that made me dream good dreams? You told me when I was scared of the dark, when I was scared of the monsters. It always worked, Davey."

Dave did remember the magic. "But that wasn't real magic, Tommy. That was just kids' games."

"No, Davey. It was real magic 'cause it worked. That's the same magic you have to use to stop the bad people."

Dave felt a hot tear run down his cheek. He sat and looked at Colleen, her eyes still rolled back into her head. "I don't understand," Dave said, his voice still shaking.

"You have to stop them."

"Tell me how."

"Use the magic."

"I don't understand."

"You have to stop them," the childlike voice called to him. It seemed to be the only response to Dave's lack of understanding.

"What do I have to do?" he asked again.

"Use the magic."

"Tell me how," Dave begged. His voice was displaying both urgency and annoyance.

"I can't right now, they're coming for me."

"Tell me quickly," Dave said.

"You'll have to come back when they aren't coming, then I'll tell you."

"Tell me what you can now, Tommy."

Colleen's head began to shake from side to side. Her eyes, still white, rolled back and forth as if she were looking around frantically.

"Tell me what you can," Dave repeated.

"I'll have to come back, Davey," the voice answered. "They're here now."

"Run away, Tommy." Dave stood up, still holding to Colleen's hands. "Run away from them and tell me what I have to do."

"I can't!" The voice was becoming frantic. "I can't get away. They're all around me and they want me to stop talking to you. They're going to hurt me, Davey."

"Get away, Tommy!" Dave called out.

But his words were interrupted by the scream of a child which melted into the scream of a young woman. Suddenly Colleen's eyes returned to their beautiful brown coloring, but the screaming did not stop. Her hands pulled back from Dave's. Then the room went black as the magical glow disappeared.

Colleen's screaming stopped. Then Dave heard a shuffling noise and suddenly he felt Colleen's arms around his waist. She had climbed part of the way across the table and was making her way over it.

"Don't go," she called to him. Her voice was shaking and her grasp seemed frantic.

She lost her grip on Dave and fell to the floor at his feet. She was up in an instant holding onto him again. She stood holding him tight and close. He could feel her whole body shaking.

"Don't go," she repeated.

Dave held her. After a few minutes of silence she spoke. "I've been somewhere," she said. "Somewhere horrible." He felt her arms loosening. "Let's get out of this room," she said.

She led Dave to where the door should have been.

But there was only a smooth, black wall.

Her mind rebelled and she began to grow frantic.

"Where's the door?" she cried out.

Dave did not know how to answer, and her question brought further unease to him.

She felt out for the door again, and again found only wall.

"I'm still there!" she screamed out. "I'm still in that place, and you're here too!"

There was too much panic in her voice. Dave felt her fingernails digging into his palm. He released her hand and put both of his hands on the wall.

"Don't leave me!" she called out.

"I'm right here," Dave answered.

He felt her hands on his back, then around his waist. She held on tightly as he made his way along the wall to the first corner. He felt along the second wall until he came to what felt like a door. He felt around for the knob, then turned it when he found it. A dull light made its way into the room.

Then things began to become familiar again.

"You were just disoriented," Dave explained as he walked out of the room. She still held tightly to him. He walked to the nearest light switch and flipped it on. No light came on.

"I don't think so," she said. "I think that for a moment we both really were in that place."

"The lights are out again," Dave said.

Then Colleen screamed and Dave looked over his shoulder. He saw the face staring through the hall window. It was a white face with white eyes. And it was laughing.

Then the light came on and the face disappeared.

Dave turned around to face Colleen. Tears covered her face and there was a little blood on her cheek where she had struck the table when she fell.

"What's going on?" he asked her.

"I don't know," she replied. Then she put her arms around him again and buried her face in his shoulder. "But it's scaring the hell out of me."

"So you haven't really experienced anything quite like this?" he asked.

She pulled back and looked at him with an expression of incredulity. "Are you kidding?" she said. "I'm in over my head."

"So now what?" he asked.

She looked beyond him for a moment as she thought. Then she let go of him. Her confidence was returning and she didn't like appearing vulnerable as she had in excess for the past several moments.

"Now," she said, "now you tell me what happened in that room and we go from there."

"Do you want to know now?" he asked.

"Right now," she replied. Then she walked past Dave and toward the living room.

Dave looked at his watch. It was after one o'clock. Tomorrow was going to be hell.

He followed Colleen back into the living room where she sat in the chair opposite the couch. A certain coldness had returned to her demeanor. Dave sat down on the couch.

Then he told her exactly what had happened in the power room.

When he finished he sat in silence as she looked again somewhere beyond him. He waited while she thought for a moment.

Then she looked to him and spoke. "I'll have to go back," she said.

"Back where?" Dave asked.

"To that dark place I went to before."

"What is that place?" Dave asked.

"Apparently its where I go while my body is in use by your brother."

Dave thought for a moment. "Tonight?" he asked.

"No," she answered, "I think your brother has made it clear that he is under some restraint. We'll have to wait until he is able to tell us what we need to do."

"When do you think that will be?" Dave asked.

Colleen tilted her head slightly. "I'm sure he'll find a way to let us know."

The room grew silent and uncomfortable.

Colleen spoke. "For tonight, however, I think we're done."

Dave understood her meaning and stood up from the couch. He walked past Colleen on his way to the door and she walked behind him as he went.

He turned to face her at the door, his hand on the knob behind his back. "I'll call you if anything else happens."

"Okay," she agreed.

"You'll do the same."

"Of course," she agreed.

Then he leaned forward and kissed her. She did not resist, but neither was she warm.

He opened the door and walked out of her house. He walked to his car without looking back as she closed the door behind him.

VIII
1

She actually smelled him before she saw him.

Donna looked up and saw Crazy Joe walking toward her teller window. He always chose her window, even if there was someone in her line and another window was available. She figured it had something to do with her breasts since he looked at and spoke to them instead of her. She was very self-conscious about it, but there wasn't really anything she could do. She had confronted him once, but he had simply chuckled and continued to stare.

Today there was no one in line so Joe walked directly to her window. She tried not to grimace at the stench.

"I need to withdraw some money," Joe explained. His breath smelled like something dead.

"Which account?" she asked him.

He thought for a moment, then said, "The big one."

"Do you have the number?" she asked.

He looked at her incredulously. "Are you joking? No. Just look at them and take this from the biggest one."

Joe pushed a piece of folded paper across the counter to her. She was reluctant to touch it, but equally reluctant to offend the man for fear he might take his business elsewhere. Too many people had closed accounts lately. She looked at the piece of paper. Her eyes widened a little. Usually Joe's withdrawals were small, never more than fifty dollars. He seemed to be able to make that last him months at times, especially in the summer. She assumed it was because this was when people throw away the most stuff. Today Joe wanted over a thousand dollars.

Donna walked to the computer behind her and pulled up Joe's four accounts. All but one held in excess of a hundred thousand dollars. She couldn't begin to guess where the money had come from, and there were all kinds of rumors. All that was known for certain was that one day, many years ago, a filthy bum who seemed too young to be a bum had pushed a shopping cart full of cash into their bank and set up in their town. Since then he had lived off of less than the interest, and the accounts had grown accordingly. He never received statements, and didn't seem to care. He probably didn't even know that he had exceeded the maximum insurable amount some years ago. Sometimes when he would request his small amounts of money he would look concerned, as if he would find out that there was no more. But Joe had more money than all but a few of the wealthiest of Cisco's citizens.

She took the number of the account with the largest balance and returned to her counter. "How would you like that?" she asked Joe.

"What?" he asked.

She noticed that he was looking beyond her today, not at her breasts. He seemed distracted, more so than usual. "Would you like hundreds?"

"Oh," Joe said. "Yea, sure. Hundreds is good. Sure."

She counted out his money to him and watched as he took the money from the counter, stuffed it into one of his large pockets, and turned away without saying anything further.

2

Joe walked to the front office of the salvage yard. He walked to the front desk where a young man looked up at him with an expression which showed both disgust and fear.

"We don't have anything for you, old man!" the boy said harshly.

"I want to buy something," Joe explained.

"We don't have anything to sell you," the boy said, then returned his eyes to the buxom brunette on the hood of the Corvette in the auto magazine before him.

Joe counted out five hundred dollars and slapped it down on the page the boy was reading. The boy looked at the money, then back at

Joe. He didn't know where Joe had gotten this kind of money, but he figured he must have stolen it.

"I want to buy the old white delivery truck," Joe explained.

The boy looked at the cash again, then back to Joe. He reached forward to take the cash when he heard a clicking sound. He looked back to Joe and saw him holding a gun and pointing it at him. So now he was going to be robbed? Great.

"Leave the money alone. I want to buy the white delivery truck. Get the owner."

The boy kept his eyes on Joe as he walked from behind the counter and out a small door which led to the yard. When he left Joe put his gun away and took the money from the counter. He folded the money up and put it in a pocket while he waited. A minute later the owner came through the small door the boy had left through. He was a big man who wore loose jeans and a dirty white T-shirt, his normal attire. Though Joe could not see it the man carried a gun tucked in the back of his pants, just in case Joe meant trouble.

"What do you want, Joe?" the man asked.

"I want to buy the old white delivery truck. I'll give you five hundred dollars."

"There's a lot of old delivery trucks out there. Which one do you mean?"

"I mean the white one."

"They're all white!" the man exclaimed. "Why don't you show me?"

Joe started to walk around the counter.

"Wait," the man said, "my boy says you got a gun. No guns back here."

"He tried to take my money," Joe said in a flat tone. His eyes wandered.

"That may be, but that doesn't change the rule."

Joe didn't trust the man. Who's to say he wouldn't take his money as soon as he had taken his gun? Who would believe Joe if he claimed he had been robbed of over a thousand dollars in cash? Not the police, that's for sure. Certainly this man had figured the same thing.

"I'll just go somewhere else," Joe explained. He turned to leave.

"Wait," the man called to him. "You can take your piece, but you have to show it to me first."

Joe just stared at the man. Finally the man lowered his eyes and walked back out to the yard. Joe walked around the counter and out into the yard where the man stood waiting for him.

"Okay," the man called out, "which one?"

The big man walked slowly over to the old white truck and the stinking bum. He hadn't really even thought of that particular truck, mainly because it had been in the yard for twenty years. It had set right where it now rested and had only been stripped of a few parts. It had become a landmark of sorts, a permanent part of the yard. It was just like the crazy old fart to pick that truck. Joe was offering twice what the stupid thing was worth. But Joe was crazy, and there was no telling what he needed the thing for. Whatever it was Joe probably thought it was quite important. Maybe important enough to pay even more for. All of this ran through the big man's head as he walked to where Joe stood. As he took another look at the old truck it looked somehow different to him. He had thought that it was in much worse shape than it now looked to be. In fact, he remembered more than one discussion about how that side door would have been useful if not for the big dent, which now seemed to be missing. He dismissed the oddness of these things and merely added a few dollars more to the price.

"Oh," the man said with mock surprise. "You meant this old truck. I'm sorry, Joe. I can't sell you this truck. It's like an antique, a landmark of sorts."

"Cut the shit," Joe said. "I'll give you five hundred dollars, which is more than the thing is worth."

"I mean it Joe," the man said. "It's not for sale."

Joe simply turned away and began to walk back toward the office. After about ten paces the man called out to him, "Of course I might be persuaded to take a thousand for her."

Joe didn't slow down a bit.

The big man walked after Joe and explained to him the great value of the vehicle, and how it would break his heart to see it go. He dropped his price to nine hundred as Joe reached the office door. This continued until Joe was completely out of the yard and walking down the sidewalk in front of it. The big man stood in front of his office shouting to him that seven hundred would probably do the trick.

Joe stopped and turned around to face the man. The man stood with a big smile on his face and sweat running across his forehead.

"I'll give you five hundred dollars," Joe repeated.

The man stood and said nothing for a moment. Then he said, "Look, I've got to pay the bills around here. I'll be losing money to sell it to you for less than six-fifty."

Joe said nothing. He turned away and resumed his walk. He was another twenty paces away when the man finally gave in and called him back. Joe grinned before he turned back around. He loved to win.

3

Sandra opened her eyes slowly. The room seemed too bright. As it slowly came into focus she realized that it was not her own and became disoriented. The bed was unfamiliar with its stainless-steel rails and white sheets. Then she saw the tube running to her arm and remembered what had happened and realized where she was.

She looked quickly at herself to see what damage there was. Her right arm was lying straight and had the I.V. stuck into it. Her left arm was in a sling. She wiggled her toes and moved what she could move. There were some aches and pains, but there didn't seem to be any casts. Her neck and back hurt, and there was a funny dull feeling on her face. She could not move either arm far enough to feel for what it might be. But she could reach the alert button with her right hand so she reached out and pressed it. A few moments later a nurse appeared.

"So, you're awake," the nurse observed.

"Have I been sleeping?"

"Just out for a little while. I let the doctor know you were conscious. He'll be here in a few minutes. In the meantime I'd like you to tell me if you have any sharp pains."

"No, but there are a lot of dull ones."

"Of course. They would probably feel a lot worse if we didn't have you hooked up." The nurse pointed to the I.V. bottle when she said this. Sandra smiled weakly and the nurse returned the smile though it was somewhat cold.

"Can you tell me where I am?" Sandra asked.

"Sure," the nurse replied. "You're at Memorial."

"I mean what city?"

"Oh, they brought you back to Springfield."

"Who did?" she asked.

"The ambulance, I guess. Have you been out since the accident?"

"Yes, I guess so," Sandra answered.

Then the door to her room swung inward and the man Sandra correctly assumed to be the doctor walked in. He was looking at some information inside a manila folder as he approached. The nurse stepped back but did not exit.

"So, Sandra, how are you feeling this afternoon?"

"Not great," she answered, "and what afternoon is it? Are you here to tell me that I've been in a coma for five years and my boyfriend is married?"

The doctor smiled at the reference to an obscure movie he remembered seeing once. "No, actually your little accident was last night. You suffered a mild concussion, a couple of sprains, but nothing serious considering what might have happened."

"Nothing broken?" she asked. "My legs still work."

"Of course," the doctor replied. "It's just a matter of keeping a watch on the pain and the brain activity for another twenty-four hours or so to make sure there are no surprises."

"So, I'm stuck here for a while?" she asked.

"Just until tomorrow evening. Then your sister will be here to pick you up."

"My sister?" she asked. "Which one?"

"I think her name is Audry," the doctor replied.

Audry. She hadn't seen Audry in almost five years, and they hadn't spoken in three. "Did you tell her that it wasn't that serious?"

"We told her exactly what I've told you, and we told her that someone would need to drive you back to Saint Louis since your back won't be up to the task for some time yet, and you don't have a car."

"But I'm not going back to Saint Louis," Sandra said.

"You really need to go home and stay in bed for a while before resuming this trip," the doctor explained.

"That's fine, but I really need to go where I was going. Just give me the pain pills I need and I'll deal with the rest myself."

"You have some torn ligaments and a strained disk that needs some time to heal..."

"I don't have that luxury!" she shouted out. She found herself leaning up from her pillow and noticed that her neck was shaking. She settled back into the pillow and took a deep breath. "I'm sorry, Doctor. I just have to sort all of this out. Why don't you do what you can to get me out of here as soon as possible, and I'll try to get a hold of my sister to let her know not to bother picking me up."

"I'll do what I can," the doctor explained as he lowered the folder to his side, "but we definitely need you here another twenty-four hours to make sure that there wasn't any more serious damage to the brain than we suspect."

"Okay, thanks."

Sandra sat and listened to the rest of the doctor's explanations and instructions. The nurse removed the I.V. from her arm and left some pills with her that she was to take at prescribed times for the pain as explained by the doctor.

Finally the man left. He was pleasant enough, but he didn't understand what her priorities were, nor could he. Of course all she would really have to do was play along for another day or so, then she could get back to her original task. One day couldn't be so bad.

After a few moments of tending to the patient in the next bed the nurse also left the room. Sandra sat looking at the wall before her, wondering just how much danger lay in store for her, and whether or not it was worth taking the risk. Then she heard an old and raspy voice coming from somewhere inside the room.

"You were in an accident?" the voice asked. It was coming from behind the curtain which separated her bed from the bed of another patient.

"Yes. A truck hit my car."

"Are you all right?" the voice asked.

"They tell me so."

"That's good," came the reply. After a pause the speaker introduced herself. "I'm Maude Stanfield."

"I'm Sandra." Sandra didn't mind the discussion; it would help to pass the time.

"This is my third time in here this year, and it's only the summer," the old voice explained with some dismay. "I keep telling them to just let me go. It's getting so damned expensive to keep bringing me back, you know, and I'm ready to go. But the damned fools at the nursing home don't want me to leave just yet, not until my savings and insurance run out. And the hospital feels the same way too, you know. So I keep having my little strokes, and they keep on bringing me back here. It's all very tiresome."

"I'm sorry to hear that," Sandra said. She felt awkward, knowing she had no way to understand what the old woman was going through. "I hope things turn out for you as you want."

"Ah! Yes!" the old woman exclaimed. "Now if we could just convince my doctor and the nursing home of the same. Perhaps if I called up my insurance company and cancelled my policies they'd let me go."

"I don't know," Sandra replied.

"Oh sure you do. Anybody can see how the system works these days. You don't have to pretend you're naive with me. I've seen the world as it is for too long."

There was silence for a little. Then Maude spoke again.

"I can't even get visitors in here during regular visiting hours. Seems the folks still living are not as interested in me as those that wish to keep me living. You, on the other hand, seem to be able to get visitors even at odd hours. You must be some lady."

Sandra was puzzled at this. Had she had visitors, or was the old women senile or imagining things?

"I've been unconscious until a few moments ago, so I was unaware if I had visitors. Has someone been here to see me?"

"Oh, yes," the woman replied with some excitement. "I assumed it was your little boy."

"A little boy?" Sandra asked. "Are you sure?"

"Oh yes, of course. I couldn't see much of him, and he wouldn't speak to me. He seemed very concerned at your state. He was with you all last night except for a couple of hours, I'm not sure what time that was. I really coaxed him to talk to me, but he wouldn't. You say he's not your son?"

"No ma'am," Sandra replied, "I don't have any children."

"Oh, my. I wonder who it was then?"

"It may have just been a friend."

"Are you not from these parts?" the woman asked.

"I'm from Saint Louis. I was on my way," she thought for a moment. She wasn't sure exactly where she was on her way to. "I was on my way south, through Tulsa."

"Visiting relatives?" Maude asked.

"More just driving around. Seeing the countryside. Going wherever the road took me. That kind of thing."

"Oh, that's nice," Maude answered. "In my day a lady couldn't do such a thing. I wish I could have been a young lady in your day. Not quite so stuffy, you know. I would have even settled for the higher crime and all for a little more moral freedom. Oh, I got into a little trouble in my younger years for things which children do nowadays almost with their parents' consent. The world has certainly changed."

"Yes it has," Sandra replied. She wanted to know more about the boy, though she was already certain of who it was. "How did the boy get in?"

"I'm sorry? Oh, yes, the boy last night. Well, I never..." she broke off and went into a fit of coughing. "Sorry," she apologized, "can't seem to shake that cough. Anyway, I never actually saw him come in or leave. He was just there sometimes when I woke up. I never really got a good look at him, just glimpses around the curtain. I would have loved to get out of this bed and taken a look, but I can't really do that on my own these days. So I didn't really see him, but I guess a friend of yours or his must have let him in the regular way. I asked the nurse about it this morning and she didn't seem to know anything. Oh, my," Maude went on, "I hope I haven't ruined anything for you. I mean I hope they aren't watching for him if he wants to come back. Perhaps you should call him and let him know you're awake now. He would probably love to see you."

"I'm sure my family's been notified."

"So he was probably a nephew or something?" Maude probed.

"Must be."

Sandra didn't sound certain, but Maude decided not to probe any further. So the discussion turned the other things, though Sandra's thoughts remained on the boy and the urgency of her task.

4

After a few hours of conversation and debate the pain grew. Sandra took some pain pills and an hour later she drifted to sleep as Maude continued her soliloquy on individual rights, past and present. Apparently Maude had been quite a 'swinger' in her day, or at least wished she had been. When she realized Sandra had fallen asleep she stopped talking and fell asleep from exhaustion within thirty minutes.

Several hours later Sandra awoke to a dull pain in her neck and shoulders. The room was dark. She had no idea how long she had been sleeping, but the pain had awakened her, so she reached for her pill bottle.

Then she saw the shadow in the corner and remembered her dream. It had not been a strong dream, but for most of the time she had been asleep she had seen someone in the distance calling to her, trying to get her to awaken. Now she was awake and as she looked toward the shadow she knew from its outline that it was the same little boy. Even the shadow was mangled and tattered. The boy did not speak, but sat silently in a visitor's chair, watching her. She tried to speak to him, but he would not answer. She did not know if it was because he could not or because he chose not to. But she knew why he was there, and she made the decision that it was more important than some cautious observations. They had her insurance company name and policy numbers now, and they knew where to send her belongings that survived the wreck. Maybe her sister would pick them up for her when she showed up the next day. Probably not when she discovered that Sandra had snuck out during the night. Nevertheless, she could wait no longer.

Sandra sat up in her bed. Pain shot down her left shoulder and pounded at the base of her neck. She knew now exactly which disk had been strained, and which ligaments had been damaged. She sat still and got used to the pain which softened but persisted. She picked up the pain pills but did not take one. A few hours from now she would be driving again, and she could not afford to fall asleep at the wheel and end up back here or worse. She stood slowly. The pain grew but did not force her back into her bed. She shuffled slowly across the room to a small closet which she opened. It was dark, but enough light made it in from the hallway so that she could see outlines. Inside the closet were a few of her belongings. The rest were most likely in a storage room somewhere. The closet held mostly clothes, her purse and a makeup bag. It would have to do. She took off the blue hospital garb she had been given. It came off easily as it was designed to. Her clothes, however, were not of the same design. She put on some pants and a shirt. The process was a slow one, especially with the sling and her injured arm getting in the way. She had to put on one of her casual oversized T-shirts and pull it over her arm. That would have to do for now. As she tucked the shirt into her pants she heard some rustling beyond the curtain.

"Sandra, are you all right?"

Sandra froze. She could not answer from where she was, and she could not sneak quietly enough back to the bed. Then she heard Maude speak again.

"Okay, I just thought I heard you moving around."

Sandra was puzzled. She looked back to her bed to make sure it was empty, and it was. Then she looked back to the little boy and saw he was staring straight through that curtain to where Maude must have been lying.

"Okay. Good-night then."

Sandra waited a few moments, then resumed getting dressed. When she had pulled on her slippers she took her purse out and looked through it. There were only a few items missing, things which had probably fallen out in the wreck. Her wallet and checkbook were still there. She took the purse, makeup bag, and a few sets of clothes. This was all she could comfortably carry over one arm for any period of time and still be able to open doors and push buttons. She would have to buy the rest of her needs on the road.

She shuffled across the floor to the door and worked with the knob until she got it opened. Then she worked her way around it and into the hall. She shuffled down to the elevator where she pushed the down button and waited. Five minutes later she was standing in front of the hospital waiting for a cab. The woman at the front desk had gladly called it for her. Sandra had expected some trouble, but apparently not too many people snuck out of the Springfield hospital at two in the morning. She had seen the clock over the counter as she left.

Ten minutes later the cab pulled up. She told him to take her to the nearest car rental facility. She figured with the right luck she could be back on the Interstate within the hour.

IX
1

Dave sat on the edge of his bed looking toward the window. From where he sat he could see that there were lots of stars out tonight.

It was three in the morning. He had been awakened by the voices again. This was the second night that the voices had plagued him. Both nights the voices had begun as whispers as he had started to drift to sleep, then had become louder as his sleep had deepened. When he would come suddenly awake they would stop. Then it would begin again. On the previous night this had allowed him only four hours of sleep, and none of it had been deep. Tonight he could not get past that part of consciousness where the body relaxes and the mind begins to wander. When the whispers would begin his mind knew that they would only grow louder and eventually wake him, so he would come awake before they grew from their soft beckoning. Finally he had become unable to take any more and had gotten up out of bed. He'd wandered to the bathroom where five minutes of digging uncovered a long-expired box of Sominex. He had taken two of the chalky blue pills and returned to his bed where he sat down on the end and put his head in his hands.

He sat now looking to the skies, wondering again what was going on and why he had to be involved. Why couldn't it have been someone else? Why couldn't it have been somewhere else? He had seen and heard more in the past few days from a world he did not understand than he had ever imagined possible. He believed that what was happening to him was real, but he didn't think he would have believed it if someone else had told him that these things were happening to them. He had seen hints of this strange world and heard much more of it in his youth. But much of that he had written off to the naivete of the young mind. Now, however, he realized that perhaps it was more the flexibility of his young mind than the naivete that had allowed him to believe what he had seen then, and what he was experiencing now.

He just wasn't sure what it all meant. Believing was one thing; understanding was quite another.

He sat pondering these things for about thirty minutes. Then he realized that he was becoming very tired. His whole body was relaxed and he felt as if he could crawl under the covers and be asleep in no time. The effect of the pills combined with his lack of sleep pulled at his conscious mind, urging him into the realm of sleep. He smiled a soft smile as he crawled to the top of his bed and under the top sheet. A blanket and his comforter lay in a pile on the floor. It had been too warm the past few nights for anything but a sheet. He crawled under the sheet and rolled over onto his side. He felt the relaxation run through his body.

And he also heard the whispers.

He fought them, but this time they did not pull him away from his restful state. He felt himself slipping to sleep despite the voices, but he also heard them growing louder as he slipped slowly away. They got loud enough that he could actually make out words.

Then he remembered why he did not want to hear the voices.

But it was too late. As he slipped solidly into the world of sleep the words became clear to him again.

Only this time he could not run from them.

2

"You will know death. You will know it very well before we are through with you."

The voice was deep and dark. It had no face, and it came from everywhere.

Dave knew he was asleep. He knew he was not in any place other than his own mind, but it felt like a very foreign and very evil place right now. And he didn't think that he was there by himself.

"You will know death," the voice repeated.

"Your mother will know death very soon."

This was a different voice. It too was deep, but it seemed like a feminine voice. Dave despised the voice, recoiled from it, but could not get away. Suddenly he knew what the voice meant. He knew when and where his mother would die. It was soon. He even knew what would happen, and hoped he could remember it when he awoke.

"You will know death," repeated the first voice.

"Death will brush near to you soon," came a third voice.

Dave knew for only an instant what this meant, then that knowledge slipped away from him. There was something he was not meant to know. Even those voices which tormented him did not wish for him to know. He struggled to regain the knowledge; he knew that it was vital, but it was gone for good.

"You will know death." The first voice returned.

"Your brother knows it now." A new voice. "He knows it well. He knows it as one who lingers near it."

Dave understood this voice too. It was as if there was much more being said than the mere words revealed, and this knowledge was coming to him. His brother was dead, but his soul was still where it did not know the difference between life and death. Tommy's soul was trapped. It lingered in a place between worlds as it had for twenty years.

"And many linger near it."

This new voice brought with it a new and horrible knowledge. Tommy's was not the only soul which lingered between the worlds. There were other souls, many other souls who lingered. Many were lost. Many were not lost. Many knew where they were and longed to return to the world of the living, though Dave's understanding here was incomplete and he knew it. There was something horrible about these souls, something which had to do with the things that had been plaguing him the past week. Things which would become critical soon. And somehow he played a role in all of this. He and Tommy both played a role.

Then there was a new voice. It was soft and less threatening than all the others. It spoke carefully, choosing words which revealed as much as possible, but at the same time hid things from him. It was Tommy's voice. Dave knew this for certain. He also knew that his voice was being allowed to talk. A price had been paid somewhere and Tommy had been allowed to get through. A sacrifice of some kind had been made. Dave knew this too. But the words which were getting through were being watched. Even those possibly benevolent forces which allowed or perhaps even assisted Tommy in getting the message through were limiting what could be said and what could be heard.

But when it was all over Dave knew what he had to know.

The knowledge was a horrible thing, one he wished he didn't have. Because with the knowledge came the knowledge of things which no man should know, things which would stay with him for the rest of his life, things which would haunt the rest of his waking hours as well as his sleeping ones. Never again would sleep bring him the kind of peace it had brought to him for the first thirty-one years of his life. From now on there would always be this background noise from the other world.

Perhaps this was part of the price that had to be paid.

Then the voices stopped and true sleep returned.

But his sleep was filled with the echoes of the voices which would haunt him for the rest of his life.

3

When Dave awoke his body ached and he felt exhausted. He saw that he had kicked his only remaining sheet completely from the bed.

He also saw the sunlight filling his room, which was not a thing that normally happened until afternoon.

He shouted his curses as he saw the clock. It was afternoon.

He jumped from his bed and hurried into the back bedroom. The light on the answering machine was blinking. He listened to his messages. There were five. Two were from Katy, his boss's secretary. Two were from customers and one was from Colleen. He cleared his throat and returned his customers' calls first. He would have to call Katy from the office. Colleen would have to wait until tonight.

As he shaved and showered his mind returned to the things he had learned in his sleep. As he pondered on them he realized that these were urgent matters, things which had to be acted upon immediately. As he stepped out of the shower he decided that he was going to call Katy from home after all and explain that he was sick today. His need to act on his new knowledge outweighed his obligation to the company. Today that need outweighed many things. He knew that he had become the key to the future of the town of Cisco, and maybe more. He had become a pawn of sorts in a supernatural game of chess, and the opponent was well positioned. Now was not the time to rationalize or reason; it was the time to act.

He phoned Katy and explained that he was quite ill. Then he phoned Colleen. She was home and waiting for his call. Apparently her sleep had also been touched by the otherworld, though not nearly so strongly. Dave spoke only briefly of his night of dreams, saving the details for an in-person discussion.

"I've already showered; give me a few minutes to get dressed and put some gas in the car," Dave said. "I should be over in about half an hour; then we can discuss this in more detail."

"You said there were some things which had to be done," Colleen observed. "What kind of things, and when?"

"I'll tell you more when I come over. It's pretty important though. We're going to be busy tonight."

"Dave?" Her voice sounded uncertain.

"What?"

"I'm not so sure I can do this."

"What do you mean?" Dave asked.

"I mean, I'm not sure I can do this. I don't think I'm strong enough."

"Bullshit," Dave exclaimed. His voice showed his edginess. "You've been doing this kind of stuff for years. Why get scared now?"

"It's never been this real before," she explained. "I've always been safe. I don't feel so safe on this one. What if I go to that place again tonight but can't get back?"

"You'll get back." Dave assured her.

"Says who?"

"You'll get back," Dave repeated, "trust me."

"So you're an expert at this now?"

"No," Dave said. "I didn't mean it to sound that way. Listen, I'm just as scared as you about all this, but we've got to do it."

"Says who?"

"What do you want to do?" Dave asked. "Run away?"

"That doesn't sound so bad," Colleen admitted.

"You'd run and leave the people around here to face whatever it is that's coming from the other side?"

"I don't know. I'm just not sure I'm so ready to sacrifice myself for this stinking town."

"Who said you have to sacrifice yourself?" Dave asked. "You're just going to be required to participate in a little ceremony, that's all. When this is over we'll be heroes, except nobody will know it but us."

Silence for a moment.

"I don't know, Dave."

"Look," Dave replied, "I'll be over in thirty minutes. Then we can talk about it some more. Maybe when I tell you everything I know it won't be so hard for you."

"Okay," she agreed. "I'll see you in a bit. Then we'll talk."

"Great."

They said good-bye and Dave finished getting dressed. Then he got into his car and headed into town.

4

He showed up at her door at a little after three o'clock. She smiled, then let him in. She looked visibly shaken.

"Crazy Joe hasn't been back by, has he?" Dave asked.

"Funny you should ask."

"He has?"

"I think so," Colleen answered. "But I'm not sure. I woke up three times last night and heard something outside my window. When I got up to turn on the light it sounded like someone was running away."

"Have you told the police?" Dave asked.

"Sure, but they just drive by every once in a while. They never see anything. And it doesn't really make me feel any better."

They walked together into the living room and sat down on the couch. Dave thought about the last time they had been on this couch together and looked into Colleen's eyes to see if she was thinking of this too. Her gaze was distant, but he sensed just a hint of that remembrance.

"So, what else is there?" Colleen asked.

"Well," Dave began, "apparently there's a spiritual gate of some kind around here."

"Is it an Indian thing?" Colleen asked. Cisco lay deep in Comanche country.

"No, it's older than that. I don't really know the source; I just know that it's here. It's a kind of doorway between worlds, only the door is locked and bolted."

Colleen's dreams of the ivy-covered ground and large paneled door came into her mind. Last night she had been to this place again, only this time she had been unable to keep the door from opening. Terrible things had come through, things which had shaken her resolve.

"I've seen this door," Colleen explained, "or a representation of it anyway. There are terrible things behind the door."

"Exactly," Dave replied. His eyes sparkled and Colleen could see that he was excited about this. "The door is opening. Apparently there are certain times when it is more likely to open than others. It hasn't opened in over a hundred years, and it's never opened as wide as it is threatening to open now."

"So what happens when it opens?" Colleen asked.

"When it opens it allows spirits to cross from the otherworld into this one."

"So Cisco gets haunted for a little while then they go away?" She brushed some of her dark hair out of her eyes. "So why not just let it happen? Maybe it'll go away without hurting anyone."

"Not this time," Dave explained. "The spirits which lay in limbo are aware of this doorway. It's like the spirits that hang around near the earth after dying are just across some barrier. Most dead people have gone on and couldn't come back if they wanted to. But some never left for some reason or another. Many of these spirits are from people who died violently or suddenly or both. Those which desire the most to get back aren't those that have loved ones behind or miss the flowers; most of the ones who want to get back are terrible souls who seek revenge."

"Revenge on who?" Colleen asked.

"Just revenge," Dave continued, "revenge in general. Revenge against humanity. Revenge against order. Revenge against life. They want to come over to wreck and destroy."

"But how can they if they're just spirits?" Colleen asked. "How can they do anything but scare people?"

"I'm not sure," Dave answered, "but I know they can do more than just scare people. Once they've crossed through the doorway they will have the ability to come in contact with objects and people of this world."

"So they'll be just like people walking around?"

"No, they'll still be spirits. In fact many of them have joined together and represent a larger, darker force than they could have individually. They hate order, they hate to follow, but they understand that by submitting to this grouping of sorts they'll be able to do more damage. By themselves perhaps they could have pushed glasses off the counter or flipped over a few radios. But together they are capable of much more."

"You said something about following. Is somebody leading them?"

"Apparently they have chosen a leader, or the leader has chosen himself. They've agreed to submit only because they know that it's only as a unit that they can have their revenge. There's some discord and some rebellion, but overall they've agreed to stay together. And together they are a serious threat."

"How many are there?"

"I don't really know. Most of the spirits have not joined. But many have. More join as they see the power the group represents. As they join they put more pressure on this door. When the time comes they'll push the door wide open. Then we'll be in deep shit, if you know what I mean."

"I'm not sure I do," Colleen responded, "but I'm not sure I want to find out either."

"So you're going to help?" Dave asked.

"Why me?"

"I can't do it alone."

"Why not somebody else?" Colleen asked.

"Who else is going to believe me? It's got to happen tonight or it'll be too late. I can't find anyone else by tonight. Besides, you're better prepared to face this than anyone else in this town would be."

"What do we have to do?"

"We just have to close the door and seal it shut."

"How are we going to do it?" Collen asked.

"We'll have to go to Abilene and get a few things. There's a ceremony that was explained to me in my vision. I can remember the whole thing like I memorized it or something; it's just sitting in my head. It will take a couple of hours, but when we're done the door will be closed and it will be taken care of, at least for our lifetime."

"We're not going to have to kill any cats or anything like that are we?"

"No."

She looked away from Dave and glanced out her window. She thought she saw something dart into the bushes. Probably a rabbit.

"Tell me about it on the way to Abilene. Then I'll decide for sure."

Dave stood from the couch. "I really need you on this, Colleen."

"I'll give you an answer before we get back."

"Okay," Dave answered. "Just remember it's more than a small town we'll be saving. This is much bigger than that."

Colleen stood. "I want you to tell me more about that too."

"Of course."

Colleen grabbed her purse and walked with Dave to the door. They walked out into the warm afternoon together. Collen flipped the sign hanging in her window so that her customers would know she was not in. Then she locked her door. They walked to Dave's car and he opened her door for her. She reached over and unlocked his side as he walked around. Then he got in and started the vehicle.

"I really need your help," Dave repeated.

Colleen just looked at him. Then he put the car into drive and headed for the interstate.

5

Dave drove toward Abilene. The highway was fairly empty.

"So we've been chosen to lock this spiritual door?" Colleen asked. Now it was she who was having trouble believing. Dave was right. She was the only one who would work with him on this, and then only because she had been through certain things which convinced her of the reality of it all.

"I don't think it's like we've been chosen. I think it's more like there happened to be a portion of the spiritual world that I was in touch with. I think that if I hadn't been here then no one would have been contacted. It's just the fact that my little brother never crossed over and I'm still around that the otherworld had a way to contact me."

"So why me?" Colleen asked.

"I guess I can't do this alone, and you're the only person in town who would believe all of the signs you've been given. Anybody else would probably have run away, or hidden."

"I'm still not sure I'm not going to run away."

Dave looked at her. His eyes showed dismay and hope. "Come on Colleen. This is too important to run away from. You could never live with yourself if you did."

"Maybe I could."

"You couldn't."

They both sat in silence as Dave drove on. After a few miles Colleen spoke.

"Why don't you tell me what's got to happen. Maybe that will help me make up my mind."

"Okay," Dave agreed. "Okay, well, we probably need to do this at your place."

"We don't have to go out in the woods or anything?"

"No, your place will do. We just need to be in town. The doorway isn't in one specific place, it's just in town. I supposed if we could go to the center of town that would be ideal, but I don't think we could do this in the city park."

"And your place is out of the city limits?"

"No, but it's on the fringe. Besides, I feel like your place is better suited to this kind of thing."

"So the spirits didn't tell you exactly where to do this?"

It sounded as if she was being sarcastic. Dave checked her expression to be sure she was not. "No. I didn't really get any instructions from 'spirits', I really just heard from my brother with their consent."

"The spirits that want to come over allowed him to tell you how to stop them?"

"No, it wasn't them. He was protected somehow. I know a price was paid, but I don't know what that price was."

"Your brother paid it?"

"I don't know that either. There's a lot about this that I don't understand."

"Yet you feel comfortable doing this ceremony?"

Dave sat looking down the road and thinking about the question. He was not exactly comfortable with it at all, but he knew something had to be done. "I don't think that I have any choice. I couldn't walk away from this, not knowing what I know now."

Colleen knew she couldn't either. But inside she knew that she must. She had a terrible feeling about it all, one she could not shake. She supposed this came from her fear. Most of her fear came from her experience in the dark place. She knew she would have to go there again. Even if she knew she would be back she was terrified of the prospect. The dark place was so empty and so final. Even thinking back on her last trip to that place gave her chills that ran all the way down her spine and tickled the back of her brain.

"So what exactly do we have to do?" she asked again.

Dave looked to Colleen and then back to the road. They passed milepost 350 which meant that he had about twenty minutes to explain what had to be done. It would not be enough to include every detail, but it would be enough to give Colleen a good idea of exactly what would be expected.

"All right," he began. "First we'll need to make a triangle out of thirty-six tall red candles. The triangle will need to be about ten feet on each side."

Dave explained the ceremonies and Colleen listened intently.

By the time they reached the exit for the loop she had a good idea of what was expected of her.

And she knew as well that she had no choice now.

She had to do it.

Dave looked at her one last time before taking the exit and he knew what she had decided.

"Thanks," he said.

She didn't answer but simply stared ahead, not really seeing anything before her but thinking instead about the hours that remained before nightfall.

X
1

For the past two and a half hours she had been driving down two-lane highways and passing through small towns. The towns seemed to be spaced too far apart and too far from any major cities to be surviving. But they were there, and though there were remnants in each of bigger and better days they all had their fair share of empty buildings and worn out roads. She stopped in Graham to get gas. The gas seemed pretty expensive, but it was on the state highway, and there weren't many options. She supposed that this was exactly why it was so expensive. She also had to pay for full serve since maneuvering a gas nozzle around with one arm in a sling was not something she wanted to worry with. It was worth paying the extra money to have someone else do it.

She had left the interstate in Wichita Falls, which was less than twenty miles inside of Texas. She had not seen the child there, but that no longer mattered. She knew that she was getting closer now, and she knew which way to drive, but she still did not know how much longer she would be driving. From the strength of the disturbance, she had thought that her final destination would be in Oklahoma. But she'd driven on, and the intensity of the feelings had continued to grow. Now as she passed through Graham she began to wonder if this was something she should be pursuing. If she did not reach her destination within a few more hours then whatever was calling to her was much too big for her to be able to do anything about. She could be rushing to a useless task, or perhaps a very dangerous one.

But she also felt compelled. She knew that she could not stop now. Now she had to know what was happening. She wanted at least to have some answers about what was happening, or about to happen.

While in Oklahoma she had experienced another illusion. Once again the white truck had appeared on the highway before her. This time it was the middle of the day. There had been more traffic on the road, and the car travelling behind her had swerved around her and honked its horn when she hit her brakes. This time, however, she did not lose control of the car. She let up on the brakes when she saw that the car which had passed her had gone right through the front fender of the white truck. Sandra passed through the truck at around thirty miles per hour. Though there had been no impact it felt very cold when she passed through the ghostly vehicle.

She was very tired. She had been driving for almost twelve hours and the pills she finally took for the pain also made her very sleepy. She had to stop every hour and buy a can of Coke. By the time the next hour rolled around she had to stop anyway to use the bathroom, then she would buy another Coke. The caffeine and the need to urinate helped to keep her awake. The last stop had taken more than an hour due to the spacing of the small towns, and she had begun to grow concerned that she might have to pull over to the side of the road somewhere, but then the town of Graham appeared and saved the day.

It was only six o'clock in the evening, but it felt much later. She had picked up the rental car at a little before three o'clock that morning, then driven to a cheap motel where she laid down for a couple of hours. Her dreams and the pleas of a small child had urged her back into the car. Now she felt exhausted. She knew that she wouldn't be able to keep this up for more than a few more hours anyway, even with the dreams. Even if they would not let her sleep, she could not risk falling asleep at the wheel and driving into somebody's ranch fence or a deep bar-ditch. She decided that she would have to stop before dark since the dark would lull her to sleep quickly. This gave her a maximum of two more hours.

Sandra took Highway 67 toward Breckenridge. It was the next town of any size and it would take her about half an hour to get there. She looked at her map and saw that if she continued southward she would be at Interstate Twenty in about an hour. She would stop and eat then. She would also decide then whether she should lodge in one of the towns along the interstate, or continue her drive southward. The only good road which continued southward after Breckenridge was State Highway 183. This led to two small towns on the interstate, Cisco and Eastland. There was no telling how large either of these towns was, but certainly she would find a restaurant since they were both on the highway. After the interstate the roads southward continued through small towns which were spaced far apart. The small towns she had been through so far had not seemed to have any decent lodging facilities, so there was a good chance she would stop in either Cisco or Eastland and try again to get some sleep.

She passed the small green sign that marked the city limits of Graham and turned her radio back on. From here she could catch some of the Dallas AM stations. She listened to Bruce Williams explain to a young man what a fool he was for not having a lawyer as she drove southward toward Breckenridge.

2

"I know it, I know it!"

Joe argued with himself as he walked again around the white delivery truck. All of the work that had been done had required all of the cash he had withdrawn from the bank the day before. All he had to show for it now was a big white truck which was of no use to him. What could he do with it now? He didn't even have a driver's license and certainly couldn't ever get one. He rubbed his hands nervously along his pants legs as he debated with himself.

"Okay, so what am I supposed to do with this now?"

He felt lost. He had not heard from the White Man nor had he seen any new signs or received any new gifts for two full days. Now the truck was just like the White Man had asked for it to be. But the White Man had abandoned him. Where had he gone? Why had he left? He had given no warning that this might happen.

Joe had gotten Fats from the repair shop to drive the truck to his place and park it behind the big old store. It had been sitting there for two hours now, and Joe had been walking around it and talking to himself the entire time. Every so often he would look around, half expecting to see the White Man standing there with his new instructions or a new gift. Even the good dreams had gone. No more dreams of women who wanted him, large-breasted women who had yearned for him every night since that first night. No more fantasies which seemed like reality and carried him through his nights. Now there were no dreams, not any he could remember anyway.

He looked into the driver's side again. The inside of the truck still looked dirty. Springs poked through the rotted seat cover on the passenger's side. The driver's side had been patched up. The dash was cracked and peeling and he could see the foam beneath the vinyl covering.

"Okay so it's ready now." Joe looked up into the sky. "It's ready now, okay! You can come get it now!"

His eyes returned to the truck then darted back and forth.

Then he saw the White Man.

It startled him and his heart raced. The man appeared in the truck only for an instant, then was gone.

Then Joe knew what was expected of him.

"How can I do it?" he said. "I haven't driven a truck in over twenty years, how am I supposed to do this?"

He waited but heard no answer. Then he opened the door and climbed into the truck. It complained as he sat down in the seat and took the steering wheel in his hands. He looked down at the stick shift. It was old and the markings were faded. He didn't even know where to find the gears. Even if they had been marked it would have been a formidable task to drive the thing. The faded markings just made matters worse.

He pushed in the clutch and turned the key. The moves were instinctive and he began to wonder if maybe he would remember how to drive. A puff of black smoke appeared in the rearview mirror and the truck began to shake. The fuel gauge showed full. He had requested that it be filled and had left enough money with the repair shop.

"I don't know, I don't know," Joe said to himself. He sniffled and ran his sleeve across his nose. Then he let slowly up on the clutch.

The truck lurched forward and died.

"Too fast. Okay. Too fast."

He started the truck again and killed it two more times before getting it around the back of the store. Then he pulled onto the road and pushed the stick downward into second gear. The change was not smooth, and it jerked him around some, but the engine did not die.

"I think I got it now. Okay."

The gears whined as he gained speed. He shifted into third.

"Okay," he said again. "Okay, okay."

He looked around at his surroundings as they passed by him at a speed that he had not experienced in a very long time. He had trouble keeping the truck on his side of the road and ran off onto the shoulder once. But after a few minutes he was driving well enough that the police car he passed did not pull him over for reckless driving.

Then a sly grin crept onto his face, and he began humming as he headed toward town.

3

When Sandra reached the city limits of Breckenridge she knew that she was getting close. She could tell that there was something significant about the town, something to do with the small child. She felt that she needed to drive through Breckenridge and continue southward, but something else called to her. As she reached the tall Citizens National Bank building she did not turn left and take 183 as she had planned. Instead she went straight through the light and headed for the residential areas off the main road.

She drove past the fast food joints and gas stations. To her left she could see a number of older homes just a block off the main road. After only a minute of driving down the main road she turned left onto one of the residential streets.

She saw a strange contrast of homes as she drove. Some were made of native stone and looked to be a hundred years old, while others were constructed of relatively new red brick. There seemed to be no pattern. Some of the run-down homes were sitting next to some of the nicer ones.

She headed down the road until it came to an end at another road. Across from her was the elementary school. It was late, but there were children playing on the playground equipment. One child looked odd to her. The child didn't seem to be paying any attention to the other children. She was pale, and she kept walking around the horizontal bars. It took Sandra a second to realize that this child was not living. She had died here recently, probably on the bars she now circled. There were red marks around her neck, and she carried a jump rope in her right hand. Sandra looked at the forlorn child and felt sorrow. The image had no significance to her current journey, but it was disturbing for her nonetheless.

She turned right and found that she didn't really know where she was going. She knew she was close, but now she wasn't sure which way to head. She decided that she would just drive around a little and look at the homes while she waited for some direction.

She drove around the residential streets on Breckenridge for about half an hour. She saw some pretty lawns, but most were not real lawns; they were more an agglomeration of grasses and weeds. She looked at the houses and the lawns and the people as she drove. The people all seemed to have a sense of purpose, even the ones which just sat on the porch and waved at her as she drove by.

She made a right turn and suddenly there was the white delivery truck right in front of her. This time it was moving. She swerved to avoid it, but it passed through the left front quarter of her car before turning onto the road she had just come from.

THE THRESHOLD

Her heart raced as her car came to a stop. The big oak tree now in front of her had blocked her view of the truck. Now she looked in her rearview mirror, half expecting not to see it.

But she did see it. And she saw the child, only he was not mangled. And she saw the older child running after him.

She turned around quickly in her car and saw the street behind her differently than she had moments before. Now it was lined with newer looking homes and older model cars parked in the driveways. The road was paved differently, and even the sky looked different now. She watched as the familiar dream was played out in the theater before her. From her angle she could not see the child as he was struck, but she did see the trail of blood which the truck left behind it. Then she saw the truck strike the older boy as it came to a stop. Then a man got out of the truck and ran off down the street, disappearing quickly between houses.

She looked at the scene which seemed frozen except for the soft shaking of the white delivery truck. It was not in gear, and the brake had been set.

She got out of her car and began walking toward the scene. There was no one else there, just the truck and the two boys. As she walked toward the truck she could see the little boy's missing arm lying on the road to the side of the truck. Then she saw the twitching body of the dead child underneath it. She could smell the smoke from the exhaust mixed with the blood and death of the child.

She approached the truck and saw that this was the same child she had seen in Saint Louis, only now he was not communicating with her. Perhaps he was not here, only the old image of his death. Then she looked to the older boy who lay sprawled in the bushes beside the road. She knew that this boy was his brother. Suddenly she also knew that he was still alive, and that he was the one she needed to get in touch with.

She heard screaming and looked up to see the image of a young woman standing at the door of the house closest to the bushes. She was a pretty woman, despite the contorted face and terrified eyes. She pointed toward her dead child and screamed even as her house began to age before Sandra's eyes.

Sandra looked back to the child in the bushes. She studied his face, trying hard to memorize the features and put some age on them. She did not know exactly how much age, but she could guess by the cars and his clothes that it would be around twenty years.

"Is there something I can help you with?" came a voice.

Sandra looked up and saw an older version of the screaming woman standing in the same doorway. Only now the woman was not screaming; she was looking toward Sandra with a questioning gaze. Sandra looked carefully and decided that this was the mother of the man she now sought. She also understood that this was the very street where the nightmare had taken place in reality.

"Maybe so," Sandra called back. She walked to the driveway of the small house, then up to the front porch. "I'm Sandra MacElroy." She extended her right hand and the woman took hold of it while she glanced quickly at the sling which held Sandra's left arm. Sandra tried to think quickly of what she would say. "I'm looking for someone who can tell me a little about the accident that happened here about twenty years ago."

The woman's face fell a little and she looked suddenly years older. "Why do you want to know about it?" she asked. Her eyes no longer shone and they wandered about.

"I knew the older boy that was involved and I wanted to talk to him about it."

"Where do you know Dave from?"

Dave. She finally had a name. Now she just needed a location.

"I met Dave a few years ago at a social gathering. We talked briefly about the accident. I recently began putting together an article on the effects of childhood accidents on the adult life and I was going to see if he might be interested."

"Oh," the woman said, "I see." The woman looked around again before returning her gaze to Sandra. "Well, he has been having a little trouble with it lately, but I suppose it should be his decision whether or not he wants to talk to you. Did you say you're a reporter? What newspaper?"

"Oh, I write for magazines," Sandra explained. "I just do freelance work. I just write stories I think are interesting and hope that someone will be interested enough to buy it. I've been working on this one for three months and I've only got two more people I really want to talk to. Dave is one of them."

Sandra didn't care to carry any lie this far, but she knew that the truth would not have gotten her any closer to the man. Dave's mother seemed very uncomfortable. She began unconsciously to wring her hands and her eyes spent most of their time wandering about the horizon, not fixed on any one object.

"Can you tell me where to find Dave?" Sandra asked.

Dave's mother was so distracted that it did not even seem odd to her that Dave would tell this woman where his mother lived, but not provide his own address or number.

"He's living in Cisco," she explained. "On 14th Street, near the west end of town."

"Do you have his address?" Sandra asked.

"Sure, it's in the house."

Dave's mother did not even excuse herself but simply turned around and walked into the house. Sandra waited for what seemed like a very long time. As she waited she turned back around to look at the street. All of the homes now looked older, and the only cars from the seventies were worn out and broken down, not new as they had looked a few moments before. Now the bushes by the side of the road were much taller.

But she thought that through the bushes she could still see the red stains where the blood had been on the road.

The sound of the door opening again startled Sandra. Dave's mother came through the door with her hand extended. In her hand she held a piece of paper with some writing on it.

"Here," she said, "I wrote it down for you."

Sandra took the paper and looked quickly at it. "Thank you Mrs. Chatburn," Sandra said. She got her last name from the sheet of paper.

"Certainly," Mrs. Chatburn replied, her eyes still wandering about.

"You have a nice evening," Sandra said as she stepped back from the porch.

Mrs. Chatburn smiled a weak and unconvincing smile as Sandra waited for the reply which never came. Then Sandra turned and walked back down the street to her car. She heard the door of the house open and close again as she walked. She sighed in relief.

Sandra got into her car and looked at the sheet of paper. Dave Chatburn. This was the older boy from the dream, and he was still alive. She knew that he was involved somehow in the things which had drawn her to this place and hoped that he would have some answers for her when she found him. Mrs. Chatburn had written his phone number on the sheet as well. Sandra started her car and drove out of the residential section of Breckenridge. She found her way back to Main Street and stopped at the first gas station where she called Dave from a pay phone. It rang three times, then an answering machine picked up. When it finished its announcement she left a brief message.

"Dave, my name is Sandra MacElroy. I've come down here from Saint Louis because I've been receiving messages from your deceased brother. Something very bad is happening, and I'm wondering if you might have any ideas about what it might be. I'm in Breckenridge right now and I'm heading your way. It's..." She paused and looked at her watch. "It's a little after seven o'clock now. I should be in Cisco by eight. If I don't catch you tonight I'll be staying at a hotel in town. I don't know which one yet so I'll leave you a message when I find one. Thanks. Bye."

She hung up the phone and got back into her car. She wondered if perhaps she had been too direct. Perhaps she had revealed too much and this would simply scare the man away. Then again, if he didn't know what she was talking about he probably wouldn't be much help anyway. She started the car and headed east on Main Street until she came again to the big bank building. This time she turned right onto State Highway 183 and headed toward Cisco.

She left the city limits of Breckenridge and the land quickly became again dotted with cattle and mesquite trees. The houses were few and far between. The road ran up and down the terrain. The variety in the terrain surprised her; she had always thought of this part of Texas as being flat. There was actually quite a bit of variety. The countryside was also very green. There had been a lot of rain this year, and it had made the grass, trees and weeds grow more than in most years. The cattle she saw looked fat. They seemed to be beneficiaries of this wet weather.

Half an hour later the road began to twist and curve. The corners were not sharp, but she had to slow down a little for some of them.

Then as she turned one of the corners a little too fast her can of Coke turned over and began emptying to rest of its contents on the seat beside her. She reached quickly and tried to grab it, but it rolled into the floorboard where she couldn't reach it.

"Great," she exclaimed as she returned her eyes to the road.

There it was again.

Only fifty feet in front of her the white truck sat across the road.

She went for her brakes but did not hit them hard. Just before she hit them she remembered what the white truck represented. If she tried to stop she would run off the road or get in some kind of accident. In that split second she decided to just drive through it.

As she made the decision the sun which hung low in the sky reflected off the right front fender of the truck. This sent off a warning in her head and then she did push down on the brake.

But it was too late.

She was still going forty-five miles per hour when she struck the vehicle.

Her body snapped forward against the seat belt and her left arm flew out of the sling and struck the dash. She ran into the truck on the passenger's side, about a foot behind the door, almost squarely in the middle. The truck slid back a few feet. The tail end of her car slid around to her right and onto the shoulder of the road. Then it raised up a little. It felt as if the car had completely left the ground, and she felt the impact when it came back down.

There was the sound of breaking glass.

She opened her eyes slowly. Her head felt as if it were going to split. Her left arm felt numb; she was sure she had broken it. Her right collarbone hurt too, where the seat belt had pulled her back to the seat. Maybe it was broken too.

The pain in her head was tremendous. She looked ahead and saw the dent she had put into the white truck which sat on the road about six feet in front of her.

Then she saw some movement out of the corner of her eye. She turned her head slowly, and it hurt to do so. When she looked she saw a man approaching. He was a short and filthy man. Probably a bum, she thought to herself. He wore too many clothes for this warm day, and as he approached she could smell his stench.

Then she saw that he was carrying something with him. In his right hand he held a small hammer. As he approached her he raised the hammer slowly. There was a sly and terrible grin creeping onto his face.

She tried to move away from the window, but her movements were slow and pained. The man brought the hammer down on the window next to her. The top quarter of the window caved in, showering more glass around her throbbing arm. He raised the hammer again and brought it down hard. This time it broke away most of the remaining glass. She grabbed the seat belt release with her right hand and pressed it. The seat belt came loose but did not slide back into the door as it should have. She tried to react quickly despite the pain and disorientation, but it was very hard. Her back and neck screamed out at her.

She looked to her assailant as she tried to move away. He reached into her car with the hammer and brought it back before her eyes. She screamed and closed her eyes as the man prepared to crush her skull.

Then she heard a loud horn and felt the hammer fall onto her left leg then to the floorboard. She opened her eyes and saw another man rushing toward her car. She looked for the bum, but could not find him. Then she looked down and saw the hammer resting against the accelerator.

"Miss, Miss, are you all right?" the man asked as he rushed toward her.

She tried to answer the man, but she could not get the words to come out. She felt suddenly very sick and very lightheaded. Then she watched him fade away as she slipped into unconsciousness.

XI
1

It was almost midnight when Sandra had her most vivid and most terrifying dream. In the dream she stood naked in the dark room again. It was cold and she could feel the evil souls inside the darkness as they pressed up against her and enveloped her. Then the strip of light appeared in the distance and the darkness left her. It rushed to the crack and pressed up against it. The small boy with the missing arm and bloodied face stood next to her. He spoke to her, and this time she understood what he said.

"They're getting out."

"Where are they going?" Sandra asked.

"They're going out, to the other side."

"Why?" Sandra asked.

"Because they want to hurt and kill."

Sandra looked back to the slit of light which seemed to bulge and grow larger.

"Will they get out?" Sandra asked.

She always asked this question. Before tonight there had been no answer. But this time the small child looked to her with tears in his eyes and spoke. "Yes."

Then there was a loud explosion and a rush of warm air. Sandra looked up and saw a blinding light and an opened doorway. On the other side of the doorway she saw a scene of ivy and sunlight. A young girl lay sprawled and bloodied in the ivy as the darkness rushed past her and on through the doorway. Pieces of the doorway were strewn around the girl. The girl's face and left arm were covered in fresh blood, and there was a deep red stain in the center of her white blouse.

Then Sandra stood alone in the room. It was empty now. The doorway lay open and the door was in pieces.

And she realized that until tonight it had never gone this far.

Then the light faded and left her once again in darkness.

2

Sandra opened her eyes and could only hear the sound of her heart pounding in her ears.

She could remember. For the first time she could remember what the child had said. She could remember all of the dream this time. What did that mean? She feared the worst. The child had probably been allowed to give the message because now it was too late. It didn't matter if she remembered it or not, there was nothing she could do.

Sandra tried to call out for some help, but she could not keep her eyes opened. The dream had awakened her and she knew something terrible was about to happen, but the drugs she had been given pulled her back to sleep.

As her eyes closed a tear ran down her cheek.

3

Colleen stood in the center of the power room. She was clothed entirely in black. Thin black scarves hung from the belt which held the dress to her waist. Her hands rested by her side and trembled slightly. Red candles were arranged in a large triangle around her. Dave walked from one candle to the next, lighting them carefully as he went. The candles were tall and each stood in a small brass holder. At the base of each candle lay a sprig of dried rosemary and a dime. The dimes were all dated before 1965 and were therefore silver. This was the quickest way Dave could find to get the small amount of silver needed. He had bought them at a rare coin store in Abilene. They had been in a box which held dozens of the coins.

The triangle was made of thirty-six candles. This meant each side was composed of thirteen. As Dave lit the final candles the room actually seemed to become darker, as if the flame of each candle had been turned down. Eerie shadows danced in unfamiliar patterns across the walls. The shadows seemed not to reflect the objects which were physically in the room. They seemed instead to cast the shadows of images from the otherworld as they waited for their time to cross over. Dave stood and looked at these shadows. He wondered if he and Colleen would do everything right. He wondered if they would be able to shut the spiritual door tightly. His mind was still fresh with the chants and movements he had been given. But his faith now was at a low and would sink lower as the ceremonies proceeded.

Colleen had to memorize the chants and her role in the odd play. When she had decided that she did in fact have a responsibility to participate she made Dave walk her through it half a dozen times. Then she sat down and wrote it all out and studied it until an hour before the ceremonies began. Then she had relaxed in a sort of preparatory meditation until a few minutes ago. Now she stood, waiting for her cues. She was glad she had only been required to memorize just a few sentences in Latin. The rest were in English. All brought specific images to her mind, as they were supposed to do. It was the images, not the words, which were crucial.

Dave walked back to a table at the edge of the darkness. On the table he had placed the various supplies he had acquired earlier that day. He pressed the play button on the small tape recorded which rested on the table. After a few seconds there was the sound of a drum beating steadily and softly. Dave looked at his watch which also rested on the table. It was too dark to make out the time. He grabbed it and walked to the nearest candle. Ten more minutes.

He let the tape run while he waited for the starting time.

Colleen just stood still with her eyes closed and relaxed.

What seemed like only moments later she heard the soft cymbals which signaled the start of the ceremonies.

4

"Who stands at the door?" Colleen said. It was more than a whisper yet less than speech.

"We are here," came the reply. It was Dave. He stood at the edge of the candlelight, where Colleen could only make out his outline.

She waited a few moments then asked again, "Who stands at the door?"

"We are here." It sounded different this time. It was still Dave who spoke, but his voice had changed somehow.

She asked again. "Who stands at the door?"

"We are here." This time there were distant whispers, voices which chimed in with Dave. Dave's own voice had faded.

She was only to ask three times. She bent down and picked up the small cross which rested in the items at her feet. It was a simple cross, made of two thick twigs held together with twine. She held it before her upside down.

"What do you want?" she asked.

"To cross over."

She repeated the question three times, and she heard the reply three times. Now she could not hear Dave at all. She wondered if this was the reality of it all, or if she had slipped into some kind of trance. Dave had told her she would become somewhat entranced, though always aware. Her perception seemed warped, like she had taken a small amount of a hallucinogenic drug. But she had not. It sounded like there were dozens of quiet voices, and there seemed to be a light in the room which did not emanate from the triangle of candles.

She laid the cross down at her feet. Then she picked up a small bowl which contained a dark and smelly liquid. The liquid was a mixture of herbs and spices in water. She walked to the border of the triangle and began sprinkling the mixture just inside the line of candles. When she had completed the triangle she walked back to the center and tossed the remains of the liquid toward the western wall. The liquid turned red where it hit the ground, and it doused the flame of one of the candles. Colleen watched as the candle's flame returned. She looked for Dave, but could only see his shadow. She wanted to call to him now. She had become frightened. But she knew that if she did she would ruin the ceremonies. Instead of crying out she returned her eyes to the wall before her and recited the words she had memorized. Many of them formed sentences which made no sense, and most of it she did not understand. But she did feel the power growing as she spoke, and the flames of the candles began to stir with the breeze which came from everywhere. It was a soft breeze and she could feel its coldness on her face.

When she finished the chants she heard the voices again. They came from Dave's direction, but they were not from Dave. This only increased her fear and she began to doubt whether she would be able to complete what she had begun.

She listened to Dave's words. They sounded strange. They did not sound like words meant to repel but more like words to invite. She had not known ahead of time what Dave would say, only her cues. As she listened she became puzzled. She remembered that Dave had told her that they would need to lull the spirits into comfort, to relieve some of the pressure which lay on them at the threshold before slamming the door in their faces and bolting it shut. But the words Dave uttered seemed too inviting. They seemed to call to the spirits in a manner in which they could not refuse. She began to wonder just how wide the door would open before they would slam it shut.

Then there was a bright flash of light. Dave had warned her about it, but it still terrified her when it hit. It lit the room so brightly that the brilliance was all she could see for that instant. She could not see Dave, nor could she see any of the items which were in the room with them. When the flash was over she could see nothing at all. It seemed as if she had been taken from the room completely.

Then she began to panic. She began to wonder if she had been transported again to the dark place. She dropped to her knees and felt the floor before her. The objects she had placed there were still at her feet, and the soft glow of the candles slowly reappeared. Her blindness passed, but her vision was not completely restored.

It was time for her to say something, but now she could not remember what it was. She remained on her knees and looked around her. The disorientation was getting bad. She knew where she was, yet it all seemed unfamiliar.

Then she saw a face in the western wall.

She covered her mouth to muffle the scream which escaped from her.

She watched as the face took shape but did not become distinct. The entire wall became a milky substance which seemed to churn and flow. The face did not come out of the wall but remained an image inside of it. Colleen stared at the frightful image, forgetting altogether her responsibility.

Then she heard Dave's voice.

"Stand up," he said.

She stood up, but did not take her hand from her mouth.

"Put your left arm out," Dave said in a rough voice.

Colleen put out her left arm and looked at it. She stared, remembering now what she was supposed to do. She looked back at the wall and realized that they had come too far. She had to be strong now, or there would be dire consequences.

"Pass to the door, come to the door, but not through," she chanted in a monotone voice. She stared ahead at the wall as she spoke, unable to take her eyes from the face before her. Its mouth opened and closed as if it would speak, but could not be heard.

Colleen reached down and retrieved the small knife from the floor. Then she stood and faced the wall. The candles between her and the wall suddenly grew brighter, and the flames grew until they seemed more like flames from gas torches than from candles. She could hear the two-foot-tall flames as they burnt the wick and the wax, and she watched the candles as they shrank before her. As this went on she slowly reached out and drew a line across her arms with the blade. Her fear had subsided some. She felt the tranquility slowly run through her veins as if she had been injected with a soothing and calming drug as she drew the line and her blood began to run. It ran down the sides of her arm and dripped slowly to the floor before her.

"Come you spirits, come now, come through." Her voice sounded strange even to herself.

"We come," came the answer. The sound of the voice came from Dave's direction. The face in the wall mouthed the words.

Colleen dropped the knife and picked up a small chalice which held some dried leaves. She let some of her blood drip from her arm into the chalice. It made a sound like water in hot grease when it hit the leaves, and a small stream of smoke came from the concoction.

"We come," repeated the voice.

Now she could not tell if the voice came from Dave or from the wall before her. She could no longer see the wall, and the image before her was beginning to take on a third dimension. Smoke billowed outward from the edges of the image but were reabsorbed before they could enter the triangle.

Colleen carried the chalice to the edge of the triangle closest to the western wall. She stood before the flames which continued to reach upward from the base of the candle holders. The candles on this row were gone, yet the flames burned on. She held her arms out over the flames. Instead of warmth she felt a biting coldness which covered the portion of her arms closest to the flames.

"We invite you," she chanted. "Come."

It was getting close now, close to the point where the chants would be reversed and force the spirits off guard back into their world. Then they would be farther from this place than they had ever been, and they would not be able to return within Colleen's lifetime. She watched the wall and waited for her signal.

The face on the wall became more solid. She could see into the white eyes. There was destruction and hatred in those eyes, hatred of a hundred years. There was desperation and cold intent. These things struck deep within her soul, but the fear was kept at bay. She knew she should be terrified, but the terror would not come. Instead she stood entranced as the face before her began to smile.

She closed her eyes and emptied the chalice outside of the triangle. This was to be the beginning of the end. This was the breech of the ceremonies, the element of defiance which would break the chain and send the spirits deep into their own world.

There was another flash of light and the sound of an explosion. A cold wind struck Colleen's face and pushed her back with enough force to knock her down. The chalice clattered against the floor and bounced off a candle holder behind her.

Dave waited for the effect of the flash to wear off so that he could see. When the room came back into view he saw that Colleen was lying inside the triangle with her feet facing the western wall, her legs spread slightly apart. Her arms rested at her side and her eyes were trained on the ceiling. The wind which had come had knocked him against the table, but not to the floor. He looked to Colleen. Now was the crucial moment. Now was the time to send the spirits back.

But she seemed to be in some kind of trance.

He looked at her, waiting for the words. As he waited he saw the face in the wall as it grew in its reality. There was no wall now. Smoke came from all sides of the image, still turning back at the wall of flames created by the candles which had gone wild. Then he saw another, smaller face. Then another. The faces began to overlay one another, and dozens of them were appearing.

They were coming through. They had been invited.

It was time for the final words.

But the words did not come.

Instead the door into the room burst open and a man jumped in. His body was covered in rags and he leapt over the row of candles landing inside the triangle with Colleen. The man knelt down beside her and lifted an object over his head.

It was a long bladed knife with a silver handle.

He uttered the final words of his own.

"Come now, great spirits. Come now and wreak your revenge."

"No!" Dave shouted.

Then the man looked up and Dave saw into his wild eyes.

It was Crazy Joe.

Dave ran toward Joe. He tried to jump over the candles which still burnt with small flames then found himself lying on the floor, his head pounding. He had jumped, but he had hit some kind of wall. He felt the electricity of it still flowing through him.

Then he remembered where he was and looked up.

As he looked he saw the blade descending.

It sliced cleanly through Colleen's chest above where her heart lay. Dave watched in horror, frozen in his place as Crazy Joe moved the blade surely and quickly in a triangle of his own making. Then he reached down and pulled the pulsing heart quickly from the body.

Dave tried to cry out but could say nothing.

Joe held the heart before him.

"The sacrifice has been made," he said. "The door awaits!"

With this he tossed the heart toward the western wall.

It sailed through the air, directly toward the main face which could still be clearly seen amidst a hundred other faces. Its mouth opened and the heart sailed through.

Then there was the sound of thunder, and the candles which stood between the western wall and the center of the triangle suddenly went out.

The wall was down.

The door was opened.

Dave could see the faces coming out into the room. As they passed him by he could feel an icy chill which covered him completely.

As the spirits passed through the triangle the remaining candles were extinguished. The room fell to utter darkness. Then he heard the sound of glass exploding in millions of pieces.

He could hear the screams of the souls as they came through and he knew that the true terror had just begun.

XII
1

The true terror had begun.

Sheriff Jim Walker drove through town on his way to the medium's place. A disturbance had been called in. The house was not next to any other houses so either someone had been walking by and noticed a problem or it had been a substantial disturbance. He figured that it was the first of the two. He also figured that either the girl who lived there was holding some kind of dramatic ceremony for people who did not wish to be seen there in the daytime, or someone had just decided to harass the girl again by sending the police to wake her up in the middle of the night. There were plenty of people in town who still did not accept that the VanZandt girl had set up a shop of this kind in their town. Living in Cisco was an odd enough experience by itself without the help of the medium. Some of the people even blamed her for the fact the toasters never worked long, batteries never lasted, and transformers always blew out. But these things had been going on long before Colleen VanZandt had turned to the darker practices. In fact, Cisco had been like that for as long as Jim could remember. He remembered asking his grandfather once many years ago about Cisco and all of these odd problems. He simply said that it had always been that way. Jim's grandfather was the first Walker to settle in Cisco. He had moved down from Oklahoma after the first world war, when the only road to Dallas was a dirt trail. There had been oil then, and Cisco had been a much larger town. But even then there had been problems. Even then getting oil out of the ground became more of a chore the closer you got to town. There were always more downed rigs and injuries within the city limits.

He drove past one of Cisco's four auto shops. For a town of six thousand it had plenty of auto repair stores, and each of them was kept quite busy. From the end of the block he could see the house. It looked dark and quiet. He turned the corner and drove to within a hundred feet before stopping. He left his engine running and stepped out of the car. Jim could hear the cicadas singing in the trees. It was a warm and peaceful night. He decided that he would not knock on the door. He didn't care for Colleen VanZandt's particular line of work, but he respected a person's right to do what he or she pleased as long as it didn't break the law. She seemed to do just fine living off what the people of the community paid for her services. He supposed that the harassment which came to her was just part of the job. But he did not wish to compound her problems. So from time to time, when he got the disturbance calls, he would just take a look at the house and drive on if it was dark and quiet. Colleen was a pretty girl, and he did not mind seeing her in her T-shirt in the middle of the night, but he also respected her privacy and did not wish to disturb her.

He stood looking at the house, listening to the sounds of the night.

Then he noticed something strange.

The house was dark.

He had seen this right off, but had not noted the significance. Usually Colleen left a light or two on. He had never understood why, but she did. Tonight the house was completely dark, and too silent. He looked up the street to see if the power had perhaps gone out again, but the nearest streetlight burned as brightly as ever. He decided that he would take a closer look.

Jim shut off his engine and walked cautiously to the front of the house. He could not see any signs of a disturbance, but he was careful nonetheless. As he approached the door he felt glass as it crunched under his feet. He shined his flashlight down on the walkway and saw that it was covered with glass. Then he turned his light onto the house and saw that the nearest window had been broken. But he was still a good thirty feet from that window. How had the glass been thrown so far? He flipped open the snap on his holster, but did not withdraw the gun from it. As he approached the house he continued to step on broken glass. He inspected the outside of the house carefully with his flashlight and saw that every window had been broken, apparently from the inside. He listened, but there were still no sounds. He walked carefully to the front door and knocked. When he did the door swung slowly inward and he saw that the frame of the door had been broken and that the door was cracked from top to bottom. Had someone forced their way in? It looked more like they had forced their way out. He drew his gun.

Jim pushed the door the rest of the way open and turned the beam of the light into the house. It was a mess. The floor was covered with items which had been on shelves or on the wall. It was as if someone had run through the house and knocked over everything standing. Pictures lay on the floor with their frames broken and their glass shattered. He shined the light down the hallway and saw that the mess continued. He listened very carefully, but still he heard no sounds. He felt a cool breeze and knew that either there were more broken windows or a back entrance was open.

Was it a burglary? It looked suspiciously like one, yet there were things which didn't make sense. There were too many items of value left. It was more like someone had just ransacked the house. It had probably been a couple of kids who knew Colleen was gone and whose parents had given them the idea over the years that things like this just happened to evil people.

Jim debated on whether or not to go back to the car and call for backup. The situation was odd, but it did not appear particularly dangerous. He listened, but he could hear no activity inside the house. He looked back to his car. He decided he would have a look around. If he saw or heard anything which made the situation more threatening, then he would exit the house and call for backup.

Jim called out to Colleen, but there was no answer. He flipped the first light switch he came to, but it did nothing. He made his way cautiously down the hall, toward the living room.

When he reached the living room he could see that it too had been vandalized. A small television lay in the center on the floor, its screen shattered. The windows here were broken too, but none of the glass lay inside the house. All of the windows had been broken from the inside, and with enough force that most of the glass lay some distance from the house. It was as if there had been a terrible explosion, only there were no signs of burning or scorching. In fact, it felt cooler inside the house than it had outside, much cooler. He noticed then that his breath was turning to steam before him. This made no sense. It was nowhere near cold enough for this to be happening, at least not outside. He saw nothing in the living room which would help him solve the mystery, so he headed back through the hall.

There were two doors off the hallway before it turned back to the left into a bedroom. He opened the first door and discovered a small bathroom. Not much was disturbed here except the mirror which was shattered. Whoever had been through the house had been thorough when it came to glass breaking. He walked further down the hall and opened the second door.

The air from this room was very cold. It felt as if he had opened the door to a meat locker. He shined his light into the room. First he saw the burnt candle holders with no candles in them. Then he caught the edge of some black fabric so he trained his light on the object.

Then he saw the body.

He took in a deep breath of the freezing air as he looked at the bloodied body of Colleen VanZandt. There was a lot of blood. Some of it came from her arm. Most of it came from a gaping hole in her chest. The blood formed a circle around her body and it reflected his flashlight beam in a glistening red hue. Her eyes were frozen upwards, on the ceiling. Her arms and legs were spread out.

Jim decided to go call for that backup.

Then he heard a sound to his left.

He pointed his gun and his flashlight toward the source of the sound. Then he saw the man, sitting on the floor. He looked both terrified and weary. His face was an unnatural pale color, and there was a small amount of blood on his clothing. His mouth moved in contorted attempts at communications. Jim's first and only conclusion was that this had to be the killer.

"Lay down!" Jim called to the man. "Lay down and put your hands behind your head!"

The man closed his eyes and lowered his head. Then he forced words from his cold and numb lips.

"Please go. Now."

Jim looked at the man in puzzlement. How could the man expect him to leave the scene of this hideous murder, especially when the killer was sitting right in front of him?

The man looked back into Jim's eyes. "Please," he said.

For a moment Jim understood. For just an instant the words made perfect sense and he began to lower his gun and leave.

But then he heard another sound.

Jim turned quickly to his right just as the man leapt toward him. He fired into the man five times, but still the man came. He seemed to be floating toward him in slow motion, flying across the room, laughing as he came.

Jim hesitated then fired his last shot.

And still the man came.

Then the man was before him. His face was dead white, as were his eyes and hair. The terror stood before Jim, looking into his eyes, filling him with all the horror possible before smiling again and reaching for him.

Then the door behind him closed.

He tried to use his flashlight as a weapon to keep the man away, but it was as if the man was not solid and the flashlight passed right through him.

Then he felt sharp claws closing around his neck.

He dropped his flashlight which rolled a few feet and came to rest against a candle holder. The light shone in his direction. He tried to grab onto the arms of his assailant, but they seemed to have no substance. Then he grabbed his neck as he felt the claws digging into his flesh. He dropped to his knees and pulled at the claws, but they would not let loose. He tried to gasp for air, but he could not.

Then he heard the hideous laugh again as the blackness around him became even colder and his neck grew numb. The pain pounded inside his head, then faded away as he dropped to the floor.

Dave leaned back against the wall in the utter coldness. He had not seen the assailant, but he knew what had happened. He crawled slowly toward the door. He knocked over a few of the candle holders, then picked one up and hurled it through the darkness. It crashed against the western wall, the wall from which the terrors had come, then fell to the floor. Dave crawled until he came to the body of the officer. He felt for the man's hands which were still holding tightly to his own neck. Dave had watched as the man had fired into the darkness, then grabbed his own neck and strangled himself. Dave checked for a pulse. There was none.

He wondered if this was what awaited the town.

And how much further it would go.

And if it would ever stop.

He crawled past the body to the door which he managed to open. Air which felt warm to him brushed his face. He had been stuck in the freezing room for over an hour. He crawled into the hallway and then closed the door behind him. He sat with his back against the closed door, looking down the hall to the shattered window at the end of the hallway.

Then he lowered his head into his hands and wept.

2

Despite the fact that the entire left side of the vehicle was pushed in, the white delivery truck still ran. The left front tire wobbled a little bit, but not so much that it kept the vehicle from working. Getting it away from the scene of the accident earlier hadn't been that difficult. The man who had stopped had put the woman in his car and taken her to the hospital himself. When they had left the scene Joe simply got back into the truck and drove off. The man had checked the truck for people, but had not taken down the license number or anything like that. Joe had kept the truck hidden until tonight.

Now he sat at the end of a residential road. He sat and waited, his engine running. Joe held onto the steering wheel and watched the road for activity.

But there was none. Not yet anyway.

He ran a sleeve across his nose which had been bleeding earlier that night. It had begun bleeding shortly after he had sacrificed the witch woman in her dark room. There had been a terrible cold blast, and his head had begun to ring. He had escaped while the commotion continued and was long gone by the time it was over. Then he had gone home and gotten the truck.

Now he sat and waited as the night dragged on.

3

Betty Chatburn tossed and turned in her bed. She had taken sleeping pills tonight. She did this more often than not, finding that she had become dependent on them to put her to sleep. But tonight she slept lightly despite the pills. Her light sleep was filled with vague but horrifying dreams of death and disaster.

She saw the road again.

It was the aftermath as she had seen it twenty years ago. There was a truck and there was lots of blood. One son lay in the bushes, was he dead? The other she could not see, not until she approached the truck and saw the mess he had become.

The dream was elusive and repeated itself in different forms.

Then she awoke again to the cry for help.

This was the fourth time. The first time she had gotten up and looked around, sure that the voice had not been within her dreams. By now she understood that this was exactly where the voice lay. It awakened her as if it came from the conscious world, but she knew that it did not.

But then she heard it again.

This time she recognized the small voice and it frightened her badly. She lay still, listening for any movement or any more speech, but there was none. She rolled out of her bed and put on her slippers again. She walked back through the hallway to the room which had belonged to her son Tommy, and in many ways still did. She walked to his room on not much more than instinct, as she had the first time the voice had awakened her.

But this time when she opened the door she took a step back at what she saw.

The room was clean and fresh looking.

It was always clean; she always saw to that. But there was something new to the cleanliness this time. The sheets on the bed were not so faded. Neither was the paint on the wall nor the carpeting she had never changed. The toys which were out looked newer than they should have. There was no rust now on the tool set which rested on the edge of Tommy's dresser. The room was in exactly the same order she had left it, the same order it had been in on the day of Tommy's death, only now everything looked new again.

"Help, mom!" came Tommy's voice again.

A light glow came through the bedroom window. Betty walked to the window and looked out. There was light outside, even though it was still night. The darkness had been invaded by an eerie glow which made it look like morning, perhaps as it appeared on another world. She looked around the outside and saw that it had changed too. It too was fresher. The Jacobsons' house across the street was a different color, and the car which sat in front of it was the same one which had sat there when the Thompsons had lived there twenty years earlier.

In fact the whole street reminded her of that time.

Then she saw Tommy as he came up the sidewalk on his Big Wheel. She saw him riding around carelessly, and she knew what was going to happen.

"Hey mom!" Tommy called. She could hear him, even through the closed window. "Look! I'm back! I'm back and alive, and you get a second chance to change everything!"

Tommy turned the Big Wheel around and headed back down the sidewalk. He stayed on the sidewalk, but Betty knew that he would eventually head out into the road. She was being given the chance to do something, to change the past.

"Oh, dear Lord," she said to her God, "what should I do?"

She knew inside that she should leave the past alone. Things had happened the way they had happened for a reason. She had come to accept that. God had a reason for taking her son.

But it was her child, and she loved him so. Watching him ride again down the sidewalk brought tears into her eyes. She knew it didn't have to happen. Who was giving her this second chance? Was it God or was it Satan? She didn't know. She didn't care.

Tommy turned back around and she knew that her time was growing short.

Betty ran through the house to the front door. She threw it open and ran out into the front yard. Tommy was riding quickly up the sidewalk, approaching their driveway.

"Tommy," she called out, "stay out of the street."

Tommy looked at her, but he just smiled. She remembered that smile, and she knew what it meant. It was Tommy's 'I hear you, but I don't hear you' smile. He was going to go out into the street. Why did it have to be so hard?

She rushed across the yard to meet him at the driveway, but he was riding too fast and he passed not ten feet in front of her as he turned off the sidewalk and into the street.

"Tommy!" she cried out. She ran out into the street and called after him. "Tommy, get out of the street right now!"

Tommy looked back at her with a questioning gaze.

Then the white delivery truck came around the corner.

The truck looked wrong. It was dented up, and it was shaking as it drove. But this was not important.

"Tommy!" she shouted. "The truck is coming, get out of the road!"

Tommy just looked back at her as the truck approached. Then he stopped his Big Wheel and got off. It was changing. She was changing the past.

Betty ran toward her son, trying to get him before the truck did. Tommy just stood looking at her with that puzzled gaze. She hurried, but she didn't think she was going to make it. The truck was picking up speed, and she was a tired old woman.

"Tommy!" she cried out one last time.

Then the truck was upon him. She stopped running and put her hands to her head as the truck struck her small son from behind. His head snapped back and blood splattered the grill of the truck.

But the truck did not slow down. Instead it picked up speed. She looked at her mangled son, now stuck to the front of the vehicle as it sped toward her.

She understood all too well what was happening. She had messed with fate, and now she would have to pay the price.

Then she saw that the man behind the wheel of the truck did not fit the picture either. She had seen him before, but she couldn't remember where. He was a crazy man, and there was a glimmer in his eye.

Then the truck struck her.

There was no scream.

Bones snapped and broke, and blood began to flow.

Joe stopped the truck and looked out the window behind him. It was still dark out, but his brake lights provided enough light for him to see that his job was done. A small line of blood ran away from the body and toward the curb.

Joe pulled his head back into the vehicle and headed down the road.

He knew that there was a present waiting for him at home.

4

It was four in the morning when Virgil awoke. He had been in a restless sleep which had included some odd and horrible dreams. But now he was awake and he could hear the clock on the wall as it ticked the seconds by.

Virgil was alone. He had been alone for the past seven years. Before then he had shared his life with Thelma. He had done so since their marriage in 1925. Since then there had been a great depression and a world war. There had been assassinations and resignations of presidents. Korea and Vietnam had come and gone.

But none of these events had been as earth shattering as the death of Thelma seven years ago. Living as one half of a duo was all he had known since he was sixteen. That's when he had married Thelma. They had been good together, a team despite the bickering. People had always commented on how much younger than their actual age they each appeared to be.

But nobody said that to Virgil. His age had caught up with and passed him by. A part of him had died along with Thelma, and now it looked as if the rest of him was wilting away. He had always been a stout man. Now he was frail and the lines of old age covered his entire body. He had withdrawn from his friends, feeling inadequate without the rest of him, without Thelma. He spent most of his time in the small apartment, taking care of himself as best he could. He paid for some help with the mundane chores and errands. He spent most of his time watching television or reading second-rate detective novels which were all at least ten years old.

Virgil lay still, listening to the ticking of the clock. It reminded him again of the beating of his heart which seemed to go on endlessly despite his wishes to the contrary. He waited for death, but he did not rush it on, at least not consciously.

He heard a faint but familiar sound. At first he could not place it. He lay still listening for it, but it did not repeat. Then he heard another sound. This sound brought to his mind a picture of a dress being thrown onto a bed.

Virgil and Thelma had moved into the apartment ten years ago. It had been their way of leading a simpler life which did not include yard work. The apartment had been constructed from part of a big old house. There were a few cacks in the walls, and the rooms were lit by light bulbs dangling from brown cords which came from the ceilings. But all in all it was a decent place, and somebody else did the yard work. Virgil's section of the house had two bedrooms. The bedroom Virgil lay in now had once been the guest room when Thelma was alive. When she died he had moved out of the bedroom they had shared for three years and into the guest room. He hoped that doing so would help him to escape some of the memories that rested in the floor and the walls of that room. It was from that room that these sounds were coming.

Then a light came on in that bedroom. He could see its reflection in the hallway. Somebody was in the house. Virgil's son was the only other person who held a key, and he had not said he would be coming over. Virgil decided that it was probably a burglar, and he wondered what he should do. He was no longer agile nor strong enough to overpower the burglar. There was a small caliber pistol in the nightstand by the bed, but this might get him into worse trouble if he confronted the burglar, especially if the man was armed. Virgil decided that he would get the gun, then hide on the side of the bed away from the door. If the burglar tried to come in Virgil would shoot from behind the bed. Perhaps then the burglar would take what he had gathered and leave. Virgil cursed himself for not hooking up the phone his son had put on the nightstand three months ago.

He pulled the drawer of the nightstand slowly open, then stopped when he heard the music. It was an old but familiar tune. It was the tune which he and Thelma had claimed as theirs over fifty years earlier. There was an old radio in that room, once they had bought new in 1956. This was the only source he could imagine that the music was coming from. Then there was a faint but distinct smell of a perfume he had always called his favorite, but only when Thelma wore it.

He listened. There were a few more rustling sounds. The music and the smell toyed with his mind. He wanted to go to the room and look. But his mind told him that it would be dangerous, that he should wait until the intruder left.

"Virgil? Can you come here for a moment?"

His eyes grew wide and the gun fell to the floor. It was definitely Thelma's voice which called to him. For a moment he hesitated. Then he decided he should go look. He walked slowly to his bedroom door, listening to the sounds which came from the old room. He reached the hallway and could see the shadow of someone in the other room. The door, which was always closed, was halfway opened. From where he stood the music and the perfume were stronger, and they pulled him into the hallway and up to the door of the old bedroom.

He reached forward and pushed the door the rest of the way open. As the door swung in he saw that the room did not look like it was supposed to. It did not look like a guest room with their old furniture in it, which was what he had made it. It looked like a room that was being lived in.

Then the woman stepped from her place near the closet. He looked up at her and took in a breath.

It really was Thelma.

"Thelma?" he said, not sure just how to respond. Was this really Thelma? Was this a body, or a ghost?

The woman looked at him with eyes that showed disappointment. "Virgil!" she exclaimed. "We've got to leave in twenty minutes and you're not even dressed!"

"What?" He looked her up and down. Not only was this Thelma, but this was the shapely and pretty Thelma of many years past. She looked to him now as she had when she was in her forties.

"We'll never make the show on time if you don't get on the ball!"

Virgil looked down at himself. He was still wearing his pajamas, but something wasn't right. Then he saw his hands. The black spots were gone. He held his hands up and looked closely at them. Then he pulled up his sleeves and looked at his arms. The hair was thick and black, and the blue veins had gone as well.

"Thelma?" Virgil asked. "What's happening?"

Thelma looked at him with concern. "Don't spoil it, honey," she said in a pleading voice. "It's all so wonderful here."

He stepped into the room, towards Thelma. He missed her so. He wanted her so. He crossed the room to her and reached out. He didn't know if he would touch her, or if she would disappear.

But she was real. He could feel her skin, though it seemed oddly cold. But when he touched her his world changed. His mind worked to accept things as they were. They were so much happier than what they had been. He turned and looked at the dresser across the room. The mirror revealed a man half his age, and the man smiled back at him.

The new world worked its way into his mind and he accepted it, hoping that by doing do it would become and remain his new reality.

Then he noticed his clothes laid out on the bed. They were his 'going out' clothes. He turned back to Thelma and gave her a kiss.

"Why Virgil!" she exclaimed. "You're going to make us late!"

This was a cue of some kind which aroused an old excitement within him. He removed his clothes so he could change into his good ones. As he stood in his underwear he saw that his excitement was strong, and he turned back to Thelma who stood looking at him with a slight blush. Her eyes wandered down his chest and to the evidence of his excitement.

"Oh, Virgil!" she said again.

Then he laid her out on the bed and made love to her like he had not in many decades.

When he was done Thelma looked into his eyes and smiled. "We can still make the show if you hurry."

"Yes," Virgil agreed, "of course we can."

Virgil put his underwear back on and began to dress in the clothes she had laid out for him. In his bewildered mind he wondered what movie they were going to see. He wondered what world he would see when he stepped out the door. Would it be the new one or the old one?

He put on all his clothes but his tie. Why had she forgotten his tie?

"Honey?" he called to her. She stood behind him, near the closet. "Where's my tie?"

When she did not answer he turned to look at her. She had a mischievous look on her face and she was pointing toward the ceiling. He turned back around and saw that she had somehow attached his tie to the ceiling. He smiled back at her, then jumped up on the dresser where he could reach the tie. He did not jump down right away, but stayed on the dresser while he placed the tie around his neck and tied it in the best knot he knew how. She watched him and smiled as he tied the oddly shaped knot. The tie felt odd in his hands and was not as flexible or cooperative as he thought it should be. But finally he got it tied.

Then he smiled at Thelma and held his arms out. "Ta-da!" he said. She giggled at him.

Then he jumped off the dresser.

He flew toward the floor, then stopped about a foot before he reached it. His head snapped back and the electric cord tore a few inches from the ceiling. Pieces of white dust showered around him and the bulb at the end of the old cord burst and cut into his neck. The cut was not deep, but deep enough to send a trickle of blood across the brown cord.

The force of the fall was enough. He did not grab at the cord. His eyes rolled and his feet twitched a little, but he was dead with a broken neck within seconds.

The room was dark and empty except for the old man who swung gently at the end of the light cord in front of the dresser.

XIII

1

"The damn town's gone crazy." Sheriff Pritchard sat in his car talking to his best deputy. "Sure, we get a weird case from time to time out here, but I want to know what the hell is going on, know what I mean?"

"Yessir." Deputy Sharp wasn't one to contradict or even contribute to the sheriff's comments, at least not until he was asked. That was one of the reasons he was the sheriff's best deputy.

"I should be sitting behind my desk, seeing to the smooth operation of this department. Instead, I'm out running around Cisco because we're suddenly shorthanded." The tall but too thin sheriff spit out the window as he drove. "Did you know there's been ten people killed in the last twenty-four hours in this county? Did you know they've all been in Cisco? Not everybody was from Cisco, but that's where it all took place. Doesn't that strike you as odd, Sharp?"

"Yessir."

"Car accidents, home accidents, and three suicides." The sheriff looked to his deputy and held up three fingers, shaking them for effect. "Three damn suicides! That's more than we've seen in the whole county in the past two years! And all in one night!" He turned his eyes back to the road and returned both hands to the wheel. "They found an old man swinging from a light cord in his apartment this morning. His son found him. They say he shouldn't have even been able to climb up there. He was even wearing some old clothes he had gotten out of storage somewhere. That was the first one. There was the Parkins girl..."

"Sherry Parkins?" Sharp asked, forgetting for a moment his place.

Sheriff Pritchard flashed him a disapproving glance. "Of course, Sherry Parkins. Are there any other Parkins in Eastland County?"

The deputy had gone to school with Sherry. Her father had been a police officer. Sherry had been bright and energetic. The only time he had ever seen her down was when her father had died of a heart attack at a young age. He found it hard to believe that life had gotten so bad for her that she had seen no other solution but suicide.

"They found her in the garage," the sheriff continued. Sharp didn't really want to know the details. "She'd wandered in there and blowed her head off with one of her daddy's old service revolvers. Her mother was in bed when it happened."

"Who else?" Sharp asked.

"Dewey Harper."

"The old welder?"

"Yep."

Deputy Sharp just looked at the road. Apparently the sheriff didn't want to talk about this one. Sheriff Pritchard had known Dewey since childhood. They had not spoken in several years, but at one time Dewey had been the grandfather Gordon Pritchard never had.

After a few moments the sheriff spoke again. "All this on top of what happened to the city patrol officer. It just don't make any sense." He emphasized the "don't" with a slap on the steering wheel.

Sharp had not heard the complete story on the city cop they had found in the VanZandt house. What he had heard was a little on the bizarre side. "Do they know anything more about what happened there?"

"Nope. It looks like he stumbled onto the scene of some bizarre ritual killing and strangled himself."

"How could somebody strangle themselves?" Sharp asked.

"That's what I asked the coroner. He said a lot of words, but he didn't really tell me anything." The sheriff spit out the window again. "The place has been pretty well worked over. I was there early this morning. I don't know where that one is going to lead, but I don't like it any better than all this other stuff." He turned the corner onto Conrad Hilton Drive. "It just don't make any sense."

As he turned the corner a young girl ran out in front of his car. Pritchard hit his brakes instantly. His car came to a quick halt. Still, he struck the girl and sent her to the asphalt. He jumped from his car and hurried to the girl who was already trying to sit up. The sheriff helped her into the sitting position and looked her over quickly. He discovered only a broken arm. A less aware driver, or one who had a habit of driving faster would probably have done more damage.

He called back to Sharp to call the incident in and get an ambulance to the scene. He would have taken her himself, but they were short-handed today and he felt he needed to be available for more serious calls. When he saw the girl was fairly cognizant he asked her if she was trying to get herself killed, or if she just had a lapse of reasoning.

"I saw my grandmother," the girl replied. Her eyes seemed to wander around.

"Where?"

"She was across the street."

The sheriff looked to where the girl had been headed. There were a few people standing there. One of them was an old woman. He called out to her, "Are you this child's grandmother?"

The lady looked startled. "No," she replied. She was just a gawker, like the other two.

"She isn't there now," the sheriff replied. "Why would she leave if she saw you get hit by a car?"

"Because she's really dead anyway," the girl replied.

"What?" Sheriff Pritchard asked.

"She's dead. She died two years ago."

"But you saw her across the street?"

"Yea." The girl looked back to the opposite side of the street to where she had seen her grandmother standing. Now there were other people there, but her grandmother was gone.

Sheriff Pritchard was beginning to wonder if this girl was sane. "Have you ever seen her like this before?"

"No, of course not." The girl seemed indignant, as if she were being accused of the insanity that the sheriff suspected.

"Where did she go?" he asked again.

The girl started to cry. "I don't know. I guess she'd dead again."

The sheriff felt awkward. He wasn't good with kids, and he didn't know what to do about the crying stuff. He held onto the broken arm and looked back to the people on the sidewalk. "Move on now!" he told them in a sharp tone. They obeyed. A few moments later he heard the sirens of the ambulance which came to take her to the hospital.

When the mess had been taken care of to the sheriff's satisfaction he got back into his car and resumed his patrol.

"I wonder how much of that's going on," he said.

"Excuse me, sir?"

"There's so much big stuff going on that we've become preoccupied with it. I wonder how much little stuff is going on. I wonder how busy the hospital is with broken arms and cuts and things like that."

"I couldn't begin to guess, sir."

Then a call came over the radio about a swimming accident at the lake. The sheriff waited for a moment. There were two other cars which should have been closer. They did not respond. He turned on his siren and headed toward Lake Cisco, which was just outside the city limits. The deputy called in the response as the sheriff cursed the situation once again.

"If this keeps up we're going to have to start running double shifts. We're not even getting much local help."

"I imagine they're pretty busy too."

"Of course they are," the sheriff exclaimed with exasperation. "They're always too busy to help out."

"We could always ask the state for help if this gets out of hand," Sharp suggested.

"I spoke with the state trooper's office this morning. They complained about being busy, but said that they would help out if it got any worse. Hell, it's already worse. A lot worse."

They rode silently for a while. The deputy wanted to know more about what the sheriff was thinking. He had his own theories about what was going on. Sharp figured that all of this stuff was related to the cult killing at the VanZandt place the night before. Something bigger than just a double murder had taken place there. Something had been let loose in Cisco, something which had been waiting for a very long time. He knew the history of the small town. He had been brought up just thirty-four miles away in Albany. He had heard the strange stories which had always surrounded Cisco. Now something big was finally happening. And it all had to do somehow with the killing of the VanZandt girl.

"So," the deputy began, "do you have any theories?"

"I'd say it was a full moon, except that it's worse than it's ever been on any full moon, and the moon isn't anywhere near full." He looked pensively out the window as they passed the city limits sign. "I don't know. Just a lot of weird coincidences, that's all."

The sheriff also believed that this was all linked somehow to the cult slayings, but he was more skeptical of those things he didn't understand. He knew that the first indications of any trouble had been the murders at the VanZandt house the previous night. After that all hell had broken loose. He knew that the killings had been the first of many odd events, but he did not yet believe that the girl's killing was the root cause.

But in time he would.

2

When Sandra awoke she knew that she had failed.

The sun was already in the sky when she finally awoke. She found herself once again in a sterile environment. Her head and back hurt, and her arm was in a new sling. Apparently she hadn't broken it as she'd feared. Whatever it was that had finally gotten free had managed to keep her out of the way long enough. She knew that there was now a breach between the two worlds she was in contact with. She also knew that she was not as close to it as she had been the day before. She remembered the accident with the white delivery truck at the edge of Cisco. She remembered the horrible dreams she had experienced in the night. She also could now remember dreams which had previously been partially or completely blocked from her memory. Now it didn't matter. She had a fairly good idea of what had happened. There was a breach now between the worlds, a tear through which the malice and hatred of hundreds of years was slipping through. It was slipping through in pieces, and it was spreading like a moldy spot on an orange. Now it was bad. Later it would be much worse.

She pressed her call button and waited for the nurse. When the nurse arrived, Sandra asked about the whereabouts of her belongings and the severity of her condition.

"Your stuff is all here. The man who brought you in came back later with your things. He was a very nice man."

"That's nice." It really was nice. She thought for a moment that in Saint Louis it probably wouldn't have happened that way. Perhaps it would have in a small southern Missouri town. "What about me?"

"The doctor will be in here in a while. His hands are kind of full right now. Seems everyone in Cisco decided to get injured at the same time. He'll tell you what he found."

"What he found?" Sandra asked.

"Bad wording." The nurse smiled. "I just mean he'll tell you how you're doing. I don't think you have any broken bones or anything, but I'm not sure."

The nurse was obviously new at her job. Sandra found it refreshing. The girl had not yet acquired the coldness which many in her profession eventually displayed. She smiled a sincere smile and seemed genuinely concerned.

"What's going on in Cisco?" Sandra asked. Perhaps the girl's openness would be of some further benefit.

"There just seems to be a lot of people coming in from over there. More than usual, a lot."

"Where are we?" Sandra asked.

"Memorial."

"Where's that?" Sandra asked.

"Oh, we're in Eastland. I forgot you're the one from out of state."

Sandra smiled back. "What kinds of things are going on in Cisco?"

"Mostly accidents. Some broken bones and a few burns. One or two were pretty serious. I think one even died in a car wreck."

"Is that all?"

The girl looked over her shoulder for a moment to make sure no one was around. "I hear rumors that there were some suicides and a couple of murders. Weird stuff. And I think there were more fatal accidents they're not telling us about yet."

"That is weird."

"Yea, and you know what else?" The girl was becoming visibly nervous.

"What's that?"

"I hear there was one of those weird cult slayings with dead animals and crosses and stuff."

Sandra listened with interest. In small towns people talked a lot for excitement. But this could have something to do with what had been haunting her for over a week now.

"Where did you hear this?" Sandra asked.

"My best friend's boyfriend's brother is a cop, and she says he says that a cop was killed last night at some witch's house. Her boyfriend said there was a girl killed there too, that she had her heart ripped out and no one could find it so they think it was eaten or something."

"That is weird," Sandra agreed.

"No shit, oh sorry," the girl blushed slightly at her professional faux pas. Then she looked at her watch. "I gotta get outta here," she exclaimed. "We're really busy today. Maybe I'll stop by later. Oh, I almost forgot, are you okay? Do you need anything?"

"A glass of water would be nice."

"Sure," the girl said. She hurried out of the room for a minute then returned with a small glass and a bottle of Tylenol. "I know you gotta hurt, so I got you some aspirin. Tell the doctor you asked for it."

"Okay," Sandra agreed. Then she took two of the pills as the girl fluffed her pillow roughly then turned to leave.

"Come back and tell me if you find out any more," Sandra asked the young girl.

"You got it," she answered as she reached the door.

"Oh, one more thing."

"Yea?"

"What time is it anyhow?"

"Oh." The girl looked at her watch again, even though only five minutes had passed since her last glance. "It's a little before noon."

"Thanks."

"No problem. Doctor should be here any minute."

"Great."

The girl flashed a good-bye smile and left the room. Sandra drank some more of the water. Her throat felt dry. She looked around and saw that she was in a very small room with no real furnishings. There wasn't even a chair for visitors. She supposed that this meant her stay would be short, and she hoped she was right. She did not wish to sneak out of another hospital.

The question now was what to do. Should she try and find Dave Chatburn? If she did try, would she still be a target of those forces which had been working against her? She doubted this since she was probably not seen as much of a threat, and the forces which had finally escaped were busy now with other things. If she found Dave perhaps she could learn enough to become a threat again.

The trip down here had been a long one, and she decided that it was not going to be wasted. She also decided that this was a chance for her to do something really constructive with her gift. This was an opportunity to do something more than provide a little comfort to an old lady or some peace of mind to some terrorized folks. This was her chance to do something substantial.

Perhaps this was what the gift was all about. She felt that there might even be a touch of destiny involved.

She knew she would stay and look for Dave. From there she would simply have to play it by ear.

She lay back and waited for the doctor as she thought carefully about her options.

3

Dave sat in his mother's home, his head in his hands. What had he done? Colleen was dead. Though the police did not know it yet, he was the prime suspect. He wanted to go to them and tell them his story, but he didn't know where to start, and he was sure that they would think he was using Crazy Joe as a scapegoat. It had been tried before. Joe was crazy, but he had never proven himself a threat to anyone. At least not until last night. And an officer had been killed as well. Apparently no one had seen Dave with Colleen. Perhaps someone had and the police were looking for Dave now.

And his mother. His mother too was dead. He had found out when he had showed up at her house early in the morning and found her missing. The people across the street, the Jacobsons, had told him about it. As they told him he remembered that the voices in his dream had told him this would happen, but he had forgotten until he heard the news. Then it had all come back. This only added to the guilt.

Apparently Mr. Reay, who lived two houses down, had found Dave's mother in the road as he returned home from his rounds at the night clubs on the edge of town. He had called for an ambulance. When it came the Jacobsons went out to see what was going on. Dave's mother died before the ambulance arrived. Dave had gone to Eastland and identified the body. It was awful. She had been broken and battered. The doctor said she had been struck by a large vehicle which had crushed her skull on the pavement.

Dave had come home to his mother's house after trying first to go home. After the policeman had killed himself, Dave had left Colleen's house quietly and carefully. He had gotten into his car which was parked behind her house and driven with the headlights off for about a mile. Then he had turned them on and driven home. When he arrived he found that his house was gone. In its place was a smoldering heap of burnt wood and broken glass. The fire department had come and gone. The house had burned down quickly, as if it had been made of straw. Dave supposed he knew when the fire had started, a little after the faces had come through the western wall of Colleen's power room. He was right.

Now he sat in his mother's house trying to figure out what to do. He had not yet heard about the odd things which had begun to happen in Cisco. He knew that the souls he had been trying to thwart had come through with his help last night. If only Colleen had been able to finish her chants it would all be okay. If Crazy Joe hadn't come in when he did everything would have worked perfectly. Why did Crazy Joe do it?

Then he knew. Crazy Joe had also been instructed by the otherworld. It's the only answer which made sense. Crazy Joe had been instructed when to come through and offer Colleen as a sacrifice. Crazy Joe had piggybacked on the ceremonies which Dave and Colleen had performed and had used them to set the souls free.

Perhaps Crazy Joe had also killed his mother and burnt down his house. Either way, Crazy Joe had to pay. He had certainly killed Colleen, and there was no telling what other damage had been done since the freeing of the souls. Colleen had said that the souls were waiting to cross over and wreak their revenge. What did that mean? Were they going to destroy Cisco? Was it bigger than that? Perhaps it was smaller. What was going on in Cisco now?

Dave longed to know the answer to these questions. He wondered what impact his actions had produced in the past twelve hours, and what was to come. He wanted to go back to Cisco and take a look at what had become of that town, but he was tired and scared.

He laid down on the couch again and looked around the room. It would never be the same here. Life in general would never be the same. He remembered these feelings from when he lost his father, and from when Tommy had died. It was like something which was supposed to be permanent had changed, and life would forever have this dark spot which could not be filled or removed.

And where was Tommy now? He had tried to help, but his instructions had worked against him. Perhaps little Tommy had also been used. Perhaps he had been allowed to give the instructions to the ceremonies with the intent that Crazy Joe would be involved and the ceremonies would be modified to meet the needs of those wishing to cross over. But where was Tommy now? Could he come over too? Had he already? Tommy didn't have any revenge, not unless he too blamed Dave for his death. Surely he did not, considering Tommy's attempts to help him stop the spirits from coming over.

Or were they attempts to help?

Dave began to wonder if he hadn't walked into some kind of trap which his brother was a part of. He wondered if maybe the ceremonies had never been intended to shut the door.

But if Tommy's soul was anything like it had been when he had been living, then this was not possible. Tommy was a loving and carefree child, not one to hold grudges or be hateful for very long. He was spiteful. He liked to defy his older brother; that's part of what had gotten him killed. But he was not a vengeful boy. At least not twenty years ago.

Dave lay still and listened. There were no sounds. The house was empty and silent. It reminded him of the times in his childhood when he had been left home alone. Only now nobody was going to come home. He closed his eyes and remembered those earlier days. He pretended that he was just a boy, and that in a few minutes mom or dad was going to come through the door with a surprise they had gotten for him while shopping.

But they never did come home.

Dave stayed on the couch and rested. It had been an exhausting night and he had gotten no sleep. Now sleep pulled him away from his thoughts and wishes and into its world of regeneration and dreams.

4

Sandra drove down the interstate back toward Cisco. The doctor had looked her over and told her he would like her to stay around through the night for observation, but she was not required to do so. Sandra had explained that she wanted to go. Not long after that she was standing in front of the hospital waiting for delivery of her new rental car. Apparently there was a shortage of beds and rooms. Sandra figured that's why they had gotten her out so fast. At any other time she might have stayed. Her neck and back were not in the best shape, though her arm didn't feel any worse. She turned the arm within the sling and did not notice the sharp pain which had been there the previous day. There was some new bruising, but nothing had been seriously damaged. Perhaps there were forces looking out for her, as well as those which seemed to be trying to kill her.

Only now she didn't feel as threatened as before. Those forces which had been after her had accomplished their goal. She could no longer give the warning which would keep them behind the door. But she could try to find out what had happened, and maybe she could do something to hinder them or send them back. But first she had to find Dave Chatburn.

It was only ten-minutes to exit 330 and then the city limits of Cisco. As she approached the town she could tell that something was very wrong. The town didn't look right. Many of the streets and buildings seemed to be overlain with shadows of their former selves. The town was crowded with images from the past. This was something she was used to seeing on a smaller scale. There were always images of the past which came and went with various places. But in Cisco everything was overlain with these images. She did not see any spirits, but she knew that they were here. As she drove through the town she saw the cars and the people from the present. Occasionally she would catch a glimpse of an object which did not belong in the present, but usually it would disappear when she tried to look directly at it. The images were everywhere, but they were fairly weak. She had the awful feeling they were only going to get stronger. Normally this would not be a matter of concern, but she knew there was evil and malice in the images and that the town was in great danger.

She drove to the west end of town where she knew she would find Dave's house. When she turned the corner onto 14th Street she knew something was wrong. As she drove down the road she saw a house which had recently burned down. She drove to the mound of rubble and stopped. The next house was two blocks down. She looked at the mess that used to be a house and though she hoped otherwise she had a feeling that this pile of rubble was the house she was looking for. She got out of her car and walked to the driveway where the mailbox stood. 'Chatburn' was spelled out in adhesive black-on-gold letters. Sandra walked up the driveway to what used to be the garage. She kicked aside some of the scorched roof tiles as she looked into the heap of burnt wood, scarred metal and ashes. It was a warm day, but already she could feel the coolness of what was happening to Cisco. She had to get in touch with Dave and find out what he knew. He was the key. If the terrors which were here and growing were to be stopped then she had to find him.

She thought about where he might have gone. Perhaps he had a friend in town who he might stay with. But how could she find out? She figured that Dave would probably have gotten in contact with his mother about the situation. Perhaps she could be of some help.

Sandra got back into the car and drove to the gas station on the corner of 14th and Main. There she called directory assistance to get the phone number for the only Chatburn in Breckenridge. Then she used her calling card to make the call to that number.

It rang several times. She held on and waited. Perhaps the woman was outside working in her flower bed, or maybe she was in the bathroom. Sandra let it ring and she waited. After about ten rings the phone was lifted from the receiver and apparently dropped. She listened as the phone was fumbled around. After a few moments there was a man's groggy voice on the line.

"Hello?" it said.

"Is this the Chatburn residence?" Sandra asked.

"Yes," Dave replied.

Sandra had assumed that Mrs. Chatburn lived alone. Perhaps her number was unlisted and this was the wrong number. She realized then that she did not know Mrs. Chatburn's first name. "May I speak with Mrs. Chatburn?" she asked.

"She's not here," Dave replied. "Who's calling?"

"This is Sandra MacElroy. I spoke with Mrs. Chatburn yesterday about getting a hold of her son Dave. Apparently there's been a fire at his house, so obviously he's not there. I was hoping she could help me find him."

"This is Dave," he replied. "What are you trying to get a hold of me for?" Dave racked his groggy mind but could not recall a Sandra MacElroy.

"Dave Chatburn?" she asked.

"Yes."

"Dave, I've come down here from Saint Louis. I've been seeing your little brother in my dreams and I know something terrible happened here last night, but I'm not sure what and I need your help."

Dave sat in silence for a moment. How could this woman know about Tommy? Had she really been dreaming about him, or was this a trick of some kind? "What do you want from me?" he asked.

"I want to find out just what happened last night. I need to know how you are involved and what can be done. I tried to get to you before all of this happened, but something's been trying to stop me. Yesterday just before I got to Cisco I hit that white delivery truck from the dream, only it was real. There was an old bum that tried to kill me, but he ran off when someone passing by saw the wreck. I just got here from Eastland, from the hospital. Could you meet me somewhere so we could talk?"

She was saying a lot of things and she was saying them too fast. His mind raced with her words. "Crazy Joe," he mumbled.

"What?" Sandra asked.

"It was Crazy Joe that tried to kill you." Dave thought for a moment. The white delivery truck? Had Joe gotten hold of an old white delivery truck? If so, what was he using it for? Had this been the vehicle which had struck his mother? Dave began to suspect that this was so. "Why don't you come back to Breckenridge, to my mother's house? That's where I am, and I plan to stay here for a while."

"But the problem is here, in Cisco."

"I want to talk about it here, you'll understand better when we've had a chance to talk. Come on over. I'll wait here for you. If we need to go back to Cisco we'll do that later."

"Okay," Sandra agreed. "See you in about an hour."

"Okay."

Sandra heard the phone click then she hung up the pay phone. She looked up at the odd-looking gas station which appeared to have a shadowy image of a newer station from the past laid over it. She knew that she was the only one who could see this, at least for now.

Then she heard a scream.

She turned to look and she saw a woman standing in the middle of the road. The woman was pointing at the side of the road opposite Sandra and she was screaming. A man came running out of the gas station to see what was wrong. He looked at the woman, then across the street. There was a puzzled look on his face. Obviously he did not see the mangled man who stood on the other side of the street, beckoning the woman to come closer. The man looked terrible. The lower half of his body was exposed, the pants had been torn off of him. His legs were covered with blood and hanging tendons. His thighs were burned and his penis was missing. His shirt was covered with blood, and his head was cocked at an odd angle. It looked as if he had been in a burning wreck, which was exactly how he had died four years earlier. The man stood, calling to his wife. She simply stood in the center of the road, holding her head and screaming. Her groceries lay on the pavement in front of her.

Then a car came around the corner. It swerved to avoid hitting the woman but clipped her right leg and set her to the ground. The woman continued to scream as her eyes returned to the gruesome image which now began to walk toward her.

Sandra watched as the people rushed to the woman's aid. Her leg was oddly bent and obviously broken. They tried to comfort her and get her to hold still, but she kept trying to get to her feet as the horrible man approached. When he reached the woman he simply stood before her and watched the terror as it took control. The man who had come from the gas station went back inside to call the ambulance. When he came back out Sandra heard him explaining that there were no ambulances available and someone would have to drive her to the hospital.

Sandra turned from the scene and returned to her car. She got inside and drove around the mess. She looked in her rearview mirror at the hysterical woman and the malevolent spirit. She knew that this was the kind of thing going on all over town, and that this was nothing compared with what was to come.

XIV
1

Sheriff Pritchard sat in his car in front of the VanZandt house. He had looked at it early that morning only briefly. The city cops had done most of the work and seemed at that time to have everything under control. Now he wondered if this was so. In the early morning sun, he hadn't seen the severity of the destruction which had taken place. Sunlight now reflected off the shards of broken glass which lay strewn about the house. The house was surrounded by the yellow 'police line' tape which was intended to keep out the curiosity seekers. Often it served as an invitation to the young kids who were both curious and daring. He had been like that once. Now he was a lot less curious and a lot more careful.

Since the drowning incident at the lake he had been to four other accident scenes. Only the drowning had been fatal. At one of the remaining three incidents the victim had been badly injured and rendered unconscious. At each of the other two incidents the victims had claimed they had seen someone from their past, someone who was supposed to be dead. The sheriff's mind had returned to the incident with the young girl earlier in the day. Something odd was going on, and he was beginning to believe that it might have something to do with the cult slayings from the previous night.

He had called back to the office and spoken with some of the officers who'd been out. There were questions which were best not asked over the radio, too many citizens with police band radios would be listening and the questions he had were not those the police force should be heard asking. He found out from the two men he spoke with that they too had run into a few cases where people claimed having seen people from the past. In each case nobody used the word ghost. Apparently all of the victims believed they had seen a real person, though sometimes the person they had seen had been in a state of decomposition which suggested they were not truly living. After these discussions his thoughts had returned to the VanZandt house. He had left Deputy Sharp at the last scene to be taken back to the station by another officer. Deputy Sharp would then return to Cisco with a car and run his own patrol. All but one car was now being used, and the sheriff had been forced to place only one man in each car. Then Sheriff Pritchard had taken his own car and driven here, to the VanZandt house.

The sheriff walked up to the concrete path to the front door of the house. He lifted up the yellow tape and passed under it, crushing broken glass under his boots as he walked. He approached the front door which was not locked. It would have been meaningless to lock it with all of the windows blown out. He saw that a large crack ran from the top of the door to its bottom, as if someone had hit it on the inside with a sledgehammer. He pushed the door inward and walked inside. Sheriff Pritchard had not been inside the house until now. When he stepped in he noticed immediately that it was cool. If the windows had not been broken and the air conditioning had been running it would have made sense. But the windows were opened, and there was no electricity running to the house. It seemed darker in the house than it should have been, but he was still able to see enough that he did not need his flashlight.

He looked briefly around the house. It was a mess, just like he had heard. Everything made of glass had been broken. He walked to the room where the murders had taken place. There was more tape across the doorway, and the door was closed. He reached out and opened the door. A cool breeze came from the room, despite the fact the room had no windows. Sheriff Pritchard ducked under the tape and walked in. It was somewhat dark, but he could still see into all but the farthest corners of the room. There were lots of bloodstains. Most of them were in the center of the room, in the middle of the triangle outlined by the brass candle holders. He had heard about the condition of this room but had not pictured it right. His mind had left out most of the blood. He saw something on the floor near his feet. It was metal and rectangular. He bent over and picked it up. It was the name plate of the officer who had strangled himself in this room that morning. Then he heard a creaking sound and he looked up quickly.

There was a man standing before him. How had he gotten there? The sheriff grabbed onto his gun but did not withdraw it from its holster. The man was wearing a police uniform. On his breast was a city badge with the name plate missing. The man looked pale, and there were bruises around his neck.

"You found my name plate," the officer said to him.

It took the sheriff a second to understand what was being said. This was the officer that had been found here this morning. "You're dead," Pritchard observed.

"Yes, of course," the man replied. "I died in here this morning."

Pritchard was frozen with fear. His heart began to race. Now he knew why the people he had talked to had not spoken of ghosts. He could see this man. He was not a shadowy image, he was a man, and he smelled like a dead animal.

"What do you want?" Pritchard asked.

"I want my name tag. And I would like out of here."

The sheriff looked down at the name tag. It said Walker. "You're Officer Walker," he stated. Then he looked back at the man before him. "How did you die?" he asked.

"I strangled myself. I heard the people who were here earlier say so."

"Why?" Pritchard asked.

"Because I saw terrible things which I couldn't bear. Things which made it better to be dead."

The man took slow but deliberate steps toward the sheriff. When he came to the edge of the triangle his foot struck a candle holder. It fell over and clinked to the floor. Pritchard looked down at it and realized that the thing he saw did have substance. He also realized that he didn't wish for it to come any closer. He drew his gun.

The dead officer stopped approaching the sheriff and laughed. "What are you going to do?" he asked, "Kill me?" He laughs again. "You can't kill me. I'm already dead."

"Then I'll kill you again. Just stay where you are."

The man stood where he was with a grin on his face. "I want my name tag."

The sheriff threw the tag at the man. The ghostly image grabbed it as it sailed through the air. Then the dead man put the pin back on his shirt and patted it. "That's better," he said.

"What's going on?" Sheriff Pritchard asked.

The dead man looked up from his name tag. His eyes were cold and hard. The room grew colder.

"Now I want out of here," the officer said.

Pritchard pulled the hammer back on his pistol. "I asked you what's going on."

"Well," the dead man began, "the door has been opened. The rift has been breached. This town is doomed."

"What do you mean?"

The dead officer resumed his walk toward the sheriff.

"Just stay there," the sheriff warned.

The man ignored him and continued to approach. He continued to display a wicked and purposeful grin. The bad smell grew stronger.

"Stay there, damn it!"

But the dead man wouldn't stop.

Pritchard was scared. He pulled the trigger.

He saw where the bullet went into the flesh, just below where the dead man's heart was. The man let out an 'ugh' and took a step back. Then he resumed his approach. The sheriff saw malice in those cold eyes so he raised his pistol and aimed between them. He fired again and the dead man's head jerked back. Grey matter flew from the back of his head and a large part of his skull disintegrated into bone fragments. Then he stood straight again and faced Sheriff Pritchard. The sheriff could see the man's brain which lay exposed and mashed. There was no blood, but there was bone and puss. The sight and the smell were sickening.

"I want out of here," the dead officer repeated.

Then there was an icy cold breeze and the door shut behind the sheriff.

There was a sound of a scuffle in the darkness, then Sheriff Pritchard cried out. "No!"

There was a loud report as the sheriff's gun went off, then another. Then came the sound of a body falling to the floor.

Then there was silence.

2

Dave had expected someone older, and not as pretty as the woman who now stood on the porch just outside the door.

"Come on it," he said.

The pretty woman with fiery red hair and a slim but well-rounded figure walked through the doorway into his mother's home. She walked with grace despite the sling around her shoulder and her eyes glanced once around the room. He could tell that in that one glance she had taken in more than most people would notice after an hour of observation.

"I'm Sandra MacElroy," the woman explained.

"Nice to meet you," Dave said, not sounding particularly convincing. "I'm Dave Chatburn. Please come in and have a seat."

She walked to the couch where Dave had been sleeping when she had called. Dave walked to the chair his mother always sat in when he was talking with her. Only that would never be so again. He suddenly was embarrassed about his appearance. He was unshaven and wearing the same clothes he had been wearing for the past day and a half. They were well wrinkled from his nap.

"You'll have to forgive my appearance," he exclaimed, "I've been through a lot in the past day or two."

"I'm sure you have." She smiled and held the sling out in front of her. "I have too."

The room fell silent and tense for a moment. Sandra did not know where to begin. Dave did not know what to expect.

"So," Sandra began, "has your mother gone out?"

"No," Dave explained. His eyes wandered for a moment. "She was run over last night. She died."

The news surprised Sandra. "I'm sorry," she said.

"Yeah." Dave looked around the room, trying not to tear up. "I think it must have been a large white delivery truck."

"That's what did this," Sandra explained, holding the sling out once again. "I saw it a couple of times as a ghostlike image." She made a motion with her hand. "Passed right through it. The first time I encountered it my car was hit be a semi and I ended up in the hospital. Yesterday when I saw it on the road I thought it was another false image, but it wasn't. I hit it and ended up in another hospital." She shifted to get more comfortable. "Luckily both times I didn't do any serious damage, though my back feels like it's been twisted a thousand different ways." She looked at Dave. He seemed very distant. He was still thinking about his mother. "As I mentioned on the phone," Sandra continued, "I went to your house in Cisco from the hospital." Dave's eyes finally returned to hers. "So, you said something about a guy named Joe?"

"Yea," Dave answered, "Crazy Joe. He's a bum. He's been in Cisco for as long as I can remember. He lives in an old store past the junk yard at the end of town. He's probably the one after you."

"What makes you think that?"

"Well," Dave explained, "you said that a bum was trying to kill you, and he's the only bum in Cisco. The cops run the rest of them out of town. Also because he's somehow become involved in this thing. It had to be him. He probably killed my mother too." Dave's eyes wandered again, and this time they glazed over with moisture.

"So what do you think this thing is?" Sandra asked Dave.

Dave looked back to Sandra. "I was hoping you could tell me."

"Well," Sandra said, "I'll tell you what I know."

Sandra explained in detail everything she could remember from the past week that involved Dave's brother and the malicious spirits. At times she could see Dave's eyes widen with recognition, especially at her descriptions of some of the dreams. As she spoke Dave began to better understand exactly what had happened, and he was beginning to understand that he was responsible for much more than he had suspected.

"So that's why I'm here," Sandra concluded. "I've been drawn by this thing. And now it's happened and I'm hoping you can tell me how to sop it or reverse it. I feel a little responsible for not getting to you in time. Now I want to help."

Dave looked to Sandra. A tear slipped from his eye. This tear was for his brother.

"I've been having dreams about my brother too," he explained. "At first it was the same dream I had when I was younger, just the terrible scene as it happened twenty years ago. But then it started to change. There were things which were different about the dream. Then I started hearing voices on the phone, voices from my past. From there it just got stranger."

Dave explained how he met Colleen in the library, and how she had helped him to work with the messages he was receiving from the other side. He explained how she too was having the dreams and visions, and how she became more and more involved. He explained their first seance and what become of it, and then he explained the dream which had revealed the ceremony to him.

"This was revealed to you in a dream?" Sandra asked.

"The whole thing."

"Incredible," she replied. The ceremonies were not familiar and ancient. There were elements which she understood, and those which she did not. The one thing that was most clear to her was that the ceremonies had never been intended to close the door. They had been intended to throw it wide open. She let Dave speak, however, anxious to hear what had happened.

Dave told her about the ceremonies. He explained the details as best he could remember them. Last night they had been etched on his mind. Now they were distant images, difficult to remember or comprehend. He left out some of the actions and some of the words, but he remembered all of the climatic events.

Then he told her how Crazy Joe had come in and killed Colleen. He watched as this time her eyes widened. Dave told about the faces coming through the western wall, and the cold air that had rushed though the room.

"There where brilliant flashes of light," Dave explained, "and these things were rushing past me." Sandra could see remnants of the terror as it returned to his eyes. "They were icy cold. I tried to get up, but I couldn't. I saw all kinds of terrible things in those faces. Mostly there was evil, lots of it. I saw Colleen's body lying in the center of the triangle, bloodied and mangled. I watched all this." He stopped talking for a moment and she could see him trying to get control of himself. "Then it got dark. I must have gone unconscious because the next thing I remember was a police officer coming into the room. I was very cold, my face and hands felt frozen. I watched as the policeman had some kind of hallucination, then proceeded to strangle himself. When he fell to the floor I got up and left the room. I got into my car and drove home. When I got there I found out it had burned down, so I came here. When I got here I found out my mother had been killed." He paused again. Then he returned his eyes to hers. "Then I slept until you called."

Dave stopped talking. Sandra just looked at him. By the time he had gone halfway through the story she knew what had happened. Should she tell him he was responsible for what was going on in Cisco? She'd needed to make him feel somewhat responsible so that he would help to find a solution. But she wanted to be sure he did not feel responsible for the deaths which had resulted from it. That guilt could get in the way.

"So," Dave asked, "What do you think? Am I crazy?"

"No," She replied, "of course not. I work with this kind of thing all of the time. I think I understand fairly well."

"So did Colleen, and it just got her killed."

"I have been in touch with the world of the dead all of my life. It's something I have always lived with, I'm afraid that it's most likely Colleen was just a palm reader with a lot of ambition."

"But she had these dreams and the voices that came out in the seance weren't hers."

"You had those dreams. You had some pretty astounding vision. Does this make you a medium?" She asked him.

"Well, no. But I really don't think she was lying."

"I didn't say she was lying. She may really have believed that she was able to contact the world of the dead. She may even have had some very distant contact, but I'm willing to bet that the dreams came for the same place your dreams came from. The spirits used her as they used you. They knew she was more likely than anyone else in the town to be open to the idea of real communication. And they chose you for another reason. They probably felt they could influence you through the guilt you felt over your brother's death. Between the two of you there was enough belief and action to get the job done."

"So you think we were just used by the spirits to open the door?"

"Definitely."

"Do you think that the ceremonies could have been used to close the door at all?"

"I think the one and only purpose of the ceremonies was to open the door."

"So my brother's spirit was in on this?" Dave asked.

"Not necessarily."

"You mean they tricked him too?"

"I meant it probably wasn't your brother."

Dave had never considered this possibility. He had been so caught up in the whole series of events that he never once considered that the spirit might not really be his brother's. Now that Sandra mentioned it he wondered if it might be true.

"Who was it?" Dave asked.

"It may have been one or more spirits presenting themselves to you as your brother. They knew that you would be persuaded to believe and act because of the guilt. They believed that you would not question what you were told."

"Apparently they were right," Dave said, looking down, a tone of guilt in his voice. "So you don't think my brother had anything to do with this?"

"I think I have seen your brother, your real brother."

"Why you?" Dave asked. "How do you know that it wasn't another trick?"

"Because I can see the true images, and because it was him that led me here."

"So the spirit that spoke to me was not my brother, and Colleen was not really a medium."

"That's just my guess," Sandra reminded him.

"Right." It was a good guess, and Dave believed that it was probably an accurate one. "So now what?"

"Well," Sandra said, "now we try to see if we can stop this thing."

"What's started?" Dave asked.

"You haven't been to Cisco since last night," Sandra commented. She had forgotten. Dave probably had no idea of the magnitude of what was going on. "Well, it's a bit of a mess right now."

"What do you mean?"

"I think that the malevolent spirits which have come through are causing the people in town a little trouble."

"Like what?"

"I heard at the hospital that there was an abnormally high number of accidents taking place, and when I passed through Cisco on my way here I saw signs that the spiritual world was infringing pretty heavily on the material one."

"What does that mean?" Dave asked.

"What that means is that people are seeing things, mostly they're seeing people who have passed on. The spirits are working the peoples' minds against them. The spirits are appearing to people as things they are not. Most people cannot distinguish between the two worlds since they are used to seeing just one. Their concepts of reality are being altered."

"So what's going to happen?" Dave asked.

"More people will be hurt."

"Is that all?"

Sandra paused. "No. I think there's been a couple of deaths so far. If it continues to grow I think there will be more and more. There's no telling how far it can go. I've never been involved in anything this complex before, but I've seen enough to know what the potential is."

"And what's that?"

"The whole town could go crazy."

A look of disbelief came to Dave's face. "The whole town?"

"Just about everybody."

"What does that mean?"

"That means more injuries, and more deaths."

"When will it stop?"

Sandra looked at the floor. She had thought about this question all day. The truth was she didn't know the answer.

"It might never stop."

"What do you mean by never?"

She looked back up to Dave. "I mean Cisco might just melt away. Then there will be no town, and no one will want to settle there again. It will be written off as a dead town."

"What about the people?"

"The ones that survive will probably move away," Sandra answered,

"How many could die?"

"I don't know Maybe a couple. Maybe most of them."

"Most of them? How?"

"If the delusions grow strong enough they can drive people to kill themselves and kill each other."

"By just making them crazy?"

"No, by making them see things which aren't there."

"Like the police officer that strangled himself," Dave observed.

"He probably thought he was strangling a criminal, or even a monster."

"And this could happen to everybody."

"Yes."

Dave pursed his lips. "Do you know how to put a stop to it?"

"No. But I can try."

"How?" Dave asked.

"Take me to Colleen's house."

"I can't do that," Dave explained. "The cops will wonder why I'm there. I'll tell you where it is."

"I can't do this by myself," Sandra explained. "I'll need help, and you're the only one who can help me."

"What can I do?" Dave asked.

"You can point out things you've seen before, you can point me to things you know about. Besides, what am I going to do if that crazy guy shows up again?"

"Crazy Joe," Dave muttered to himself. "If I see that damn bum again I swear I'll kill him." He looked back up at Sandra. There was fire in his eyes.

"He may be after you now too," Sandra explained, "especially if you and I are the only ones who have any chance of stopping this."

Why him?"

What?" Sandra asked.

"Why Crazy Joe? Why did they pick him to help?"

"If he's really crazy then he's more likely to accept the reality as it's presented by the spirits who have chosen him. A sane person would probably have headed for a shrink. Joe just accepted the voices as reality."

"Sure," Dave agreed. It sounded good to him.

"When do you think we can go over there?" Sandra asked.

"I'd like to at least wait until it's dark. That way we're less likely to be spotted by the police, and more likely to get away if they do come around."

Sandra looked at her watch. "How much longer till dark?"

Dave looked at the clock on the wall. "It should be dark enough by nine."

"Okay. That gives us five hours. Let's spend the time wisely. Why don't you tell me again everything you did last night?"

Dave took a deep breath and let it out. Then he began his story again, trying his best to remember everything.

3

The old white delivery truck wobbled to its spot behind Joe's home. It idled for a minute before dying. Joe had been working hard today. He hadn't realized that a rough description of his truck had been given to the police by the man who had taken Sandra to the hospital. But the police had been busy today, too busy to notice the truck.

Joe stepped out of the vehicle and walked around to the back of it. There were two doors in back. He turned the silver-colored handle on the left door and they both opened. The junk inside shifted around and an old typewriter fell out. He looked down at the typewriter, then into the back of the truck. There was the best and biggest haul he had ever made. The stuff inside was perfect, most of it almost new. He had been told where to look while he rested that morning. It had been sitting in obvious places, but places he had never bothered to look. Some it was still on its owner's property, but no one ever questioned him. It was like walking into a store and having your pick of whatever you needed. And there were things here he had been trying to get hold of for some time. He picked up the electric can opener and smiled, it was going to make lifer easier. So would the toaster and the stereo. He would just have to run the generator a little longer. He had even found an antenna for the stereo.

Pushed way back, near the back of the seat, was an old cardboard box he had found by a garbage can in town. The box was full of old 'Club' and 'Fox' magazines. There must have been thirty or forty of them, each with different women in different poses. There was even a video tape which was labelled with a 'XXX' and the title 'Climatic Scenes.' The big cardboard box had been placed by the garbage cans earlier in the day by a disgruntled wife who had stumbled upon it while cleaning out the garage. It was great. Joe didn't own a VCR, but he was sure if he asked he would be told where one was.

He lugged the stuff one shopping cart load at a time to his loft. It took four trips to get it all. He positioned the best stuff immediately. The rest he left in the corner for later. He pulled the box over next to his bed and pulled out the first magazine. He flipped quickly through the pages, looking for the full-page spreads. When he found the first one he just smiled and pawed his crotch. The box was full of women like this, women who posed for him, women who wanted him.

He spent almost an hour with his women before the television came on again. He put the magazine he was looking through down and watched the static on the screen as it came together again into a familiar face.

"Hello Joe," the White Man said. That familiar evil smile was glued to his face. Joe had gotten somewhat used to the man, but the sight of him still sent chills down his spine. "A good haul?" he asked.

"Damn good," Joe replied. He was puzzled. The man had said that he probably wouldn't be needing Joe after last night. So why was he back?

"I'm back because I need just one more favor."

"Sure," Joe replied, knowing he really had no choice. "What?"

"I need you to go back to the witch's house tonight, after dark."

Joe didn't like this. He knew he had gotten away last night. He knew the police had no idea he had been involved. Now why should he return?

The police would be watching the place.

"It's okay, Joe," the man said. "I'll take care of the police. You go and take care of my problem."

"Okay," Joe said. "So what do I do?"

4

As night fell, the man who worked at the convenience store near the junior college grew nervous. There was a lot of crazy stuff going on in Cisco, he had seen some of it himself. Bill was edgy, and it showed. The store was air conditioned, still, sweat beaded up and rolled down his forehead from time to time. He watched his customers carefully, watched them for signs of the mania that had gripped the town. He even watched nervously as the police car cruised by the store at eight. Now it was getting dark. He had to work for four more hours. It had been tough enough in the daylight. Now night falling and the tension was rising.

The bell on the door rang and he looked quickly to it. It was Willy Pitman. Willy was only seven, but his parents let him run five blocks to the store for milk and bread. He did it all the time. Bill didn't think that this was such a good thing tonight.

"Hey Bill," Willy said.

"Hey, Willy."

Bill watched the door close and looked outside as the darkness fell. He listened as the kid walked back to the refrigerated foods. The sunset was producing some strange colors outside tonight, and they added to the eerie air about the town.

Then he noticed the old Monte Carlo. The paint on it was faded and the windshield was cracked. It was parked at the very end of the parking lot, near the railroad tracks. It made him nervous. He had seen a car like that once before and had been looking down the barrel of a sawed-off shotgun moments later. He had heard a few months back that the Mexicans who had done this to him had been killed by some other Mexicans who didn't like the quality of drugs they had been sold. The guy who had robbed him had been found in the lake. It had been good news.

He watched the car carefully, but nobody got out.

Then there was a rotten smell and sloshing sounds. Bill turned back to face the store and saw the impossible. There, a few feet in front of him, was the partially decomposed body of the dead Mexican. His clothes were soaked with lake water, it dripped steadily to the floor. He sported a hideous grin which was made more gruesome by the fact that his lips had rotted away and most of his teeth had fallen out.

"I'm back, Billy boy, and this time I want more than your money!"

The Mexican's voice was thick and groggy, his breath smelled like dead frogs. Bill looked at the terror and wet his pants. The Mexican pulled back both hammers on the double-barreled gun.

Then Bill remembered what he had done the day after he had been robbed by this man. He remembered thinking over and over what he would have done if he kept a gun under the counter, then he had placed one there. It rested there now, loaded and ready to go.

"Give me your fuckin' money, white boy." His voice changed. "Then come around here and I'll give you a special surprise."

Bill flinched. He had heard those last three words before, but not from the Mexican. These words had come from a man he had known in his childhood, a molester he later wished he could find and kill. Now before him stood the embodiment of both of these men. Then the Mexican held out his left hand. Bill looked at it. There were two dollars and some change. Bill didn't understand. He looked back to the Mexican who just grinned his gruesome grin and waited.

Bill dropped quickly to the floor and grabbed the gun from under the counter. He rolled behind the hot dog machine and stood up; all of his body protected by the stainless steel of the machine. He squeezed the trigger twice and watched as the Mexican took the shots to the stomach and fell back out of sight to the floor. He waited and listened, but there was no sound of any movement.

Bill walked carefully around the hot dog machine, keeping his gun in front of him. When he rounded the corner of the machine he dropped his gun and muttered, "Oh, shit."

Lying on the floor in a puddle of blood was little Willy Pittman. The bread and milk lay beside him on the floor. By his left hand lay two dollars and some change.

XV
1

Deputy Frank Sharp drove cautiously thought the night. He had been on patrol all day, and things had been getting progressively worse. There was talk, and lots of it. It seemed as if most of the accident victims who were still cognizant were babbling about dead people. The accidents were getting worse, more of them had proven fatal. The deputy had answered a call which had taken him to the convenience store by the junior college. There he had found a little boy who had been shot dead by the man behind the counter. The man had confessed and been taken into custody, but he too had babbled endlessly about someone from the dead making him do it.

Worst of all, the sheriff was missing. He had been missing for almost five hours now. His car had been found smashed into a telephone pole near the interstate. There had been some blood on the dash and the windshield had been broken, but there was no sign of the sheriff. There had been a witness to the accident, but he had only said that a young kid in street clothes had wandered out of the car and headed toward the freeway. Sharp wondered if this had been the kid they had found dead beside that very freeway a few hours earlier.

All day the mystery of the VanZandt house gnawed at him. He was sure that it was at the center of what was going on. The investigation on the house had come to a standstill mainly because the city force had been stretched so thin by the day's events. Now the day's events were turning into the night's events. With the night had come more lethal and more frequent occurrences. The deputy did not know what the body count was now, but he knew it was reaching proportions too high even for a large city, much less a small town. Already he had seen two members of the Dallas press wandering around town. By morning there would probably be more, if the town hadn't self-destructed by then.

And that's what Deputy Sharp began to believe was happening. Somehow and for some strange reason the town was beginning to self-destruct. It came back to the cult slayings at the VanZandt house, he was sure of this. All day he had wanted to return to the house and take another, more careful look. But the duties which had come with the day's events had not allowed him the time. Those duties had stretched him to the limit. All of the men on the force were being stretched to the limit. The state troopers had even sent over three cars, and there had been plenty for them to do. Ambulance services were being borrowed from three nearby small towns. But despite the emergency the men were still human and the needed their rest. Deputy Sharp had been working since seven that morning. In one more hour he would be turning in his patrol car.

But after he had turned it in he was going to get into his personal car and come back to Cisco. He was going to take a look at the VanZandt place on his own time. Then maybe he would find some answers that satisfied him.

2

Dave parked a hundred yards from the VanZandt house. He and Sandra would have to walk through an open field to get to the back door. Dave felt safest going this way, and Sandra had agreed.

They got out of the car and began walking toward the house. Dave had a small flashlight but did not plan to use it until after they had gotten inside. Sandra followed Dave across the field. They crossed a dry creek bed before coming to the back fence of Colleen's yard. It was a low chain link fence with a gate near one side of the old house. They walked to the gate and into the back yard. The yard had a couple of old oak trees, and the ground was covered with various weeds which had staged their invasion from the adjacent field. Colleen had never cared much about her yard.

Dave walked to the back door. A piece of yellow tape covered with warnings from the Cisco police department crossed it. The door was wood with a small rectangular opening where once had been a glass window. Dave tried the door, but it was locked. He reached through the opening where the glass had once been and fumbled around until he found the deadbolt which he turned. Then he pulled his arm out and opened the door. He pulled the yellow tape from the doorway and threw it on the ground.

Dave looked into the dark house. Sandra stood behind him. He could see familiar shapes in the living room and down the hall, but now they were eerie shapes. From where he stood he could see the couch where once he made love to Colleen. Now she was dead. His fear was returning, and he could not enter.

"What's wrong?" Sandra asked.

"Nothing much," Dave replied. "I'm just a little nervous after what happened here last night."

"That's understandable," Sandra replied. "Look, I'd be able to sense any trouble, at least if it were coming from the spiritual realm. Why don't you let me go first? If I see anything I'll tell you."

Dave was proud, but he was also scared. "Okay," he agreed.

Sandra walked around Dave and he handed her his flashlight which she took in her good hand. She walked into the house and looked around at the living room. It was a mess. She did see things, but nothing real, nothing solid. She saw echoes of what had been here, and there were many traces of the otherworld, but nothing was there now. Still she could feel the danger.

Dave followed Sandra as she walked slowly through the house. He watched her as she observed their surroundings. But her face remained fairly calm. She seemed to be studying the house carefully. She was.

"Which way to the room where the ceremonies took place?" She asked.

"Down the hallway. It's the last door."

Sandra walked to the hallway. The air was cool. She knew what this meant and wanted to know how strong it was.

"Does it feel cool in here to you?" She asked Dave.

"Yeah. It feels like a meat locker in here," he answered.

Was it residual from the previous night, or a warning for now? She didn't know. She watched her surroundings carefully, but there were no signs of activity. Still, that was no guarantee that there wasn't about to be some.

She walked down the hall to the door which led to the room where everything had happened. There was tape hanging to the sides of the doorway, as if it had been pulled aside by someone who had been here before them. Who would it be? Would the police have done it, then not re-sealed it?

"Dave," she called back, "the seal has been broken."

"It doesn't surprise me," he answered.

"Who do you think did it?"

"Maybe the police," he answered. "Maybe a spirit, maybe a kid. No telling. Would you like me to open the door?" He asked.

"If you could. Normally I wouldn't hesitate, but if there is an immediate problem I'm afraid I'd be less than agile with this thing." She again held out her arm which was in a sling.

Dave took the light from her and put his hand on the doorknob. The knob was icy cold. He decided he should tell Sandra.

"This knob is cold."

"Okay," she answered.

"Okay, what?" He said, hoping she could tell him more.

"Okay, it's cold."

"What does that mean?" He asked her.

"It probably means that there has recently been some kind of supernatural activity on the other side of the door."

"Could it still be going on?" Dave asked.

"Sure." Sandra was worried that this might in fact be the case, especially if this was the location where the spirits were crossing between worlds.

"Should I open it?" He asked.

"Yes," she answered. "We're not going to get any closer to figuring this out otherwise."

"I was afraid you'd say something like that," Dave lamented. "Stand over there." He pointed back down the hall.

Sandra took a few steps back. Dave stood to the side of the door and turned the know all the way. He stood holding it that way for a minute, then he threw the door inward.

The door sailed open three fourths of the way before it struck something soft and came to a stop. Dave shined the flashlight into the room and looked quickly around it. Sandra could not see into the room from where she stood, but she knew she would see something spectacular. Already she could see shades of dark color seeping from the room. They made it out a few feet before dissipating in the air. Dave could not see the purples and the blues. But he could see that the room was in an even worse mess than he had left it. Most of the candle holders had been knocked over. The dried blood was still in the center of the room. Somehow he thought this would have been cleaned up by now. His flashlight was weak and did not illuminate the farthest corners. He could see no immediate dangers. Then he turned the flashlight to the floor near the door to see what had stopped it from opening all the way. Before he was the object he saw the blood which trailed from it toward the western wall. It was the body of another police officer. His uniform suggested he was a county cop. The one who had strangled himself had been a city cop.

"Oh, shit," Dave exclaimed.

"What is it?" Sandra asked.

"Another dead person."

Sandra walked to where Dave stood and looked to the ground where the body lay. She wanted to be sure it was not an illusion. It was not. It was a real body.

Then she looked up into the room. It was alive with activity. Though she could see no spirits now, she could tell that the room had been full of them, and that they were still passing through from time to time. The passage was a hole to her, a multicolored hole in the western wall, a hole that Dave could not see. It was large, big enough for a man to walk through if he ducked his head. She had never seen one so large and so defined. She wondered if a human could in fact walk through it. She wanted to know but was not about to try.

Dave saw awe on her face and shined the light on the wall. He could see a slight discoloration of black paint where the hole had been, but that was all. "What do you see?" He asked.

"I see a door," she explained. "And it's still wide open."

"Is it that discoloration there on the wall?" He asked.

"That's where it is," she explained, "but I can see it in more detail."

"What does it look like to you?"

"It has a lot of swirling and moving colors. It's like the steam from dry ice, but it doesn't really come out of the wall. It has two-dimensional features, but it is definitely four-dimensional."

"Four-dimensional?" Dave asked.

"Sure," she replied.

Dave looked at the wall but could see no more than the discolored spot. He wondered if Sandra was telling the truth or being dramatic. Then he saw something like a shadow flash across the wall. A moment later he heard a voice to his right.

"Don't you know this area is closed to civilians?" The man asked.

Dave turned his light to the man. It was the officer who lay at his feet. Then he shined the light down to where that body should have been, but it was not there. Somehow it had gotten up.

Sandra could see the spirit. She could also see the body that was still on the floor. From Dave's reaction she assumed he could not see the body on the floor.

"Dave," she said, "it's not real. The body's still at your feet, you just can't see it."

"Oh, I'm real," the officer said as he drew his gun, "and you're trespassing. I suggest you leave."

"It's not even really the same man," Sandra explained. She could see the image beyond the image.

It looked at her sharply, a distant look of confusion on its face. Why wasn't this human deceived?

"It looks pretty real to me," Dave said as he took a step back.

"It's not," she replied.

"I am," the sheriff-thing said. "And I suggest you leave now, before something very bad happens."

Sandra saw the fear on Dave's face and knew she had to do something. She walked past Dave, towards the officer.

"You better stay back, missy," the sheriff-thing said.

She continued to approach him.

"Stop it!" Dave called to her.

"It's not real," she repeated to Dave as she approached the spirit.

The officer held his pistol out and pulled back the hammer as she approached.

Dave felt helpless. He watched as Sandra approached the dead man.

"I'll shoot," the sheriff-thing said.

"Go ahead," Sandra dared as she closed the final few steps.

The sheriff-thing raised the gun to her head as she came up to him. She felt the icy coldness of the gun which was not there. Then the sheriff-thing pulled the trigger.

There was an ear-piercing explosion and Dave saw the blood and brains as they flew from the back of Sandra's head. His eyes grew wide as he watched the sheriff-thing smile a wicked smile and turn the gun toward him.

"You're next," the sheriff-thing said.

"It's not real," Dave heard.

He looked backed to Sandra. She was still standing next to the sheriff-thing. There was a small hole in the front of her head from which blood seeped, but her eyes were wide open, and she was in no pain.

"It's an illusion," she explained.

Dave looked back to the officer. The gun was pointing at him. Dave resisted the urge to run. He just stood and watched the sheriff-thing pulled back the hammer.

The gun went off.

Then the body on the floor beside him reappeared. Apparently it had been there the entire time. He saw the shiny pistol next to the sheriff's right hand, so he reached down and grabbed it. He looked up and saw that the false spirit had reappeared in a different place. Now he stood Between Dave and Sandra. Dave pointed the gun at it.

"Don't shoot," Sandra urged. "He's not real, the bullet will pass right through him. He's trying to get you to shoot me."

Dave wanted badly to pull the trigger. He watched instead as the spirit changed before him. It became something terrible, something he had only seen before in his dreams. It grew until its head hit the ceiling, and it had several eyers and sharp teeth. It came toward him with its claws held out. Dave squeezed slowly on the trigger.

Sandra saw that Dave was going to shoot. "Aim for its head," she called to him.

Dave did. He pointed the gun upwards and fired into the creature's skull. He saw the bullet enter the monster's head. Green blood oozed down its front. But the monster kept coming. Dave fired another shot. He tried to fire a third, but there were no bullets left. Then he lowered his gun and just watched as the creature approached.

He wanted to run but did not. As he watched in terror he knew that it could not possibly be real, despite what he saw. He let the bloody monster approach and reach for his neck. He felt the cold claws wrap around that neck and begin to squeeze. He began to reach for those monstrous arms to pry them away, then remembered watching the policeman strangle himself and he stopped. He must have seen something like this, Dave thought. He rested his arms by his side and waited.

The pressure seemed real, but he was having no problems breathing.

Then Dave took a step forward and walked right into the creature. It felt like walking into an ice storm.

Then it was gone.

Dave looked up and saw the two holes he had shot in the ceiling.

"You're going to have to trust me," Sandra said.

"I guess so," Dave agreed. He dropped the gun and walked over to her. "Now what?"

Sandra looked around the room. She looked at the configuration of the candle holders and the big spot of blood. Then she walked slowly to the western wall. Dave followed, shining his light on the floor as they walked. He was careful not to walk in the dried blood. He felt that it would somehow be a desecration.

"Here's the portal," Sandra said.

"That's where they came through," Dave explained.

"That's where that last spirit came from."

"Did it go back in?" Dave asked.

"I didn't see it go in. I think it must have dissipated; it's probably reforming somewhere else in town right now as somebody else's horror."

"So the door is still open?" Dave asked.

"Yes."

"Can we go through it?" He asked.

"That's exactly what I was wondering," she replied.

Sandra looked around the room. She saw the candle holders, but she would need all of them for later.

"Do you have any change in your pockets?" She asked Dave.

"Sure," he answered. He took out a quarter and handed it to her.

Sandra walked close to the wall and stood in front of it. Then she flipped the coin at the wall. It sailed through the air and up to the wall.

Then it disappeared. There was the sound of a small explosion.

"Damn," Dave exclaimed. "Where did it go?"

"Over there I guess."

"Could we go through."

"I'm sure we could," Sandra answered, "I just don't know if we could come back."

Dave looked at the wall. "So we just have to close this?"

"First we have to get the spirits back through, then close it."

"How do we do that?" Dave asked.

"We get them back through with another ceremony, much like the one you performed last night, but with a few changes." She took a deep breath.

"Then we have to close the door on the other side."

"You mean somebody's got to go through there and close this thing up?"

"Yes"

"And they probably won't get back?" He asked.

"They definitely won't get back. Not if they're successful."

Dave thought for a moment, but only for a moment. He had to be the one. It was his fault that the door was open in the first place. He had caused death and destruction. He had to pay. This could be his vindication.

"I'll do it," he said,

Sandra didn't respond. She knew he was probably the person best suited, next to her. She wasn't ready to go just yet, and she had become involved by default. She might be more able to withstand the pressure of the otherworld, but Dave had enough determination to overcome the obstacles. He had proven that moments ago by walking into the monster.

"When can we start?" Dave asked.

"We'll need to gather some things. We should be able to get then from people here in town. We probably will need to split up and get the items, then meet back here in two hours."

"Okay, so what do we need?"

Sandra didn't answer. Instead she stared ahead as if she were thinking.

"What is it?" Dave asked.

"Shh."

Dave stood and watched Sandra. She seemed to be concentrating on something. Then Dave heard it too. It sounded like footsteps. But were they real, or from the otherworld? Perhaps that was what Sandra was trying to decipher.

Then there was a shadow moving at the door.

Dave turned his light to the doorway and saw a horrible sight.

Standing just inside the room was Crazy Joe. He had a gun and he was pointing it in their direction. Dave turned off the flashlight immediately and moved. A shot rang out and his left hand began to burn.

Sandra recognized the man in the doorway. She remembered the face from the time she had seen him coming towered her with a hammer. He had come back. This time he had a gun, and he was going to kill them both.

It was dark and Joe's eyesight was not good. He stayed where he was and watched for movement. He couldn't make out any. They were in the darkness, and they weren't moving.

"I have to do this!" Joe called out. "Just stand up and turn your light back on. It won't hurt so bad then!" He waited. Nothing. No movement and no voices.

Then the western wall began to cast a glow. It was dim at first, but as it grew the forms of the two people he was to kill appeared as shadowy outlines. He aimed at one and fired. He guessed that he missed since it remained standing.

Dave knew he had to act. The room was slowly growing brighter. Soon he would be a visible target. If he stood now and ran he might make it across the room before Joe shot him. Probably not. Perhaps he could take a bullet and still live. That would have to be it. Otherwise, they would simply both be shot.

Joe took three steps into the room. He could see the shadowy outlines, but they weren't clear enough yet to shoot at. The room continued to grow brighter. Soon he would be able to see the two targets clearly. Then he could kill them. Then he saw the figure on the right stand up quickly and lunge toward him. He turned to shoot.

3

As Dave ran toward Joe a shot rang out. He knew he was hit, but he could not stop. He took two more steps before jumping. As he leapt there was another shot. He only hoped that he could live long enough to keep Joe occupied so that Sandra could escape.

Then he hit Joe.

Joe fell back to the ground with no resistance,

Dave looked into Joe's eyes. They were glazed and distant. He felt a coolness as a shadowy figure rose up from the dead body. A second later it was gone, through the portal which still glowed on the western wall. Dave looked at the old bum and saw his own blood where it had soaked into the man's clothes.

Then he realized that it was Joe who had been shot.

He looked up to the doorway and there was a bright light. Then a voice spoke to him.

"Just stay there," it said. "I want to know what the hell's going on."

"Is it real?" He called back to Sandra.

Sandra had seen the man appear in the doorway. He too had a gun, and he had put two bullets into the bum's back. Now that man stood pointing his gun and flashlight at Dave. The room had faded to its original darkness. The portal fell again to a dull glow.

"He's real," Sandra called. "He shot Joe."

"Who are you," the man asked. "And what are you doing here?"

"Who are you?" Dave asked back.

"This house and this room have been sealed off by the police department. What are you doing in here?"

"What are you doing?" Dave returned.

"I'm a cop," the man replied, "what's your excuse."

Dave wanted to get up. The dead bum smelled terrible. "Can I get up?" He asked.

"Sure, just don't make any sudden moves and stay back."

Dave stood up.

Deputy Frank Sharp watched Dave as he stood and backed away a step. He looked back to the floor of the room. It was quite a sight. Ten feet ahead of him there was a dead bum, one he had killed. Five feet to the right was Sheriff Pritchard. He was dead too. He could see the blood that ran from the sheriff's body. It was dried. He had been dead for some time. But for how long, and by who's hand? He looked over the floor and found the sheriff's service revolver. It was too far away from the body to have fallen there from his hand. Sharp shined the light on Dave then on Sandra. How where they involved? What should he do now?

"Tell me your story," the deputy said to Dave. He saw that the man's hand was dripping in blood. Apparently the old bum had hit him once.

"It's pretty crazy," Dave said.

"I've seen and heard some pretty crazy stuff in the last twenty-four hours. I want to know what the hell's going on. Now I can stand here all night with my gun pointing at you if I have to, but I want to hear your story, and I want it to be a good one."

Dave looked to Sandra.

"Just tell him the truth," she said.

"That would be the best advice," the deputy replied.

Dave gave the deputy a pained look. Then he looked back to his hand. It needed to be wrapped. He looked back to the deputy. "It all started with some crazy dreams."

Dave told a quick version of what had taken place. The deputy's face did not change expression as he listened. The man seemed simply to be soaking in the information and reserving judgement until the end.

When Dave finished Deputy Sharp just looked at him. Then he looked again at the dead bodies. It was cold in this room. Did he believe?

Then Sharp heard some movement to this right. He turned his light quickly and saw Sheriff Pritchard standing before him, bullet holes and all.

"It's bullshit," the sheriff said to him.

Deputy Sharp took a step back and pointed the gun at the sheriff.

"Don't point that at me," the sheriff said. "They're the killers! He killed the VanZandt girl last night. They city cop stumbled in on the scene, there had been a disturbance call. That man strangled the cop, then set up all this crap to make it look like a cult killing. He killed her because she wouldn't have him, that's all there really was to it."

Sharp pointed his gun back at Dave.

"Don't listen to it", Sandra said to the deputy.

Sharp looked at her, then back to the dead sheriff.

"The two of them were here when I got here earlier. He shot me with my own gun to make it look like suicide. They brought Joe back here to kill him too, to make it look like another sacrifice. But he had a gun."

Sharp looked down at the bum, then back to Dave. Dave listened to the spirit's lies. He didn't know what to say or do. Surely the deputy saw through it all.

"They are criminals," the sheriff continued. "You'd do best to lock them up."

"And get us out of the way until it's too late!" Dave shouted.

"That's not the sheriff," Sandra called out.

"Shut up! Both of you!" Sharp shouted. He looked back to the spirit of his dead commander. Then he looked back to the two suspects. Then he decided what he had to do.

"Turn around and get on your knees!" He shouted to Dave. He waved the gun at him.

"I don't believe this!" Dave shouted.

"Shut up and do what I say or I'll kill you now for shooting my friend and put his gun in your hand. Self-defense. Works every time. On your knees!"

Dave turned around and got on his knees. He put his hands behind his head, as the deputy instructed, then waited while he was cuffed. He didn't cuff Sandra since her arm was in a sling and she didn't appear to be much of a threat. The dead sheriff just smiled and watched.

"You take care of them good," the sheriff said.

"You know I will boss," Sharp replied. Then he stepped to the side of the door. "Both of you get up and march out the door."

Sandra and Dave complied. Sharp kept the gun out and ready the entire time. Dave knew it wasn't worth trying to get away. Not if this man believed they had killed his friend. He would shoot them in a minute if he thought they might escape. Dave looked at Sandra and they exchanged a glance of despair.

"Keep moving!" The deputy commanded. As they left the room he turned to look at the sheriff. "I'll take care of them for you," he said. "I'll take care of this whole mess."

"I know you will," the sheriff replied. "You've always been my best man."

Deputy Sharp closed the door behind him as he left the room. Then he marched the two suspects out of the house and to his car where he made them get into the back seat.

He was definitely going to take care of things.

XVI

1

Deputy Sharp made Dave and Sandra get into the back seat of his car. Then he walked around the front and got in. He pulled away from the house and drove three blocks before he threw the key to the handcuffs into the back seat. They landed in Sandra's lap. She took them and looked at the side of the deputy's head.

"You didn't think I fell for that crap, did you?" He said.

Dave turned toward the window as Santa unlocked the cuffs from his wrists. She handed them over the seat to the deputy.

"So why did you bother putting on the show?" Dave asked. His left hand was balled into a fist. It was still bleeding some out the back.

"Two cops have been killed in that room. I didn't want to give whatever that thing was reason to kill a third. Apparently it was important that I lock you two up for some reason."

"Probably so we could have a fatal accident of some kind," Sandra observed. She took off one shoe and used her sock for a bandage for Dave's hand. "So where are we going?"

"You tell me. I figure if you're a threat to this thing, you must know where we need to go."

Sandra explained briefly what they intended to do, and what they would need to accomplish it.

"It all sounds like witchcraft to me," the deputy replied, "and I'm a Christian man. Still, this thing is evil. If it takes witchcraft to send it back where it came from, I'll have to hope the Lord forgives me for participating."

Sandra smiled and Dave sighed in relief.

"Now," the deputy continued, "I know a good number of people in this town who will probably have the items you said we'd need, and they'd be willing to loan them to me. It's just a matter of asking the right people in the right manner."

"That's great," Dave said.

"You don't know what this means," Sandra chimed in.

"I think I have a pretty good idea," Sharp replied.

As they drove to the first house something occurred to Sandra.

"I think maybe I should drive," she said.

The deputy looked at her in the rear view mirror. "Why's that?"

"Well," she began, "I'm kind of used to this sort of thing. If it becomes obvious that we're not headed to the jail, and that you've decided to help us, I'm afraid you might be forced from the road, or made to drive into a brick wall."

"You mean because I might see things that aren't there?"

"Yeah," Sandra confirmed.

"So that's what's been going on in town? People are seeing things that are causing them to have all these accidents?"

"That's it."

"I thought it was something like that." He pulled over to the side of the road.

"I didn't mean right now," Sandra explained.

"The sooner the better, I've seen what can happen. I don't want to take any chances now."

Sharp got out of the car and traded places with Sandra. He got into the back seat and extended his right hand to Dave.

"Name's Frank Sharp," he said. "I'm with the county sheriff's office. Sorry about having to cuff you."

Dave shook the man's hand. "Dave Chatburn. No problem."

Sandra got behind the wheel and introduced herself. She moved her left arm around inside the sling. There was some pain, but it was not unbearable. "Can you loosen that strap behind my neck," she called back to Dave.

Dave reached forward and loosened it some. She felt a little more pain in the arm, but it was still not overpowering.

"Loosen it all the way," she said.

"You're taking it off?" Dave asked

"It's just in the way. I need both arms for this."

"Sure it's okay?" Dave asked.

"I'll know in a minute."

Dave loosened the strap all the way with his good right hand. Sandra pulled the sling over her arm and off. She slowly moved her arm away from her body. She cried out once, but then it was okay. The arm was not in perfect shape, but it would have to do. She put the car in gear and began driving down the road. "Well," she asked, "where to first?"

2

As they drove around town gathering the items they would be needing Sandra filled in the details of the ceremonies they would be performing. These things seemed so strange to Sharp, but he was willing to accept them. He had grown up wary of the forces which seemed to now dominate the town. He saw no other solution, and he knew that he had to believe it or accept an odd kind of defeat.

By ten after eleven they had gathered all of the needed items. It had taken a little longer than Sharp had anticipated to find a couple of the spices, but they had eventually located them all. Sandra had driven the entire time, but nothing strange had happened to them. There had, however, been a lot of activity in the town as they had gone about their gathering. There were two more fires. One of them had burnt down an old, abandoned home that had been a landmark of sorts for as long as Sharp could remember. They had also been deterred once because of an automobile which was sitting sideways across the road and burning. The police had not made it to the scene yet, and there was only one person watching. It hadn't looked as if the people who had been in the car had gotten out. There were other signs that things weren't quite what they should be in Cisco, but they had done their best to work around them. Now they were ready to try to put a stop to it all.

Sandra turned the last corner. They could all see the VanZandt place about a hundred yards down the street.

It was if an alarm had gone off. As soon as Sandra began driving down the street the onslaught began.

First a sports car came careening around the corner about fifty yards away and began speeding straight toward them. Sandra looked carefully and made her decision. She drove straight down the road and didn't even consider swerving.

"Hey!" Sharp shouted out.

But before he could utter his warning the car had passed through them and disappeared in the rear-view mirror. Sharp sat back, his heart racing. He was glad he wasn't the one driving.

Then Dave saw a glowing object running through the open field next to the road. As it approached the road he could see that it was a little girl with her hair on fire. The girl ran out in front of the car. There was the sound of impact, and blood splattered over the windshield.

But the impact had no feel to it, and both men understood what was going on. They looked quickly at each other, and an understanding passed between them. It was a good thing Sandra was driving. Either one of them would have stopped the car by now.

Then Dave's mother appeared in the center of the road.

"No," Dave said quickly. He closed his eyes as Sandra drove over her as well. He heard the crunching bones and mournful scream but felt no impact. He decided then that he would keep his eyes closed until they reached the house.

Sharp kept his eyes opened. He watched in amazement as all kinds of people, creatures, monsters and machines appeared and disappeared. It all seemed like a frantic attempt by forces he did not understand to keep them from their task. It was as if these forces had opened up their toy box and where just throwing out everything they could find.

Sandra had decided to drive straight to the house, regardless of what she saw. The objects appeared so quickly now that she could not discern whether or not they were real before she hit them, but she knew that none of them would be real and was willing to risk everything on that.

Finally she got to the driveway and pulled up onto it, despite the dozens of crying and wiggling babies that lay across it. She gritted her teeth as she drove over them. She could hear the crushing bones and see the blood as it ran down the driveway. It hurt, even though she knew they were not real.

She stopped the car and turned in her seat.

"No matter what you see, just do as I say," she explained.

The men just nodded their head and got of the car.

Dave got the flashlights out of the car and handed one each to Sandra and Sharp, keeping one for himself. Dave carried the bag of things they had gathered. Even the big black plastic bag had been borrowed.

"Let's go," Dave said. He was anxious to get to it. He was ready to go now. He didn't know if he would feel this way when his time came to step through the portal, but he hoped that he would.

Sandra led them up the walkway and to the front door. She looked at the handle and saw that it was glowing. She could feel warmth coming from it. She knew that she was supposed to fear this, that she was supposed to think that the knob was too hot to touch. But underneath the image of the red-hot knob was the image of the real knob. This was an indistinct image which she doubted that either Dave or Sharp could see. She reached forward and touched the knob. There was the sound of burning flesh, and even a faint smell of it. But her hand felt no warmth. In fact, the knob felt cold. She even heard a woman's scream.

Sharp stood behind Sandra and watched as she grabbed the hot knob. He saw flame dance around the edges of her hand and heard her cry out. But then she turned around and looked at him. There was no pain on her face. He understood that he had seen another illusion, and he wondered how many more there would be, and how terrible they would become. What if she became a monster? What if a moving wall appeared between them and he could no longer see her? What if there was a loud scream which wouldn't stop, and he couldn't hear her instructions.

Dave watched the incident with the glowing knob and wondered very similar things himself.

Sandra opened the door. She held the flashlight in her left hand. The whole arm had loosened up since she had removed the sling. She shined the light into the house. The walls and ceiling looked fairly normal. The floor, however, had disappeared. She looked down and saw that there was now a pit about fifty feet deep. At the bottom of the pit was a black substance which flowed and bubbled. She tried to concentrate and soon she saw a fuzzy image of the floor where it should have been. She shined the light down the hall. "Here it goes," she said. Then stepped in.

For a moment she felt as if she was going to fall. But then she felt the floor beneath her feet. The illusion remained, but she walked over the top of it. She walked in a few feet, the turned around. Sharp stood on the edge of the imagined precipice. He looked down into the black ooze, then up at Sandra. He saw her floating above the ooze, and he understood that the floor was really still there.

"Come on," she said, "it's not going to get any easier."

The deputy knew she was right. He stopped out onto the floor. He felt the adrenaline rush through as his foot hit the floor he could not see. Dave watched this, then walked in behind him.

Then one of the walls disappeared.

There was nothing behind it but blackness. Dave shined his light into it, but the beam disappeared where the wall used to be. Sandra reached out until her hand came into contact with the wall which she could still make out. She felt her way down the hall with Sharp and Dave close behind. Beneath them the ooze continued to boil.

"How bad is this going to get?" Dave called to Sandra.

"I don't know," she said. "But there are certain things which will not happen," she said. "Your sight may be deceived, sometimes your hearing, and once in a while your sense of smell. But your sense of touch will not be disturbed. Just keep that in mind."

"Okay," Dave said. Sharp just looked at Sandra and wondered why this had happened to him.

Sandra felt along the wall until she came to the door which led to the room she sought. As she touched the knob the floor and the wall appeared as they should have. Sharp lost his sense of balance and took a step back. Then Sandra opened the door.

When the floor had disappeared, that had been hard to deal with. But now the forces which sought to stop her tapped into the very roots of her fears. She could see the floor undulating when the door came open. She shined her light into the room and saw that it was covered with snakes. They were everywhere. There was no place where the floor could be seen because of the snakes.

She knew they were not real.

But it was still very hard for her to step into them. She stood and stared.

"What is it?" Dave asked.

"Snakes," Sandra answered.

"Snakes don't bother me," the deputy revealed. "Let me go first."

Sandra agreed and stepped aside as the deputy walked passed her and into the room. She saw one of the snakes strike out and hit the deputy in the leg. Another wrapped around the second leg and crawled up it. He walked on unaffected as snakes squirmed and crunched beneath his feat.

"Do you need me to go in next?" Dave asked.

"No, I'll go," she replied.

She took in a deep breath and stepped into the room. Immediately a snake struck out at her and she really did scream this time.

"Sorry," she said to the two men, "I'm terrified of snakes."

"It's okay," Dave replied, "I'm sure we're each going to face something which terrifies us before the night is over. Maybe having three people here is a good thing. That way there might always be one of us who isn't afraid and can reassure the other two."

"Yea," Sandra agreed.

Finally Dave stepped into the room.

The door closed behind them. Dave reached out and felt the door. It was solid.

"It's really closed," he announced.

Then the room grew colder. The spot on the wall began to cast an eerie dark glow. Shadows danced in and out of it.

"Is that the doorway?" Sharp asked.

"Yes," Sandra answered, "and those shadows are really the spirits. You can only see them for a moment just after they pass through the portal, then they are invisible until they wish to be seen."

The room was silent for a moment. Then Sharp asked the question that had been on his mind all evening.

"Are you a witch?" He asked.

Sandra smiled. "No," she answered. "I'm just a person with a gift. I can see just a little more than the average person, that's all. It's a special sight I've had all my life."

"So how do you know about these ceremonies and stuff?"

"I wanted to learn everything I could about my gift so that I could make the best use of it. I read a lot. A lot of what I know about the supernatural I learned from books. Some of it I learned from the other side. It's just what I grew up with."

"I think the girl that lived here messed with black magic," Sharp observed. "That's probably how she got involved."

"I don't think so," Dave observed. "I think she was just a palm reader who wasn't even very good at that. I think she was a victim of her own deceptions."

They had all become comfortable standing amongst the snakes which they could all see, but none of them could feel. The snakes vanished and the room became familiar. The tipped over candle holders appeared, as did the two dead bodies which were really there.

"So," Sandra said, "now a taste of reality."

"I wouldn't exactly call it that," Sharp observed. He felt uneasy.

"First let's set up the candle holders like I described."

Dave put the bag down and took out the new candles.

"Hey," Sharp exclaimed, "the candle holders are gone."

Sandra could still see the faint outlines of the holders. "No," she explained, "it's just a stall tactic. Feel around for them, they're still here."

The three of them felt around for the holders and set them up in the circle. From time-to-time Sandra had them move the candle holders they had found since she could just barely see them. When they had finished she picked up the candles from where Dave had placed them on the floor. She walked around the circle and put a candle in each holder. They seemed to stand alone in the air. As she inserted the last candle she instructed Dave to light them and place he silver coins at their bases. When he had finished doing this the holders reappeared. Then there were snakes on the floor again for a moment, but they disappeared almost immediately, as if someone or something had remembered that this trick had been tried once already.

Then the candles were lit the room was bright enough that they could turn their flashlights off and set them next to the black bag. The bag was outside of the circle, near the southern wall of the room, where Dave had stood during the ceremonies of the previous night.

"Why did you kill me?"

Dave turned around abruptly. Standing in front of the hole in the western wall was Colleen. There was a large hole in her chest, and blood covered her front.

"Why did you kill me Dave?"

"I guess this one's for me," Dave said He looked to the other two in the room with him, He needed their support. He had killed Colleen. That's why he was here now. He was going to make up for it all.

"Why did you kill me?"

Now the voice was his brother's.

"Are you all right, Dave?"

Dave stood staring toward the portal. A tear ran down his face.

"You've got to put it all aside now, Dave." Sandra explained. "Now is not the time to grieve. Now is the time to act."

Dave looked to Sandra and saw the strength in her face. Then he closed his eyes and willed for the image to be gone.

When he opened his eyes it was still there, but its power over him was broken.

"Why did you kill me?" It asked.

"I haven't killed you yet," Dave said to the thing he knew was not Colleen VanZandt. "But I will be removing you form this place soon."

The image began to melt and change. It appeared as a formless lump of flesh, then melted into two images in one, two people he did not know who seemed to be intertwined.

"You have no idea what you will face on the other side," the voices said. "There are terrors there that your feeble mind is unable to comprehend. You will be tormented, and you shall never escape." The momentary wavering of faith showed on Dave's face. "It's not worth the price," it said. "Leave this place now. Leave this town with your life, and you will live happily. Come to the other side and close the door and we will be waiting there for you. There you will burn, but you will never die."

The image broke into tandem laughter then changed to a black shadow which fled into the portal.

Sandra looked at Dave. She watched his face carefully. She needed him. She didn't know if she would have the strength to go through, and she would be needed on this side.

"I'll be okay," Dave said, sensing her concern.

Sandra did not know if she could believe him, but she had no choice but to take him at his word.

Dave and Deputy Sharp walked over to the southern wall and Sandra entered the circle.

3

Dave beat softly on the small drum he had borrowed from the Carter household. After fifty beats the deputy hit the lid of a frying pan with a spoon. They had been unable to find cymbals, but it was the substance and not the materials which mattered.

Dave watched Sandra as she held her arms out before her and turned in a circle. She made no sound as she moved. Her faced seemed angelic. Her eyes were closed as she turned, then they opened as she completed it, facing the western wall and the glowing portal.

She looked toward the portal with her special vision and saw that it was like a tunnel which led down a dark and tangled corridor. The walls of the tunnel were indistinct and seemed to move. Shadowy figures darted around within the tunnel, searching for the opening they knew to be near. Once in a while one would make it out. Then Dave and the deputy saw the darting shadow as it passed out of the portal and dissipated.

"Hand me the bowl." Sandra said.

Dave reached into the bag and felt around. He found the bowl and pulled it out. When he got it out he saw that he had grabbed an odd-looking lizard with sharp teeth, and he almost dropped it. He would have done so had he not felt the cold porcelain of the bowl which in reality he held. He walked to the edge of the circle and held it out to Sandra.

"Now hand me the spices in the order."

She made her own potion which was much lighter and sweeter than the once concocted by Colleen the night before. The ceremonies were very similar, with only a few very important differences. She set the potion down at her feet and began to ask the questions.

"Who is now in a realm in which they do not belong?"

"We are." Dave and Sharp answered in unison.

She asked again. "Who is now in a realm in which they do not belong?"

"We are." This time there were whispers of other voices. There were shadowy images that flowed into the room through the walls and the ceiling.

"Who is now in a realm in which they do not belong?"

"We are." This time Dave's and Sharp's voices where only part of the harmony of voices which had chimed in.

Sharp looked around and began to see outlines of terrible things. His fear gripped him, and he looked back to Sandra. She stood facing the western wall, her hands still held out.

Sandra reached into her pocket and took out the necklaces which had been in her purse. She held the cross right side up before her. It was more a symbol of her faith than a symbol of Christ. It was her faith and the faith of the two men who stood in the room with her that would determine the outcome of the next few minutes. Sharp's faith was in a Christian God, and now he drew on that faith. Dave's faith was in himself, and he felt the faith faltering as fear took hold of his resolve.

Sandra spoke toward the portal. "What do you want?" She asked.

"To cross over," the voices responded.

There was a scream.

"Kill and maim! Kill and maim!"

Sandra did not look. The two men looked toward the door. It flew open and an old woman came rushing through with a knife in her hand. "We do not want to cross over!" She screamed. "We want to kill and maim!"

Dave watched in horror as the woman jumped into the circle. Images of Crazy Joe and the previous night flashed through his mind.

Sandra did not turn to look. The old woman disappeared as she landed inside the circle. A black shadow was sucked into the glowing portal. Dave heard another scream. This one seemed to be coming from within that portal. It was a scream of despair.

Sandra saw the shadow as it was pulled inside the portal. She saw it pass into the tunnel and become absorbed into its wall.

"What do you want?" She asked again.

There was resistance, but there was also a tremendous compulsion for the spirts to comply, so they did a second and third time.

Sandra hung the necklace around her neck. Then she picked up the bowl which contained the light sweet liquid. She walked to the border of the circle and began sprinkling the liquid just inside the line of candles. When she completed the circle she walked back to the center and tossed the remains of the liquid toward the portal. The liquid turned silver as it flew through the air. When it hit the wall there was the sound of water being thrown onto a fire, and steam flowed from the wall.

The room became icy as shadow upon shadow fell into the portal. White steam actually flowed into the room, and Sandra could see the shadows as they passed through it. There were dozens of shadows, probably over a hundred of them. She watched in awe as the spirits plunged back into their world.

Dave watched too. He felt the fear rise within him. He imagined himself walking through that portal. He imagined what might happen to him after he crossed over, after he had closed the door.

Sandra spoke to the portal. She said words which the two men did not understand. Most were English, some were not.

Then there was a brilliant flash of light and a face appeared in the western wall. It was the same face which had appeared the night before, only now it seemed to be in anguish.

There was another bright flash.

The Dave saw that Sandra was looking toward him.

"It's time," she said.

He looked to the portal. He saw the face within. There were no more illusions, but the terror remained fresh in his mind.

"I can't do it!" He called back. "I can't go in there!"

"Dave you have to!" She exclaimed "If we don't close it now, we may never be able to. You've got to go now!"

Sharp watched the face with revulsion. He knew he could not go, even if it meant saving the town. His terror was stronger than his sense of duty.

Dave fought the dilemma within. He knew he was responsible. He was willing to die to set things straight.

But what if he did not die? What if the spirits that had threatened him really were waiting for him? What if eternal torment did await him?

Sandra looked back to the wall. She knew she would have to be the one. But she would have to step out of the circle to go, and she didn't know if this would create too great a breach. It might take her too long to find and close the door, and several spirits would be able to slip back through in that time, spirits which could never be sent back.

And she would be trapped on the other side.

Then she saw a small hand emerge from the smoke.

Dave saw the hand too. Then the arm. He watched as the image of his younger brother emerged from the smoke. Then it spoke to him.

"Come on Davey," it said. "Come with me. I want to show you something."

Dave looked at his brother. Then he looked to Sandra. Sandra was facing Dave now and she spoke to him.

"It's really Tommy," she said.

Dave looked back at the image. It was different than the one that had haunted his dreams. It was not daunting or threatening. Instead it was inviting. The face was bright and seemed to be full of life. The boy's body was intact, and his arm was whole. A tear same to Dave's eye.

Dave walked slowly though the circle toward the outstretched hand of his younger brother. When he came to the edge of the mist he reached out to touch the hand.

He felt it.

As he touched the hand something about him changed. He could see more clearly who he was, and how he fit into the picture. He could see the forgiveness in his brother's eyes, and the warmth. He looked back to the room, and it now appeared to be a part of an unreal world. The world was not here, it was beyond, it was through the portal.

"I'm scared," he said to his brother.

"It'll be okay."

Dave understood those words and they gave him the strength he needed.

Without looking back he stepped forward through the portal.

Sandra and Deputy Sharp watched as Dave disappeared into the wall. Then they waited.

4

Dave stepped into a whole new world. His fear was still with him, but it no longer controlled him. The world was full of new signs and new sounds which he did not understand.

"I need you to help me, Tommy," Dave said to his brother.

"I know," he answered. "I'll help you. Then we can play, okay?"

"Okay," Dave agreed.

It was not at all what he expected. The darkness he had seen from the other side of the wall had been a shadowy deception of what he now walked though. The world was now a misty uncertainty, there seemed to be nothing solid here. Even his limbs and body felt fluid. He followed Tommy through the mist to a place where the mist was torn. Where the tear lay, there was utter blackness.

"We have to go through here," Tommy explained.

"Do I have to go?" Dave asked.

"I can't do it," Tommy explained, "I've been here too long."

"I don't want to die," Dave said. He hadn't really understood what was happening to him until that moment. He was standing on the threshold between the two worlds, standing before the tear he had created.

Dave looked into his brother's face. "You'll come with me?" He asked.

"Of course," Tommy said with a smile. "Mommy and Dad are waiting for both of us."

Dave felt both joy and fear as he looked into the rift.

Then he stepped through.

And he saw the new world.

It was glorious.

5

A few minutes later the glowing portal began to fade.

Sandra and Deputy Sharp watched the colors darken to black. Then there was nothing but blackness. Then the blackness took a form, and once again there was a wall.

They stood in silence. The illusions were finally gone.

"Where did he go?" Sharp asked,

"To the other side," Sandra answered. She tried to look, but there was nothing to see.

Sharp looked around the room which remained eerie to him despite the cessation of supernatural activities.

"Is it over?" He asked Sandra.

She looked again to the wall through which Dave had disappeared. The door was closed, this she could tell.

But she could also feel the power that waited on the other side. Perhaps someday it would rise again. But for now, it had been vanquished.

"Yes," she said. "It's over."

It was a lie, but one intended to relive the anxieties for a man who would never forget what he had seen. Surely he would relive the past few days in his dreams many times before the day when he was finally laid to rest.

Perhaps the spirits would return. But if and when they did it would not be in his lifetime anyway.

"Let's go," the deputy urged.

"Okay," Sandra agreed.

They left the house together. They both knew that a part of themselves had passed through the portal with Dave. Some day they would join him on the other side.

But for now, they had this world to deal with.

Deputy Frank Sharp escorted Sandra MacElroy across the field behind the house, back to her car.

"I'll be heading up the investigation into all this mess," he explained. "I'm not sure yet how I'm going to handle it, but I don't plan on mentioning your name."

"I'd appreciate that," she replied. "I'd like to get away from this thing now."

"Of course," he agreed. He looked at the woman a moment longer.

"Hey," he said to her, "do you do this sort of thing often?"

She smiled a weary smile. "Sure, it's just usually a lot lower key than all this."

"Right." He wanted to understand but decided that he never could. "You take care."

"Okay."

"Oh," Sharp threw in "by the way, thanks."

She smiled again. "No problem."

She closed her door and drove off toward the interstate. She was exhausted but decided to sleep in Dallas. It was only a two-hour drive, and she would feel much better when she got away from this place.

Deputy Sharp watched the strange but beautiful lady as she drove away. Then he turned and walked back to his car.

He got in his car and looked one last time at the VanZandt house. He didn't like that place. He was going to see to it that it was condemned and destroyed. It wasn't worth fixing now anyway, and he didn't think anybody would object.

After another moment of reflection and a quick prayer of thanks, the deputy drove away from the house and back toward Eastland.

Tomorrow was going to be another long day.